The Zone

GRAHAM HAMER

THE ZONE

Copyright © 2020 Graham Hamer

All rights reserved.

ISBN: 9798631723061

Graham Hamer has asserted his right to be identified as the author of this Work in accordance with the Copyright, Designs and Patents Act 1988. No part of this book may be reproduced or transmitted in any form or by any means, graphic, electronic, or mechanical, including photocopying, recording, taping or by any information storage or retrieval system, without the permission in writing from the author.

All characters and events in this publication are fictitious and any resemblance to real persons, living or dead, is purely coincidental. Except in the case of commonly accepted historical or geographical facts, any resemblance to events, localities, actual persons - living or dead - or history of any person is entirely coincidental.

Book cover design by Bruno Cavellec. Copyright © Bruno Cavellec 2020. Image used and published according to the licence granted by the artist.

DEDICATION

This book is dedicated to

Doctors, Nurses and Health Workers everywhere. And to all the other essential services who keep the country running in times of need.

We're proud of each and every one of you.

ACKNOWLEDGEMENTS

Book cover art should say something about your book. I am so fortunate to have the living legend Bruno Cavellec as designer and creator of my book covers (all twenty of them now). Bruno has an easy knack of picking out what matters and representing that thought on the cover of my books. Thanks so much Bruno, for being you and for sharing your inspiration.

Every writer needs a good 'content editor' who will advise on the plot, the characters, the title, and anything else they think needs adjusting. I am lucky to have Gina Marquita Fiserova (herself a published author) as my content editor. She has a history of killing some of my less spectacular ideas with her bare hands. And remember, before you ask anybody their opinion you need to be honest with yourself: Are you asking for advice or validation? Gina Marquita Fiserova is the queen of telling it straight. Thanks, Gina.

ABOUT THE AUTHOR

Graham Hamer was born a few years before Queen Elizabeth came to the British throne (the second Queen Elizabeth, that is). One event was televised, one wasn't. His own event happened somewhere between England, Scotland, Ireland and Wales on a funny little island where the cats have no tails and the occasional witch still gets rolled down a steep hill in a spiked barrel. He left the Isle of Man to get a life. He got one. Then he went back. You'll find him there now if you know where to look.

Accountant, pig-herder (briefly), businessman, business analyst, web site builder – hell, writing's more fun.

The following books by Graham Hamer are also available or will be published shortly

THE CHARACTERS COMPILATION
Chasing Paper – Characters Compilation 1
Walking on Water – Characters Compilation 2
Tommy Gee – Characters Compilation 3
The Zone – Characters Compilation 4

THE ISLAND CONNECTION
Under the Rock - Island Connection 1
Out of the Window - Island Connection 2
On Whom the Axe Falls - Island Connection 3
China in Her Hand - Island Connection 4
Devil's Helmet - Island Connection 5
The Vicar's Lot - Island Connection 6
Chicken Rock - Island Connection 7
The Platinum Pirate - Island Connection 8
Picasso's Secret – Island Connection 9
Travellers – Island Connection 10
Flint - Island Connection 11

THE FRENCH COLLECTION
Web of Tangled Blood – French Collection 1
Cenotaph for the Living - French Collection 2
Jasmine's Journey - French Collection 3
Taken on Face Value - French Collection 4

THE ODDBALL ODYSSEY
A Little Bit Odd – Oddball Odyssey 1
Odd Gets Even – Oddball Odyssey 2
A Little Bit Odder – Oddball Odyssey 3

You can find out more about the author and his books at
http://www.graham-hamer.com

CONTENTS

Foreword	Page 1
Chapter One	Page 3
Chapter Two	Page 15
Chapter Three	Page 27
Chapter Four	Page 39
Chapter Five	Page 49
Chapter Six	Page 57
Chapter Seven	Page 65
Chapter Eight	Page 77
Chapter Nine	Page 85
Chapter Ten	Page 99
Chapter Eleven	Page 105
Chapter Twelve	Page 113
Chapter Thirteen	Page 119
Chapter Fourteen	Page 127
Chapter Fifteen	Page 141
Chapter Sixteen	Page 151
Chapter Seventeen	Page 159
Chapter Eighteen	Page 169
Chapter Nineteen	Page 183
Chapter Twenty	Page 191
Chapter Twenty-One	Page 199
Chapter Twenty-Two	Page 207
Chapter Twenty-Three	Page 217
Chapter Twenty-Four	Page 229
Chapter Twenty-Five	Page 237
Chapter Twenty-Six	Page 243
Epilogue	Page 253

FOREWORD

It was on December 10th 2019 that Wei Guixian, a seafood merchant in Wuhan's Hua'nan market, first started to feel sick. Thinking she had caught a cold, she walked to a small local clinic to get some treatment and then went back to work.

In early January 2020, researchers in China identified a new virus that had infected dozens of people. At the time, there was no evidence that the virus was readily spread by humans. Health officials in China said they were monitoring it to prevent the outbreak from developing into something more severe.

On January 11th 2020, Chinese state media reported the first known death from the effects of the virus, which had infected dozens of people. That was the beginning of the Coronavirus or Covid-19 that has since swept the globe. The rest, as they say, is history.

Meanwhile…. one month before Wei Guixian first started to feel sick, I sat in my study at home, in front of my faithful laptop with a mug of Earl Grey, and I mapped out a synopsis for a story of – you guessed it – a killer virus. In my mind, the book would be published in the summer of 2020. By the time the Chinese admitted there was a problem, I was already typing the first rough draft. Funny how fact sometimes overtakes fiction.

At the time of first publishing 'The Zone' (early April 2020) many thousands have died from Coronavirus. Many thousands more will die before a vaccine is found. Most countries are in lock-down including the Isle of Man where nobody is permitted entry. The only transport is for food and supplies.

Well, well – whoda thunk that? Read on and you'll understand why I'm wondering if I wasn't born a clairvoyant.

Incidentally, residents of the Isle of Man and more particularly pupils and former pupils of King William's College may recognise some of the descriptions of the school buildings. I just want to say that what follows is an invention of my tortured imagination. In no way, during my time there, did I come across the sorts of masters and staff that I describe. For the most part, they were good people doing a tough job.

THE ZONE

CHAPTER ONE

I was just 18 years and 1 month old when I saw my second dead body. It came as a bit of a shock before breakfast to see a group of students standing round the hunched form of a fellow sixth-former. Braxton Boddington lay slumped at the foot of the sundial in the middle of the quadrangle and, judging from the blood-splattered hockey stick that lay next to him, his brains and the top of his skull had been removed with some considerable force. His demise had been determined at the hands of a man. A man with some strength, I would say. So much for my initial skills of detection.

I guess I shouldn't be quite so blasé about a dead body, but I never had liked Boddington, so I wasn't going to shed too many tears for him now. And anyway, back in early February of 1967, the threat of death was all around us. We'd been intimidated by death's black menace for weeks. We had almost become immune to the concept, though I admit that the blood and gore was more than I had wanted at eight o' clock in the morning.

Since that morning in early February, during my life I've seen many more dead bodies, but only one has matched the fury and carnage of that scene, and I had seen that other one just two days earlier. Death is always disquieting, even an expected death. But only yesterday, Braxton Boddington had been a living, breathing individual. Even during his short eighteen years, he had developed complex and sophisticated layers of personality and emotion. His brain, now spread across the flagstones, had harboured many thousands of computations and memories. That was yesterday. Today only his corpse remained, and even that had been defiled, dishonoured and pillaged by some unknown assassin or assassins. You'd have to hate a man quite a lot to do that to him. So much for my secondary skills of detection.

I watched from my study window as the school's principal appeared, looking haggard and distressed. I knew it wasn't just his dead pupil that was bothering him. During the last few weeks, life at Bishop's College had taken a turn that nobody could ever have foreseen. Particularly for George Godfrey Armstrong whose grip on events had weakened to the extent that he looked like a walking apparition. I remember hoping that things wouldn't get any worse for him because I didn't know what his breaking point was. I realise now that I didn't need to worry, but I didn't know that then. I took a fresh cigarette from the pack, tapping the tobacco end on the packet, as was my habit. Back in those days, I smoked with the professional determination of a true addict. Which I was.

Usually, Jack Parsons and I would sneak off to the well-ventilated toilets or behind the art school for a smoke. Despite living through extraordinary times, at that stage we still liked to pretend some semblance of normality. But today, I didn't give a damn about being seen anymore. Nobody was going to do anything while there was a dead pupil to deal with. Anyway, the praepositors - the equivalent of prefects in a state school - were more concerned with other events, and what few masters were left were skulking behind closed doors. I lit up and drew deep on my cigarette. As I exhaled, I watched the smoke rise to the ceiling defying the axiom that whatever goes up must come down. I averted my gaze to keep an eye on developments in the quad.

The principal came to a halt at the sundial. He took one look at the dead young man, belched, and vomited over Boddington's legs. The growing crowd of students moved back to give him space. Nobody wanted the Prinky's barf splattering their shoes. I heard a snigger from somewhere near the back. I think it might have been Simon Wigglesworth, but it could have been that clown Adrian Chadwick who was standing next to him. They were somewhat distasteful fifth-formers. Wigglesworth sported a face full of weeping acne, and Chadwick suffered from distressingly noxious halitosis. In addition to their immaturity and general loathsome characters, neither of those traits attracted me to them.

Rumour had it that the Prinky, as we called him, was a decorated war hero. But it seemed he might have had a weak stomach when it came to bodies with empty skulls. Or maybe all the gossip of heroism during the war had been exaggerated somewhat. He must have seen worse than this on the battle fields of Normandy. For myself, I viewed the scene with curiosity but little revulsion. I was already resistant to my emotions and certainly wasn't about to vomit on the corpse. Mind you, I'd not had breakfast yet, so things had time to change.

The Prinky wiped his mouth on the sleeve of his crumpled suit and staggered off from where he had come. I guessed he was going to contact the authorities and let them know we had another dead body. At least, if they were as quick to come as they had been when a master had died two days earlier, poor old Boddington's body wasn't going to be on public display for too long.

A light drizzle swirled in the air like pollen - what the Irish call 'soft rain'. It drifted helplessly, pushed and pulled by erratic currents of air, finding its way beneath the collars of the staring pupils and coating their clothes in a damp layer. It was the perfect metaphor for our lives since returning to school back in early January. Intrusive, out of control, unavoidable, uncomfortable, unwanted. As the drizzle collected, it slid down the glass of the window as if the morning was crying for another life lost.

But forgive me; I'm jumping ahead of myself. I'm Nicholas Quine, better known as Nick. I'm heading well into old age now and my family, in jest, call me 'Old Nick'. At least, I think it's in jest. My face has deep cracks radiating out from the centre like disused roads on an expired map. But I still remember those harrowing events of 1967. How could I forget? At eighteen, I lived through the worst horrors a human being could ever imagine. Most memories are clear like yesterday. Others have begun to fade into the grey mists of time. The intervening years seem to have slipped past almost without me noticing. Life's like that. It even keeps going when you want to put the brakes on. These were the days before mobile phones, before the Internet, before any form of electronic 'civilisation' had taken over. Selfies were a thing of the future. Nowadays, I wish they were a thing ... no never mind.

To understand the God-awful state of affairs we found ourselves in back in early 1967, I need to tell you about Coviman-12. I'll try to keep it brief, but bear with me for a few paragraphs, because it's only by doing that that you'll understand how the rest of my story unfolds. Coviman was a mean, evil, relentless virus. It was an invisible assassin which spared almost no-one it came into contact with. We had just arrived back at school after the Christmas break when all hell broke loose. This highly contagious exanthematous virus – typified by sudden skin eruptions and great weeping pustules - which the authorities called Coviman-12 had taken hold on the Isle of Man. When they quarantined the island, they were still trying to puzzle out the source of the virus, but they were getting nowhere. Some said it came from illegal meat imports to the island, others said it came from an exotic animal in captivity. Some even thought that it was a virus which had lain dormant in the soil for thousands of years and had been dug up by an innocent gardener or farmer. As you'd expect, the church said it was the work of the Devil. The honest truth was that the authorities had no idea, so they kept hinting that it might actually be a man-made virus, planned to destroy our emerging technology-based culture.

Now, with the benefit of hindsight, some people - the sort who believe that the CIA planned the 9/11 attacks - say that the British government needed to justify their uncompromising clamp down on the island, so they obscured the truth, wherever that might lie, using exaggerated threats and invented enemies. But if you witnessed and lived through Coviman-12, as some of us did, you knew that nothing had been imagined or made-up. The tough quarantine was more than justified. There was no built-in fear factor needed.

Leonid Brezhnev had taken over as leader of the Soviet Union three years earlier and was doing a splendid job continuing the politics of fear created by his predecessors, Joseph Stalin and Nikita Khrushchev. He painted threats in far darker colours than were warranted. And many believe that's what the British government did in 1967. I don't go along with that. On the other hand, I don't believe they ever located the source of the virus. Maybe some time in the future, secret government papers will be published and the world will get to know where Coviman-12 came from. But it'll not happen in my lifetime.

The incubation period was short. Very short. Anything between one and three days. Symptoms began with fever, weakness, headaches, vomiting, and muscle pains. Within 24 hours, those affected would begin to bleed from the gums and eyes, or gastrointestinal tract, or all three. Their bodies would break out in great weeping pustules. After that, their tumour-infected skin sort of melted. In fact, it began to peel off in great swathes. Their insides soon turned to liquid, and their bowels disintegrated. As you might imagine, none of that was supportive of a long life. Nor was it particularly pleasant. The Ebola virus which was first identified ten years later had nothing on Coviman. That would be like comparing the plague to a common cold. Many people, it seemed, having caught Coviman-12, decided to end their lives rather than go through the agonies of a slow death. 'Suicide Is Painless' as the theme song for the TV series M*A*S*H. pointed out in the 1970s. The effects of Coviman-12 were anything but painless, so for many, suicide was a far better option.

There is nothing so patient, in this world or any other, as a virus searching for a host. Ten years earlier, the world had experienced Asian Flu that killed over two million. In 1968, the year after Coviman-12, Hong Kong Flu would wipe out over one million people. Since then, we have seen SARS, Ebola, Avian Flu, Coronavirus, and several other contagious epidemics, but nothing that matched the severity of Coviman-12 in the first few months of 1967. Not all killers are people, we discovered.

The World Health Organisation knew that containment was the only way to control the spread. With help from the British and Manx governments, they lost no time taking all the necessary steps, and they succeeded in restricting the outbreak to the Isle of Man - a small independent island slap bang in the middle of the Irish Sea. They quarantined the whole island and enforced it with ruthless efficiency. Dictionary definition of ruthless - having or showing no pity or compassion for others. I do not exaggerate.

Looking back, the decision to quarantine the Isle of Man undoubtedly saved the world from its worst torture since the Plagues of Egypt, so graphically described in the Biblical book of Exodus. If my memory serves me right - and it should since my father was a vicar - the plagues were, blood, frog, lice and flies, pestilence, boils, hail and fire, locusts, total darkness, and death of the firstborn. I like the frogs myself. It appeals to my somewhat cynical sense of humour. My wife, who is French, would have dined well.

Being brought up in a vicarage gives you a rather different view on life. As a child, I discovered that Mother's Union and jumble sales were more important than getting some new shoes that didn't squeeze my feet so much. The Bible had a lot to answer for as far as I was concerned. But I now knew that Coviman-12 was a killer that trumped anything The Bible had to offer. The biblical plagues were nothing compared to Coviman-12. Pure amateur stuff. If God had invented Coviman-12 earlier, it would have wiped out the Israelites as well as the Egyptians, no matter how much lamb's blood they smeared above their doors.

Part of the quarantine regulations - and looking back, I have to say it was a necessary part - was that only censored news reports were being released to the outside world, so as not to cause panic elsewhere. Communications had been cut - totally. Had the people beyond our shores known the full horrors of this virus, they would have been calling for the authorities to nuke us into oblivion. Fortunately for me and the others who lived through it, they didn't.

Her Majesty's Royal Navy guarded the coast night and day, and all flights were grounded. Since our school shared a boundary wall with the airport, that meant that there were no more Dakotas, Bristol Freighters or Viscounts to disturb our lessons. We had become so used to them over the years that the new silence was deafening. After two weeks, food and supplies began to run out on the island and were being shipped in under close supervision. Dock workers wore green all-in-one hazmat suits with full face masks and breather filters. It wasn't just to protect them; it was also to protect the guys on the boats who were offloading.

The only boats allowed in port were a fleet of cargo ships leased for the duration of the quarantine. No roll-on-roll-off. No vehicular movements at all. They stacked necessary supplies on wooden delivery pallets and craned them off. Nothing was ever craned back on because any form of contact could let the virus run amok beyond the island's granite cliffs. The authorities were determined that shouldn't happen. They needed the contamination, whatever it was, kept on the island, even if it wiped out the whole population of 52,000. It would be a small price to pay to secure the rest of humanity.

The three-mile naval blockade ensured that only authorised boats arrived or left the island. Again, it was maintained with merciless efficiency. Later, we heard rumours of nosey fishing vessels having been blown out of the water when they didn't immediately respond to the orders to turn around. We never found out if the rumours were true. Maybe they were exaggerated. Maybe not.

To try and limit the spread of the virus, every town and village had also been placed in isolation, guarded by suitably attired police and army personnel shipped in from mainland Britain. Public meetings of any sort were banned. We soon came to refer to the army and police corps as street marshals. From what few reports we had, just one month after the outbreak, thousands of residents had died. The current rumour was that the old mining village of Foxdale was now a ghost town with only a handful of survivors locked into their homes. They took the bodies away on flatbed trucks and burned them on open funeral pyres. The wooden delivery pallets that could never be taken back to England helped keep the fires at the right temperatures. We could see the flames at night up in the hills. When the wind was in the wrong direction, we could smell them too. Afterwards, many said that this was inhumane but actually, there was good logic to not burying the bodies.

Historically, cholera had been a fearsome disease in the British Isles. Then, back in the 1830s and 1840s, they had buried their dead in deep cholera pits and covered the bodies with quicklime. With Coviman-12 normal burial was impossible and impractical, given the number of deaths. In any case, since nobody knew what it was or where it had come from, there was also the fear that the virus would live on underground, or contaminate the water sources. Burning was the only safe and practical solution. Nothing beats temperatures in excess of 1,500 degrees Fahrenheit. In fact, the human body burns exothermically - it gives off more energy than it needs to sustain combustion - at about 1,000 degrees. After 90 minutes at that temperature, all that is left are the ashes which are sterile so pose no health hazard. On the practical side, the more they piled up the bodies, the more fat there was to keep the fires going. Maybe you find that a little cynical, but you didn't live through those times on the Isle of Man. I did, and cynicism became second nature. We became almost immune to other people's deaths. Almost.

But we lived every single day with the very real possibility of our own deaths.

There was no cure for Coviman-12. You either lived or died. The very young and very old died. The fit and healthy stood a chance, but not much. Very few caught Coviman and lived. The sick and infirm inevitably succumbed to the virus' ravages. Pregnant women were advised to immediately abort their foetuses to give the mother a better chance of survival if the virus struck. Mostly it was a waste of time; if Coviman-12 caught you, you might as well raise your hands and surrender to the inevitable.

At Bishop's College, or just plain College as we all called it, we were restricted to the school grounds. We were only allowed within ten yards of the boundary walls. Whenever any of us looked like getting too close, the armed street marshals, dressed like zombies from outer space in their protective suits, would point their rifles at us and warn us to back off. We had no doubt they would shoot if we didn't oblige. Everybody was in danger if the quarantine regulations weren't rigidly enforced.

THE ZONE

When founded in 1843, the College buildings opened their doors with only 46 boys. In 1967, there were almost 500 of us, though the day boys were now kept in their homes so only about 300 of us boarders currently occupied the buildings. Food and other supplies were delivered to College two or three times a week by lorries guarded and driven by suitably dressed soldiers. No-one knew how long the Coviman-12 outbreak would last. We just knew it would burn itself out in due course. It had to, because the island was only 36 miles long and 12 miles wide, so once we were all dead, it had nowhere else to go. When there were no more bodies left to infect, the virus would have effectively killed itself. Meanwhile, discipline at College was in steep decline. It was destined to get a lot worse.

As I stared across the quadrangle at the bloody mess that used to be a school pupil, I couldn't help but wonder at the blatant lifelessness of the young man called Braxton Boddington. It was like some indefinable current had been disconnected and a light of awareness switched off. Even to this day, the contrast between a recently deceased and a living person never fails to surprise and unnerve me a little.

Jack Parsons, who shared the small study with me, opened the door and made me jump. I had been deep in thought. He waved a hand in front of his face. "For crying out loud, Nick, open the bloody window will you? It's like a kipper-smoking factory in here."

I let out an incoherent grumble and slid the window sash up a fraction. It was true that our study was quite small and was now filled with my smoke.

Jack looked outside. "What's all the kerfuffle out there?"

"Someone's taken a hockey stick to Boddington. Spread his head all over the sundial."

He peered over my shoulder. "Bugger, that's clumsy. That's the second body in as many days."

"And both of them messy."

"True enough." Jack said. "The whole of the top of his head has gone. Doesn't look like Boddington did that to himself."

So much for my friend's skills of detection. Neither of us was destined to become another Perry Mason. I said, "Well spotted, Jack. Anyone who can pick up a hockey stick can create death, except for the victim."

"How the hell did we get to this, Nick?"

"You want my opinion?"

"I want your opinion."

I drew deep and long on my cigarette and looked my best friend square in the face. "You already know the answer to your question, Jack. You and I bring the bloody rain, not the scattered showers. We triggered events when we caught the Prinky flobbing his old chap about, between Lesley Parke's thighs."

CHAPTER TWO

On 6th January - my birthday - we had arrived back at College for a new term, all innocent and naïve. We shared hopeful eyes, bright faces, and polished shoes. None of us then had the worry lines and prematurely greying hair that gave evidence to the horror that was to unfold.

Then Coviman-12 took hold and we were quarantined into the school and its grounds. Bang! Just like that. No fuss, no messing, no preparation.

Several days after the virus was first discovered and quarantine restrictions put in place, Jack Parsons and I had gone for our evening smoke before turning in for the night. We had built a routine the previous winter term of sneaking outside, weather permitting, to get our final nicotine fix of the day. Stopping to have a smoke is a time-honoured tradition that non-smokers struggle to understand. There was a convenient hour between the end of prep - homework - and lights out, when we kept the tradition alive. A last smoke had become an important full stop in the long sentence of a day of study. That late January evening, the moon shone bright in the sky, which posed more of a challenge than usual. We had to dodge between bushes and around trees for cover of darkness. We were used to that; we'd been doing it for years. At least, due to the quarantine restrictions, there were many fewer masters on the premises to catch us. Most of them had been at home when the shut-down was announced.

The main college buildings were only 100 yards from the beach, but the granite boundary wall that had once been but a marker of territorial limits, had now become an actual physical barrier, beyond which lay certain death. It contained and confined us. And it ensured we were never going to go for a smoke behind the indoor shooting range that was located in the dunes. It had been one of our 'safe' places before quarantine. Dodging the bullet from cancer, or a chance encounter with a master, was one thing, but dodging a real bullet from a street marshal was quite something else.

Looking back, the pervasiveness of smoking at school was simply because we had been told how it was harmless and made us more manly. Every TV and magazine showed virile men and sexy women, all clutching their Marlboros or Craven A or whatever brand turned you on. For Jack and me, it was Embassy Tipped. They used to give gift vouchers in each packet. Smoke enough to kill yourself and you could use them to buy a decent coffin. In Britain, in the 1960s and even into the 1970s and '80s, smoking was permitted just about everywhere. Smokers could light up at work, in hospitals, in school buildings, in bars, in restaurants, and even on buses, trains and planes. But not at Bishop's College.

Nowadays, where there is smoke, there is an ecologist. You can light up a spliff and no-one will bat an eyelid. But if you light up a cigarette, you risk being publicly stoned to death. Maybe it has something to do with the fact that, to a non-smoker, a smoker's breath stinks like seagulls' farts. Something it took me a long time to figure out.

Jack and I ended up behind the chapel, just yards from the principal's house. There was a cricket pavilion a little further away, but that meant crossing a small stretch of open ground in clear moonlight, so we hunched down behind a stone buttress and lit up where we were. The school chaplain had been at home, outside the school gates, when the quarantine was enforced, so the chapel was closed and daily doses of religion were, for the moment, put on the back-burner. Not too many of us minded. If anybody wanted guidance, they could come to me - I can still quote great stretches of The Bible.

In fact, all these years later I can still recite the whole Latin grace that was said before all meals at College - 'Benedic Domine nobis et donis tuis quae de tua ...' blah, blah blah. It would have meant more to all of us if they'd said, 'Bless us Lord and your gifts, which from your bounty we are about to receive...' etc. etc. but I guess some traditions die hard and I wouldn't mind betting they're still using the same grace today.

Sorry - my mind got diverted. It happens more often in my old age. Jeez, how did it get so late in my life so soon? Which is why I want to get down the facts about College during the 1967 quarantine while I can still string a coherent sentence together.

So anyway, Jack and I found ourselves huddled down against the wall of the chapel, focusing all our energy on smoking a cigarette, as if it were a job. As I lit my smoke, I wondered how we were going to get through this quarantine without our regular nicotine fixes. We could no longer leave College grounds and nip down to the local shop, or up to the airport terminal next door. It was a problem that would demand some ingenuity, as long as it didn't include quitting. There's a sort of magic in striking a match and lighting a cigarette. That feeling of peace as the nicotine hits the back of the throat. I inhaled my first draw and blew out enough white smoke to announce a pope.

A slight breeze lifted the smoke away over the high chapel roof. The antiphonal sound of police sirens wailed somewhere off in the distance. We listened as the sounds grew faint, heading away from where we were. There was nothing at all unusual about emergency service sirens in these dark times. We chatted quietly together, Jack and I, just a bit above a whisper.

Rumour had it that one of the masters, Vlad Kelsey - Vlad being short for Vlad the Impaler - was bumming one of the younger kids and that the boy planned to tell his parents. But we all knew it would have to wait. Communications to College had been cut, with the exception of one telephone in the principal's office, and that one could only make contact with the people supervising the quarantine restrictions. There was nothing technical about that. It would be a few more years before the Isle of Man got Pulse Code Modulation, so all calls were still handled by switchboard operators.

The authorities were afraid of the worldwide reactions if people discovered just how much of a threat this virus was, so there was no means of making outside contact. No physical mail was leaving the island for fear it might be contaminated. The small handful of ham radio enthusiasts had had their equipment removed. Only official communications were permitted.

This was 1967 remember. That young lad who had drawn Vlad Kelsey's unwanted attention had no way to contact anybody. As Jack and I smoked, we were still six years away from when a Motorola researcher, would make the first mobile telephone call from handheld subscriber equipment. Even then, it was a further ten years before enough infrastructure was in place to make hand-held phones a reality for the ordinary everyday guy - and, as I now remember well, the battery pack was the size of a small car. Digital cellular phones were still thirty years away when Jack and I crouched down gossiping about the rear-entry rogering of one young student. It would be over twenty years before Tim Berners-Lee would create the World Wide Web and emails as we know them today became commonplace.

Life in 1967 was a long way away from the world as we know it today. You had to have lived it to understand it. If the rumour about Vlad Kelsey was true, the boy concerned would be unable to contact his parents until the island's quarantine restrictions were lifted. That's if any of us lived through it. Many didn't, including the poor young junior. His parents never did get to know about his violated bottom. Maybe that was good thing.

But Jack and I didn't know that as we took our evening nicotine fixes. At that stage, we still held to the belief that we were immortal. We decided that, if the boy did somehow make contact with his parents, the shit would hit the fan. Unless, of course, the boy's parents felt that a good bumming by one of the masters was all part and parcel of getting a fine British education. That had happened a few times before now. Stiff upper lip and all that. How times have changed. I was just grateful that I was built like a brick shithouse and didn't have fair hair and blue eyes.

Ah, life in a British Public School, eh?

A public school, by the way, refers to private schools given independence from direct jurisdiction by the Public Schools Act 1868. Today the term is more generally used to refer to any fee-paying private school. The 'public' name links back to the schools' origins as schools that were open to any public citizen who could afford to pay the fees. They are not funded from public taxes. So Bishop's College was a public school for private students, if that clears things up for you.

Of course, the rumours about Vlad and the boy could all be a complete fabrication. The rumour mill was alive and kicking at College, where gossip was passed around like whisper-hungry washerwomen. As Jack and I were talking between ourselves, discussing the finer points of poor little Charlie McDonald's enforced buggery, Jack suddenly pointed to the living room window of the principal's house, where a light had appeared. The light, though dim, spread across his small garden, reaching out towards us like an accusing finger. We had been crouched low, but now stood, ready to make a quick escape if necessary. Then we witnessed the events that would, for us, change the way we saw the future.

From where we were, we could see that the principal, a robust and energetic man in his late forties or early fifties, was snogging a lady who wasn't his wife. We knew it wasn't his wife since Cordelia Armstrong had been visiting relatives in Somerset when the island had been placed in quarantine. She wouldn't be back until it was all over.

Jack nudged me. "What ho, Nick, what have we got here then?"

I grinned. "We appear to be witnessing our beloved Prinky, groping — Oh Jesus, look who it is."

Jack took a couple of steps forward. "Bloody hell, it's Lesley Parkes. Pete's not going to be too pleased."

Lesley Parkes was the young assistant to the principal's secretary, a crusty bit of work called Miss Partridge who had a face like an anorexic sparrow. She always wore a starched white tunic and pulled her hair back so tightly it looked like the follicles might bleed. Partridge was due to retire soon, and Lesley was expected to take over when she did. Lesley was twenty-four, stunning good looks, with a diastema - a slight, but charming gap between her two front teeth. No wonder she elicited automatic trust and amiability from those round her. It was classic psychology. A tiny flaw that made her beauty more human.

Lesley was meeting our friend Pete Scott, a fellow sixth-former, in her bedsit high in the eaves when nobody was about. Pete always returned from his nocturnal encounters looking worn out, but as happy as a dog with a belly full of piss in a street full of lamp-posts. He reckoned Lesley had tits like a Dachshund's nose - decent size, pointy, only slightly saggy, nicely tanned, with large brown erect nipples. Jack and I were about to find out as we watched the school's esteemed head undo Lesley's blouse. Our smouldering Embassy Filters went forgotten between our fingers. At some point, mine fell to the ground, but damned if I know when.

Jack nudged me out of my trance and we edged closer to the house to get a better view. It seemed to us that Lesley Parkes was not being forced to participate. If she had been even a little bit more enthusiastic, she would have sucked the Prinky's face right off. Her tongue was dancing in and out of George Armstrong's open mouth. When he had removed Lesley's blouse, he unclipped her bra like an Olympic champion. That man could undo bras for Britain. We, on the other hand, were now totally useless, standing like a pair of zombies with mouths wide open, slathering like rabid dogs.

Pete Scott's description of Lesley's upper body parts had been no exaggeration. Her breasts were perfectly shaped and, just as Pete claimed, each one was a BSH - a British Standard Handful. Anything more would be a waste. Neither of us made the conscious decision to move closer, but Jack and I had always thought alike, and now we found ourselves within a couple of yards of the window. Unknown to us, we were crushing the Prinky's crocuses. But life was far more interesting inside the house where Lesley's skirt now lay discarded on the fitted carpet, and the Prinky was busy showing us his naked arse. Not a pretty sight, but we were both more engrossed in Lesley's perfect body than our school principal's rear end. Any naked woman was perfect to us at eighteen. But looking back even now, Lesley Parkes was the stuff of many a wet dream. And I speak as somebody with considerable experience of wet dreams.

Right now, Lesley was occupied stuffing as much of George Armstrong's manhood into her mouth as would fit. Jack Parsons and I had never seen anything to match the spectacle. I'd read about it in a smuggled copy of the Kama Sutra, but seeing it in real life gave it a whole new meaning. Nowadays, kids are watching free porn on the web before they're even out of nappies. But back then the best we had was Playboy or the more recent Penthouse, and they were nothing more than erotic titty magazines that we took to the toilets with us for a bit of hand relief. January's issue of Playboy cost five shillings, a tut, and a dirty look from the crusty old lady who served me in the airport shop. I have never bought a copy since. I've never needed to.

I heard Jack whisper the words "Fucking hell," to himself as we moved forwards and leaned on the window ledge to get a ringside seat. Lesley's knickers soon followed her skirt. She lay back on the settee and the Prinky's head disappeared between her thighs. A few minutes later he was on his knees and his arse was humping backwards and forwards. He started slowly, but he soon reached the speed where a petrol engine gets valve bounce. Lesley screwed up her eyes like it was hurting her. We later realised it was undiluted pleasure that caused her facial contortions. We still had a lot to learn at that stage of our education.

When I was just a small boy, I remember one time when my father was trying to prepare his Sunday sermon and I wouldn't stop asking him questions. My dad said to my mum, "Can you not shut Nick up, Emily? When he opens his mouth, a whole dictionary falls out." It was true then, and has been true all my life, but on that dark evening in early February of 1967, I was completely speechless. I stood there in the light of the principal's living room, casting the same shadow as always, but I couldn't talk.

I guess at this stage, Jack Parsons and I should have had the good sense to back off and leave them to it. Something to chuckle about later. But in 1967, at an all-boy's school, we were adolescents, we were horny, and we were naïve. So very fucking naïve. It was a combination that attached us to the principal's window pane like the resin glue in the woodworking shop. And there we stayed, open-mouthed statues, until it was all over and the unlikely participants were smiling and regaining their lost modesty.

I nudged Jack with my elbow and whispered, "Let's get the hell out of here before we are spotted."

But I was a few seconds too late. George Armstrong turned and realised that in his haste to disrobe his young secretary he hadn't drawn the curtains. He couldn't miss the two students glued to the glass with mouths agape and eyes wide like saucers. As we fled the scene, he stormed to his front door and bellowed, "Quine, Parsons, get back here, both of you."

It was pointless running. We had been well and truly caught with our pants down. But maybe not as far down as Mister Armstrong's. We stopped, turned and dragged our heels all the way back to the Prinky's house.

"Get in here," he snapped, moving aside so we could step into his hallway.

Lesley floated through the open living room doorway with a smile on her lips. "I'll say goodnight then, Principal. Thank you for a constructive meeting." She winked at me as she passed.

"Right, you two in here," the Prinky said, pushing open the kitchen door. "He pointed at the Formica table surrounded by wooden chairs. "Sit."

We sat.

"So what do you have to say for yourselves, creeping round at night staring through people's windows?"

I was on the verge of spluttering an apology when Jack opened his mouth. Unlike me, Jack was never slow coming forward. "That seems to be a moot point, Sir. Shouldn't the question be, what do you have to say for yourself getting all close and personal with Miss Parkes while your wife is away?"

The principal's face turned from angry to nuclear in just seconds. His clenched fist landed on the kitchen table with a thump. "What the hell do you mean by that remark, Parsons?"

Jack was as calm as the USSR's Leonid Brezhnev on election day. He already knew the outcome. "I mean, Sir, that we witnessed your whole tango with Miss Parkes. We found ourselves at your window quite a little while before you spotted us. We would have quietly gone back to our study, but now you've made it known to Miss Parkes that we were there. I don't have the sense that she is one to keep that sort of thing a secret."

I stared at Jack like he was off his trolley. Nowadays, kids take knives and clubs to school. Teachers run scared of the little brats and hide in cupboards. The thugs-in-training are free to bully and rob and use violence. They are rewarded with special classes with psychiatrists and social workers speculating on the reasons for their bad attitudes. Back then, in a public school where discipline was number one on the agenda, more important even than conjugating Latin verbs, you didn't talk back to any member of the staff, much less the chief honcho.

"Of course Lesley will keep it secret if I tell her to," the Prinky snapped.

Jack laughed in his face. I'd never seen him so brazen. "Maybe she will and maybe she won't, but what makes you think that we will say nothing?"

The principal's face had a decision to make. Either it could turn puce and explode, or it could turn grey as the blood drained to his feet. It chose the second course of action and George Armstrong sank onto the hard kitchen chair next to me, his head in his hands. Jack winked at me. He raised and then dropped the corners of his mouth, the smile over in a blink, so only I noticed it. "Time for us to dicker," he said.

CHAPTER THREE

When Jack said it was time to dicker, the principal raised his head, but very slowly. His face was flushed red. I didn't know whether it was anger or embarrassment. "There's nothing to negotiate," he growled. "What the hell could I offer you that would save my job, and my reputation?"

I noticed he didn't mention his marriage.

Jack smiled. "Exactly my own thoughts, Sir. What indeed can you offer us?"

I couldn't stop myself, "Jack are you sure—"

"Shhh."

The principal shook his head. "It's no good asking for money, Parsons. I'm not a wealthy man. In any case, I would never give way to that sort of blackmail."

"It doesn't have to be money. It can be things that we need. It can be favours to make our lives easier. It can be revenge to put right those things that are wrong. I have a couple of suggestions, but first, if you have a drop of Scotch with a splash of American, I think Mister Quine and I would find that most welcome. It might also help you to see that we can have an agreeable meeting of minds here."

Armstrong stared at Jack a while, seeming to make a decision. After a few seconds and without another word, he took himself to his lounge where we had watched the action take place minutes earlier. I glanced at Jack who offered me an enigmatic smile and put his finger to his lips. He was running things, not me. We heard the clink of glass, and then the principal came back into the kitchen with a bottle of Johnny Walker Black Label and three glasses on a small tray. Either he had no ginger ale or he'd forgotten. "Ice?" he asked without emotion.

And that was the defining moment when life for us began a roller-coaster ride through extreme highs and depressing lows. If only George Godfrey Armstrong had drawn his curtains before satisfying himself with Lesley Parkes, some things might have turned out differently. Small things sometimes matter more than we think.

The principal watched as we sipped our whisky. I wasn't used to it and it burned my throat, but I wasn't going to admit to that. The nearest we had to alcohol in our house was communion wine. After a meaningful pause, Armstrong snapped, "You said it can be things you need, favours to make your lives easier, or some sort of revenge. Where do you plan to start?"

Jack rubbed his hands together. "Just two things sprung to mind while you were getting the whisky. We'll not be asking for a lot, Sir. Let's begin with things we need. I don't think you'll find our request too onerous."

"Go on."

"Well it looks like we're going to be grounded for some time until this virus is under control. It will come as no surprise to you to know that there are quite a few smokers here at College. Trouble is, most boys are already out of cigarettes. Quine and I are down to our last few packs."

"So you need cigarettes?"

"Embassy Filters. We'll need 500 each - that's 25 packs each - per week, until we're allowed out of the grounds again. Then we'll go back to buying our own."

"How very generous of you, Parsons."

"It's the only way we can get them now. I presume, since everything is being delivered to College, you can get more or less whatever you need."

"And how much will 1,000 cigarettes cost me?"

"Embassy filters are just over five shillings a pack, so 50 packs will put you back about twelve pounds."

"And what do you plan doing with so many cigarettes?"

"Sell them, of course," Jack said. "All except those we need for ourselves. I reckon we can get ten shillings a pack or more. You are presumably going to have to order supplies for the masters who smoke, so just add a few more to the order. Let College pay for them. I'm sure Lesley can take care of the paperwork for you so that the nosey Miss Partridge doesn't get to know."

I was already struggling to cope with the tone of this conversation. Had it been me, I would have accepted some form of punishment for staring through Armstrong's window, and just got on with life as normal. But then, I wasn't a fee-paying student. I had, after almost seven years at College, realised that there was a subtle difference between scholarship boys like myself and the majority whose parents were fee-paying. The fee-paying boys had a certain chutzpah about them that we lower caste boys didn't have. They dared to do and say things that we didn't. They were privileged. Us, less so. It was never uncomfortable. It was just a thing. Jack was in his element and he knew he had the principal by his proverbial balls. As Margaret Thatcher would say twenty years later when dealing with François Mitterrand and the other EU leaders, 'One should always negotiate from a position of strength'. And Jack Parsons instinctively knew that without being told.

"And does that cover all your needs?" Armstrong asked.

Jack looked at me and I nodded. I had no idea what else we should ask for. "That's all for the moment," he answered. "Though we'll let you know if anything else should crop up."

"And what are the favours and revenge?"

"Ah well those might prove a little more problematic for you."

"I don't doubt it."

"Okay, let's start with Patterson."

"What? Mister Patterson? The master in charge of Lower School?"

"Yes, that's him. Nasty horrible creature, and it's time he was stopped."

"What on earth are you talking about Parsons? Cedric Patterson is firm but fair he's—"

Both Jack and I burst out laughing. Despite my grave reservations about making demands on the principal, I couldn't help myself. I said, "Firm but fair is Mister Patterson's catch phrase, Sir. His mantra, if you like. The more he says it, the more people believe it. But it's an outright lie. Patterson is only firm, if you translate that as meaning sadistic. But fair, he most certainly is not. He's an evil piece of work, and should never have been put in charge of young boys."

The principal raised his eyebrows. He seemed genuinely puzzled by my outburst. "I don't understand, Quine. Bishop's College takes discipline seriously, but we do not stoop to sadism. That's unfair to the college and to Mister Patterson."

Jack was taking a slug of whisky and spat it back into the glass. "Sorry," he mumbled, wiping his mouth on the back of his hand. "I can't believe you said that, Sir. You must surely have some idea what he's like?"

"It seems not, Parsons."

"Mister Patterson satisfies his depraved sexual urges on young boys aged thirteen and younger. He beats them for no reason other than his own gratification, then attends chapel every morning and prays like a zealot. The man is the worst example of a round peg in a square hole in this whole outdated establishment."

The principal's face displayed nothing but honest shock. He really hadn't known. "I don't understand," he burbled. "Explain what you mean. Give me an example, so I know what you're talking about."

I looked at George Armstrong and it crossed my mind that he must have been very naïve about some of the people in his employ. He genuinely had no idea what was going on right under his own nose. Mind you, Patterson could be very convincing if you hadn't experienced his brutality for yourself.

I said, "Okay, I'd be happy to give you an example, Sir. As you know, all Lower School boys are expected to wear caps. When I was in Lower School, as we walked past the front of the building, we were all required to raise our caps to the two bay windows in case either of the housemasters were in their studies and we couldn't see them. One day, walking to chapel in the morning, I walked alongside Patterson, talking to him. That evening he called me into his study and wanted to know why I hadn't raised my cap to his study window that morning. I pointed out that I was walking next to him talking to him at the time, so he couldn't have been in his study. He replied that his wife might have been inside. Then he beat me. I saw a wet stain on his trousers even before he began."

Armstrong looked appalled. "Are you sure your memory serves you correctly, Quine? After all, that would have been five or six years ago, wouldn't it?"

"Six years, and it's burnt into my memory like a branding iron. Another time, on a Sunday afternoon, my parents pulled up in their car. As required, I went in and asked for permission to speak to them. Permission was granted, for no longer than ten minutes. I made sure not to over-run the time, because I knew what Patterson was like. But again, I was summonsed to his study that evening. He asked what I had done while I was with my parents. I responded that we had chatted for a little while and that I had stepped out of the car within the allotted ten minutes. "And what else did you do?" he had asked. I couldn't think of anything else so I said that I'd done nothing.

Patterson eyed me up like a zoo specimen and asked if I had eaten anything. I remembered that my parents had given me an apple which I ate as we chatted, and I told him so. "In this house," he said, "we share. Your actions were selfish and you need to learn that I will not tolerate selfishness. Bend down." So he beat me for not sharing an apple amongst fifty other boys. He had to have been watching me through binoculars or something. As I went to leave his office, rubbing my arse, he dragged me back and bent me over again. He beat me again for lying, because I'd forgotten to tell him about the apple. Twelve strokes of the cane for eating a bloody apple."

The principal looked aghast. He was genuinely outraged and I almost felt sorry for him until Jack added, "Patterson once beat me for having been beaten."

"Whatever do you mean?"

"I was beaten by Mister Cash because I was doing my maths prep in his history lesson. That was fair enough. I earned that. But later, after rugby, when we were in the showers, Patterson, who always made a point of watching us shower, wanted to know what the bruises were on my arse. I told him, so he dragged me off, naked, to his study and beat me for having been beaten. Clothed is one thing, but naked is something else altogether. I couldn't sit down for hours and the blood stains never came out of my underpants."

The principal poured himself a large shot of Johnny Walker and slugged it back. It was obvious to us that he could see the truth in our stories but was finding them difficult to accept. I could have told him many more. I could have told him of the day when Patterson beat every single boy in Lower School, all fifty of them, because somebody had left a turd floating in one of the toilets. Nobody owned up to it because nobody actually knew whose it was - not even the culprit. Since that day, I've always checked after flushing. I could have carried on for a long time telling the principal about Patterson's evil regime, but I judged that we'd said enough. After a while, he asked, "So what do you want me to do?

Sack him?"

"No. He can't go anywhere while this virus is rampant," Jack said. "What we want is an apology from him."

The Prinky perked up. "That seems simple enough."

"I'm not done," Jack said. "I want him to apologise one-by-one, by name, to every boy who ever passed through Lower School."

"But that would be most of the senior boarders, wouldn't it?"

"Correct. And I want him to make his apologies in public. In the gymnasium."

"And what if he won't?" Armstrong asked.

"Then we'll have to think of some other way of dealing with him. But that would almost certainly be a lot more stressful than a public apology. He has to be stopped, Sir. He has done more damage to the students at this college than any other master. And that includes Vlad Kelsey and Mister Foister, who fight over the little boys. Vlad's up to his old tricks again, by the way. The word is that he buggered little Charlie McDonald the other day."

I added, "But one buggered boy pales into insignificance compared to the permanent damage that Patterson has wreaked on innocent young kids. Not only should he apologise, but he should also be banned from ever using corporal punishment again." When it came to Cedric Patterson, I discovered that I had no hesitation in speaking my mind to the principal. My former reticence had disappeared altogether.

Mister Armstrong thought before answering. "Stopping him from ever using corporal punishment is easy. We're going to ban it from next school year anyway. Our college is part of the Headmasters' and Headmistresses' Conference, an association of the head teachers of over two hundred independent schools. We have already discussed the removal of corporal punishment, and have agreed to stop after this school year ends. It is, indeed, an outdated form of discipline."

Jack laughed. "Bloody marvellous. We get our arses whipped for seven years, and then you stop with the beatings."

"There's always a cut off point for any changes," the principal said. He paused. "I will talk to Cedric Patterson and hear his side of the argument."

Jack growled back. "I was hoping you would be more amenable to agree a date when he will make a public apology to every boy who has ever suffered his sadism. No date, no deal."

The Prinky nodded, but with little enthusiasm. "Is there anything else?" he asked, "Or is that it?"

"I think we're good for the moment, Jack said, "Unless you can think of anything Nick?"

I shook my head. I was still trying to work out if I was awake or dreaming. The permutations multiplied, serpentining their way through my mind in set upon set, angle upon possible angle. Jack was demanding stuff from the principal of this renowned public school as though they were just two good ole boys settling a minor dispute. When I look back on it now, all these years later, I wonder whether Jack had made his mind up that we were all going to die anyway, so might as well kick against authority while we had the opportunity. I didn't need him to explain to me about the sadist Patterson. The man was a brute - a deviant dinosaur.

"Fine. We'll be off then," Jack said. "Good constructive meeting. Thank you for the whisky, Sir. Very agreeable, if I may say so."

Armstrong offered an uncomfortable nod. He had aged years in less than half an hour.

As Jack and I stepped out into the cool night air, Jack lit up a cigarette, knowing full well that the principal would be watching him. I declined. I knew I would have another smoke before going to bed, but I still felt the need to hold on to the old habits. Too much change too soon was bad for your nerves, I discovered.

"We need to keep this to ourselves," Jack said as we strolled alongside the shrubbery. "Knowledge is power, and if other people get to know about the Prinky and Lesley, they will also gain the power to squeeze concessions out of him."

"What about Pete?" I asked. "Shouldn't we tell him what Lesley is up to? He's besotted by her."

Jack took another drag on his cigarette. "We can't do that, Nick. We have to keep the genie in the bottle for our own use. Pete will grow out of her, or Lesley will dump him in due course for somebody else. In any case, like us, Pete Scott will be leaving here at the end of next term. Let's leave things to work out by themselves."

I grunted. I could see the sense in what Jack said, but it seemed so unfair that our friend was being two-timed by the girl he was so obviously infatuated with.

As we strolled back into the school buildings, immune to censure from any passing masters, we were confronted by a gorilla of a student and his devious shadow. The gorilla was one Brian Williams, known to all simply as 'Bruiser'. He was loud, arrogant and large. Very, very large with a neck like the stump of an oak tree - the perfect qualifications to reign supreme as the school bully. It was a title that he had earned and took pride in. He once informed me that the name Bruiser had been bestowed on him by Vlad Kelsey, the master who liked little boys too much for his own good. It's quite possible, since Vlad was into giving everybody a nickname. I was 'Crazy Man'. Jack was 'Stupidus Maximus'. But Brian Williams wore the mantle of 'Bruiser' like a heavyweight boxer wears his title belt. He was proud to be an arsehole.

His creepy sidekick was Toby Cochrane. Small, insignificant, and wearing glasses that were always smeared in snot, where he picked his nose. Cochrane looked ruffled, like he'd slept in his clothes. He was a very rumpled student. Even his face looked like it had passed through some sort of clothes wringer. "You two been out holding hands again?" he asked, making sure to stand partly behind Bruiser.

Jack was still smoking. He blew smoke in Cochrane's face. "What's it got to do with you, Cockroach? We go where we want. We don't need your permission."

I moved to walk past them, but Bruiser put out his arm to block me. It was a large arm, and quite hairy. "Answer the question, arsehole." His voice was like crushed gravel.

"What question?" Jack said. "I heard a cockroach fart, but I didn't hear any question."

"We want to know where you've been."

"Having a smoke, and talking to the principal." He held his smoking cigarette up. "See."

"You know you can't smoke," Cochrane said. "It's

against the rules."

"Yes I can. Look." Again Jack blew smoke at Cochrane. "Unpleasant little wankers like you should be against the rules, not smoking."

"Why have you been to see the Prinky?" Bruiser asked.

"Our business."

"My business too. It's late and you've been out there for over half-an-hour."

"Christ, Bruiser, are you timing our cigarette breaks now?" Jack moved forwards and pushed Bruiser's arm aside. The look on Bruiser's face was more confusion than anger. He wasn't used to people not doing his bidding. Jack and I walked on waiting for the explosion that never came. Cockroach was probably busy kissing Bruiser's metaphorical arse. Bruiser just slung curses at our backs as we marched towards our study smiling to ourselves.

Bruiser wasn't the sort of guy you wanted to make an enemy of, but we had already done that a long time ago.

CHAPTER FOUR

Pete Scott barged into our study a few days later with two white plastic carrier bags. Pete was handsome - too handsome for some people's liking. But he was a good mate. Academically solid and excelling in sports. It didn't matter whether it was rugby, cricket, athletics, or swimming, Pete was in there, showing everybody else how it was done. He was tall with a dark complexion and dark brown hair. I sometimes wondered whether he'd been crafted as a fully-formed adult from a kit of some kind. Little wonder he could joke about having not one, but two girls running after him during the school holidays.

He dumped the carrier bags on my desk. "Lesley said to give you these. Bloody things will kill you if you're going to smoke that lot in one week."

Jack looked up and frowned at me. "Not sure what you mean, Pete."

He laughed. "These are from the Prinky. Lesley told me you pair caught him showing her the length of his appreciation the other evening."

"Shut the door," I said. "You mean you know about Lesley and Armstrong?"

Pete closed the door and perched on the edge on Jack's desk. He nodded, the smile still plastered on his face. "Lesley and I have a sort of open arrangement when it comes to sex. We don't let other people get too close to us emotionally, but physically, we have no issues sharing."

"With the Prinky?"

"To begin with it was for a reason. He told her part way through last term that he was going to have to let her go. He reckoned she wasn't up to the job."

"Bugger, that's a bit unfair, isn't it?"

Pete chuckled. "Not at all. Lesley's a great girl and fucks like a rabbit, but she has trouble hitting the typewriter keys in the right order."

"So why was she screwing Armstrong?"

"Christ, Nick, why do you think? It was so she had something on him. After she first dropped her knickers for him last term, she asked if he meant it about getting rid of her. Without too much prompting, he told her he had changed his mind and that she could work here for as long as she liked, but she needed to brush up on her typing skills."

"And did she?"

Pete chuckled. "She did, actually. She's now reasonably competent."

"But she still keeps seeing the Prinky?"

"Because she enjoys sex with an older man from time-to-time - particularly our esteemed leader. Lesley tells me he has a few good techniques. What's the problem?"

Jack scratched his head. "And you're not jealous?"

"Why would I be? Last term, while she was seducing our illustrious principal and romping all over his house with him, he thought his wife was in Douglas at some ladies' guild or something."

"And she wasn't?"

"Cordelia Armstrong was neither in Douglas nor at

a ladies' guild. When Lesley was meeting with her husband, Cordelia and I were tucked up in a room at The George Hotel in the market square in Castletown."

We both sat up. "You what?"

Pete's lips parted as he smiled. "I gave Cordelia a good time, and she reciprocated. The first time just sort of happened, like accidental sex."

"What? You mean Mrs Armstrong was lying there, you fell down, and there just happened to be an erection in the way?"

Pete laughed. "First time was up against the wall in the entrance lobby to the chapel."

"The chapel?" I said. "Christ that's ten out of ten for originality. Bloody risky too, twenty yards from the principal's house."

"No-one goes in there during the day. I think Cordelia had planned it because it just coincided with her husband holding a staff meeting. She asked me to help her move something. I never did discover what it was she wanted moved. Anyway, after that, we plotted it better. To begin with, for Lesley and me, it was like a double insurance policy. If needs be, Lesley and I had both the principal and his wife just where we needed them. But as the term progressed it became just a load of fun for both of us. Well, for all four of us if you include the principal and his wife."

"And they didn't know what the other was up to?"

"I don't think so," Pete said. "If they did, they never said anything."

"So what else did you demand, apart from Lesley keeping her job?"

Pete looked puzzled. "Nothing. Why should we? Lesley reckons he's a horny bastard and I can vouch for the fact that Cordelia Armstrong is hot as the hinges of hell. She might be old enough to be my mother, but bloody hell, with no clothes on, she's downright uncontrollable. I thought I was athletic, but boy, she's up for a marathon every time. And I'll tell you what, chaps, she's got an arse on her like two bowling balls. Firm, round—" He looked at the pair of us with our mouths wide open. "Hey guys, this is all between us isn't it? You know, the sex, the cigarettes and the Patterson bomb? I wouldn't be telling you about it except that you saw what you saw."

"You know about wanting Patterson to apologise as well?" Jack asked.

"Yeah. The Prinky told Lesley everything. Not that he needed to. She nipped round the back of the house the other night and listened in to your conversation. I hope we can keep all this to ourselves."

"So do we, Pete. So do we. We need to keep control of the information."

Pete nodded. "Lesley and I never expected to get caught. Like I said, we've been seeing to Mr and Mrs Armstrong since part way through last term. It's an arrangement that suits us both. But I don't think George Godfrey Armstrong - or 'G-G' as Cordelia refers to him - has any inkling that his good lady is anything other than a loyal, devoted spouse. I don't think he'd be too pleased if he discovered I'd been helping myself to a slice of his wife."

Jack laughed. "He may have no inkling that his good lady is anything other than a loyal, devoted wife, Pete. But no more than she thinks that he is anything other than a loyal, devoted husband. You do like to live dangerously, don't you?"

I closed my open mouth and said, "Well, well, what a bag or worms." It was a gross understatement, but it was all I could come up with at short notice. Looking at Pete, and knowing how he was built, I'm not surprised that the ladies were attracted to him. There was not a wasted ounce of meat on his body. When he worked out in shorts and no shirt, he looked like a drawing of the human anatomy, each muscle group carefully delineated. The fact he was a real nice guy was a bonus.

"You've got to understand," Pete said, "from everything Cordelia has told me, she and her husband are actually devoted to each other. Having a clandestine relationship outside of marriage has proved to be a marriage saver for many people. Folk just like the excitement of surreptitious meetings and unrestricted sex. Lesley and I feel like that too. You need some excitement and passion in your life as well as affection and devotion."

"So it seems."

"And while I think of it," Pete said, "Lesley reckoned that Bruiser and Cockroach were hovering round the chapel that evening. She couldn't tell what they were doing or saying, but she had the feeling they were looking for you two."

"Why the hell would those two clowns be looking for us?" Jack asked.

"No idea, unless it was to give you a hard time out in the dark with no-one around. You're aware that Bruiser sees you both as a threat because you refuse to lick his arse."

Jack stuck his fingers down his throat and made a gagging noise. "Just thinking about it makes me want to soil my nappies."

I chuckled. "Tossers like Bruiser and his lapdog are two a penny, Pete. They usually back down when you stand up to them."

Pete sort of nodded. He asked, "Do you two plan making any further demands of The Prinky?"

"Don't think so," I said. "You, Jack?"

"No. If we get a constant supply of smokes until the emergency is called off. And if that sadistic bastard Patterson apologises in public to each and every pupil who has ever had the misfortune to find themselves under his evil regime, I think we can say that everyone's honour has been satisfied. We'll all be gone at the end of next term anyway and the Prinky won't have to worry about his little secret."

"You're right, he won't," Pete said. "Lesley's leaving too and coming to live with me. I've already got a job lined up working for a friend of my father."

"Christ, that's a bit permanent isn't it?" I said. "We're only eighteen, Pete, and Lesley's six years older than you."

Pete laughed. "You don't get it do you? Lesley and I are great together. We think the world of each other. But we don't mind spreading it around a bit. She knows about me with Cordelia and I know about her with the principal. We sort of compare notes afterwards and tell each other the things we enjoyed about our time with Mr and Mrs Armstrong. There's not a drop of jealousy in either of us. It's the perfect arrangement, no matter what our ages."

Pete was right, as it turned out. A week or so later, with Pete Scott's blessing, I lost my virginity to Lesley Parkes, and have never regretted it. She was, as I well recall, lush and smooth, and being inside her was like being taken captive in a silk purse. I can't imagine a nicer person to have taken away my unwanted innocence.

Looking back now, I just wish I had been deflowered a year or two earlier. During adolescence, we all had worries. During my time at College, I had worried whether my trouser bottoms were too wide. The Beatles and The Stones all wore skinny drainpipe cacks and there was me with sixteen inch bottoms. Were the other kids with fourteen inch bottoms laughing at me? I worried that I wouldn't make the school hockey team. I'd been on the team for three years running, but still worried I would be dropped. Was my dick big enough? A major concern for every boy at College, except Stu Newfield who had elephantiasis of the gonads. Would I pass my scripture exams? My father was a vicar, so I could fail everything except scripture.

But most of all, every single one of us was afraid of women. We worried that we'd die spotty-faced virgins, having never experienced a good woman. Nowadays, it seems that kids are rutting away before they're even off the mother's tit. But back then, sex was a luxury that few school-age youngsters ever experienced. Relationships with females were the major insecurity of every student who passed through College. Except, maybe, the genuine homosexuals who preferred Rick Tanner's shapely arse to any woman. There weren't many of those. Mind you, there weren't too many with arses as perfectly rounded as Rick's. Casual and brief homosexual encounters were commonplace after lights-out, but it was nothing more than mutual masturbation. Boys experimenting and getting rid of their hormonal frustrations with other boys. All of these things were like extraneous shit that occupied your mind instead of learning how to conjugate irregular French verbs.

The night I went to see Lesley, I was struck by her sultry beauty. She had large, full lips and almond-shaped grey eyes. Her make-up was immaculate. Once I had fumbled my way past her clothing and done what I came to do, I noticed that I had ruffled her hair and smeared her make-up. But she still looked bloody gorgeous. Most importantly, she assured me that I had scored well on both size and performance. After that revelation, I found it easier to focus on Chaucer's Canterbury Tales. I no longer had to worry whether I would die a spotty-faced virgin, having never experienced a good woman. I wouldn't and I had. The only nagging doubt was that she had actually said 'It's not how much you've got, Nick. It's how you use it.' Did she mean I should have had another inch or two? I've always wondered, even though I've never had any complaints in that department.

Anyway, I'm jumping ahead. That was still some days in the future, but it's worth noting that, as soon as I had been released from virgin prison, I found I could study academic matters with a degree of concentration I could never have managed while my mind was still attending the local loony bin of uncertainty. And once I'd started focusing more on my studies, I discovered that I knew almost all of the stuff anyway. I was already capable of remembering the difference between a gerund and a participle. My English master, Smoothie Jones, would have been proud of me if he hadn't smoked himself to death with Senior Service Extra Strength. Smoothie Jones - real name Steven - had had a proper Oxford education and could make magazine copy for washing-up liquid sound like the Magna

Carta. He was a damn good teacher, and a fine man.

I recall once in the house plays, our house, Colman House, put on Molière's 'Le Bourgeois Gentilhomme' and I had the lead role. At one point, during the dress rehearsal, I strode on stage wearing shiny, leather-soled shoes and they slipped on the wooden boards of the stage. I ended up doing the splits, which amused no end those who were watching. The following day, I passed by Mr Jones in the corridor. He whispered, "You'd better ask Rick Tanner if he'll rub them better for you," and carried on his way. I already had a lot of respect for him. Now I placed him on a pedestal. A master who was actually human.

It was clear that not all the masters were queer, fat, or eccentric and I shall always be grateful to Smoothie Jones - who was as close to normal as any of them came. I am, when I stop to think of it, now a member of a select group: the final handful of human beings who learnt to read and write before they learnt to eat a daily helping of East Enders or Celebrity Big Brother, or play some sort of mindless digital game on a mobile phone.

But, as I say, I'm jumping ahead and rambling a bit. Losing my innocence was still a few days in the future. I'm inclined to do that as I become more and more decrepit. Rambling, that is - not losing my innocence. So anyway, rutting with the delightful Lesley - and delightful she was - relieved me of the burden of one of my major worries, leaving me free to concentrate on my studies. And though Pete and Lesley had granted me the freedom to discover Lesley's hidden charms, the pair were married six years later. Jack and I went to their wedding in Norfolk.

Few people are capable of living their lives or

expressing opinions which differ from the prejudices of their social environment. Pete and Lesley were such people. They're still together now and happy as songbirds, having participated in the best traditions of Norfolk wife-swapping all through their marriage. Whatever floats your boat, I suppose. But then I wasn't exactly a perfect husband to my first two wives.

CHAPTER FIVE

Carl Giles was a cartoonist best known for his work for the British newspaper the Daily Express. He used his cartoon family to illustrate and comment on topics of the day. Certain recurring characters achieved a great deal of popularity. Amongst those was Chalkie, the tyrannical school teacher who Giles claimed was modelled on one of his childhood teachers. Chalkie was a humourless, autocratic, walking-skeleton of a man and our Latin master, Basil Harvey, could have been his identical twin.

Known by all the boys as 'Old Knuckle Dragger', Basil could easily have modelled for the Chalkie cartoon. He was tall, skeletal and lacked even the fundamentals of a sense of humour. He was mean and authoritarian and every time I saw him, I couldn't help thinking of old, cobweb-covered tombs, dead weeds, and rotting flesh. I always wondered where he kept his shroud. Knuckle Dragger Harvey's favourite punishment was to make a pupil write out the preface to the rule book twenty times. That was for minor offences like failing to conjugate a Latin verb in the accusative instead of the indicative, the vocative, or the what-the-hell-else tense. Basil almost certainly chose the preface to the rule book since it was he who had written the damn book in the first place.

The day after Pete had dropped the bombshell about his open relationship with Lesley, Jack and I were in the fug cupboard having a quiet smoke - yes, smoking occupied a lot of our time - when all hell broke loose. The fug cupboards, there were at least two as my memory serves, were unpleasant 'rooms' about ten feet square with large bore hot water pipes circling the walls from floor to ceiling. The theory was that you could hang wet sportswear on the pipes and they would dry ready for use again the following day. The benefit to us smokers was that there were large, square open vents in the ceilings to let the humid air disperse. Those big holes served well to draw our smoke out of the enclosure.

The fug cupboards were located near the stairs leading up to Farrow Hall, the huge dining room which I am sure J.K.Rowling later used as a model of Hogwart's Great Hall in the Harry Potter series. At the foot of the stairs was a double door leading out onto the quadrangle, an open paved area about 30 yards wide and 40 yards long, surrounded by studies and classrooms. The buildings around the quad were two and three stories high, but everything was overlooked by a massive square tower with a clock face on each side reminding us that tempus did indeed fugit.

As Jack and I reached the end of our smokes, a cacophony of sound reached our ears. We stubbed out our cigarettes and rushed into the quad to find out what was happening. There, we saw Knuckle Dragger Harvey dancing a tango on a mass of twisted metal and broken glass. He shouted and screamed at the object in question then stamped on it over and over until it was well and truly dead. We couldn't tell what he said, but he turned and shouted something through an adjacent study window. Then he stormed off, face as red as the Chinese flag, as angry as I had ever seen him. Which was quite a lot.

Jack and I dived back inside before Harvey got to

us. We strode to the study adjacent to the incident, the soles of our shoes squeaking on the old tiles in the corridor. Six boys shared he study, one of whom looked to be in shock. Phil Loveless sat on one of the hard plastic chairs with a face white like bones in the snow.

"Wazzup?" Jack asked.

Rick Tanner, the guy with the shapely arse, answered. "Bloody Knuckle Dragger has just destroyed Phil's valve radio."

We all knew that Phil was in love with his valve radio. He was fascinated by electronics and had built the radio himself. To us, it looked like a load of glowing glass bulbs on a metal base with bits of wire and solder sprouting in all directions. To Phil, it represented hundreds of hours of patient, careful work. And now it lay smashed in the quad because Harvey had stamped on it.

"What the hell happened?" I asked.

"The radio was where it always was; on the window ledge," Rick said. "It's not a bad day out - bit of early spring in the air - so we had the window open a little. The radio was turned on, but not loud. Harvey walked past the window and wanted to know why it was switched on. According to the rule book, it should have been turned off ten minutes ago."

"That's a bit picky," Jack said, "even for Old Knuckle Dragger. So what did he do?"

"He stuck his hand in the works. I think he intended confiscating it or something. Anyway, the radio bit back and The Knuckle Dragger got 240 volts up his arm. Made him twitch a bit. He looked like a spastic having a stroke. He completely lost the plot, knocked Phil's radio to the ground, and destroyed it. He stormed off to go and see the Prinky. Said he was going to have all radios banned. Said they should never have been allowed in the first place. Wicked distractions, he called them."

"Bastard." Jack said.

I looked at him and could see the cogs whir and the brain tick. I knew straight away what Jack was thinking. He was going to add another condition or two to our negotiated agreement with Armstrong. I would have been willing to bet that Phil's radio would be replaced and that there would be no radio ban. In fact, the current restrictions on radio use would almost certainly be lifted completely. I'd seen it happen before with Jack. Every now and then his mind would be stretched by a new idea and would never shrink back to its former dimensions. Now he knew he could demand things from our principal, he was going to make use of that negotiating power.

I thought I could read Jack Parson like a book. I was wrong. Jack's demands went way past what I had been thinking. Later in the day, he came back from his meeting with the Prinky looking as smug as the one who laughed last and laughed the longest. "Nailed the bastard," was all he said before sitting down with a wide grin on his face.

"What have you done Jack? Break it to me slowly; I'm more delicate than you. Who have you nailed?"

"Knuckle Dragger Harvey. That Neanderthal had already been and seen the Prinky and demanded that radios be banned in future. Told him they were an unnecessary aberration."

"And I guess our esteemed leader was going to bow to his wishes, Harvey being the vice-principal and all that."

"Armstrong told me he hadn't come to any

conclusion. He felt that radios had a valuable part to play if the privilege wasn't abused. He particularly felt they helped lift morale in these somewhat unusual and stressful times."

"So what did you say?"

"I advised him that the student committee had come to the conclusion that Harvey was well out of order destroying the hard work of one of the students. I pointed out that he could have told the people in that study to just turn it off, but instead he chose to become violent."

"Hang on a minute, Jack, what's this student committee?"

Jack chuckled. "It's just you and me at the moment, but I think we could soon persuade Pete, Rick and Phil to join us. It's time there was a bit of democracy in this bloody place."

"So what did Armstrong say when you told him?"

"He sort of nodded like he was giving it some thought. He observed that communication with the outside world was important in understanding issues that affected us globally."

"Sounds like you might have fed him that particular line," I said, laughing.

Jack continued, "I also told him that the students should decide for themselves when to have their hair cut. Knuckle Dragger has been going round with his little notebook for too damn long making sure we are all shorn bald like him. It's bloody crazy. This is the late sixties, not the bloody thirties."

"And the Prinky agreed?"

"After a little gentle persuasion."

"You reminded him of what we witnessed between

him and Lesley the other evening?"

"I didn't need to. That was implicit. I said that what we were asking for was no more than simple progress and that Harvey was out of touch. In fact, I strongly suggested that Harvey no longer be vice-principal. I suggested that, when things get back to normal, Dick Curtis replace him. He's more in touch with modern society."

"That's if Curtis makes it."

Jack nodded. "It was just a suggestion."

I shook my head. Things were going further than I had imagined. "Bloody hell, Jack, that's pushing your luck isn't it? It's like we're trying to run the school."

"What can the Prinky do, Nick? We have him over a barrel so we might as well make the best of it. People like Knuckle Dragger Harvey don't belong in a forward-looking educational establishment. I mean, for God's sake, he even teaches a dead language. He's an unwanted refugee from another era."

"And you reckon he'll be removed as vice-principal?"

"Judging from what the Prinky said to me after he'd thought about it a little while, it's a certainty. Don't be surprised if Harvey walks out of here for good at the end of term, or whenever this bloody virus stops spreading."

"Jeez, how things can change in just a few days."

"Oh, and while I was there, I asked Armstrong what arrangements had been made for Patterson to make his public apologies. He said he was still trying to convince Patterson that he had to do it, but that Patterson was having none of it."

"So that one won't fly then?"

"It bloody well will, Nick. Don't underestimate my determination to see that bastard suffer the indignation of a public humiliation. You know as well as me that he should never be in charge of young kids. He's a pervert and a sadist. He made our bloody lives hell."

"And you can be a ruthless, unforgiving, and a manipulative bastard, Jack Parsons."

He grinned. "I know. But what I'm saying is fact, Nick, and you know it. Patterson made our lives an absolute misery."

I nodded and added, "Us and every other kid who went through Lower School."

While there was no doubt that what Jack said was true, I hadn't yet got my head around the idea that we could, or should, be calling the shots. In my character, a kind of wildness and a deep conservatism are wound together like hair in a braid. It was the crazy part of me that had gone along with Jack's scheme and now, in a strange way, I almost wished we hadn't witnessed what we did. I sort of wanted things back as they were, warts and all. Jack and I only had one more term after this and we were out of this hell-hole. Let the future generations of oppressed boys deal with this crap.

Jack sensed my unease. "If you are neutral in situations of injustice, Nick, you have chosen the side of the oppressor. Sometimes we have to take a stand against what is wrong, even if it's an established regime like here. You and I have the chance to make College a better place for future generations. We would be failing in our moral duty if we threw away the opportunity we now have."

"What about Phil's radio?" I asked as an

afterthought.

"Prinky agreed to buy whatever Phil needed to replace it. He said for Phil to make a list of whatever he needed, and he would have them brought over from England as soon as possible. I also told him that Knuckle Dragger should apologise to Phil. But I knew that one would never fly. Harvey is a leftover from a bygone age. He'll walk out of the school, knuckles dragging on the ground, before he'll apologise."

"That wouldn't be a bad result," I said, not knowing how prophetic my words would turn out to be.

CHAPTER SIX

The establishment of Bishop's College was funded by the Bishop Farrow Trust, originally set up in 1667 to provide education for clergy and their sons on the Isle of Man. In somewhat dubious circumstances, money allocated for a theological seminary to train Manx priests became used to fund a private educational establishment, most of whose pupils over the years have not been Manx, nor even had any connection with the island.

Knowing what I now know about Bishop Farrow, I think he may have been proud of the bullying that went on at College. Bullying was a thing at every school during the 1960's. It was particularly prevalent in the British public school system. Let me paint you a vignette - a thumbnail image as they would call it in today's digital world - of what it was like to be a student at Bishop's College in 1967. There was racism and hate, and there was bullying and harassment. I've seen cowering youngsters and towering seniors. Nowadays, it's all happening online with Internet trolls, but at College it was out in the open for all to see. And it was physical - very, very physical. I have no idea whether things are better in public schools nowadays, but I suspect most people who read this can only imagine what it was like to experience the physical torment in person. At the time, parents relied on teachers to solve the problem. That was a mistake. At College, the teachers were in many ways responsible for the problem. Either they were bullies themselves, or they looked the other way when bullying was going on right under their noses.

So, while bullying was becoming more and more a big 'no-no' in state schools, in 1967 it was alive and well in most public schools. None more so than at Bishop's College. Life is a fight, but not everyone's a fighter - otherwise, bullies would be an endangered species. I guess, then, that I need to own up to the fact that I bullied someone while I was at College. I don't have to tell you. You would never know if I didn't come clean, but I need to unload on you without withholding any facts. I need to be honest with you, and I need to feel some form of release for everything that happened in the early Spring of 1967.

In my own defence, I have to say that I only ever bullied one boy. And it was well earned. He was an unpleasant blond-haired object called Richard Barlow who, during my first few weeks at College, bullied the hell out of me. I was eleven years old and fairly robust, but I had never been picked on before, and didn't know how to handle it. One day, I snapped and landed a roundhouse punch on the side of his head. It hurt my hand, but I think it hurt him a lot more. He cried a lot and kept well away from me after that. But I caught him several times bullying other kids. In my naivety, I believed that, when a bully was held accountable for his actions, his future actions would change. I was wrong. So in the end, I decided to give Barlow a dose of his own medicine. I kicked three shades of shit out of him for almost seven years until the day the world turned upside down. But we'll come to that soon. I don't regret for one second giving him a hard time. Jerks like him need someone to put them on the right path in life.

Jack once asked me, "What if Barlow grows up to

be the only surgeon who could save your life?"

I laughed. "He's studying Geography, History and Economics. He wants to be a banker - that's with a silent 'w' in case you wondered."

"So what if you desperately need a loan and he's the only banker left in the world?"

"I'd come and scrounge some money off you."

I didn't need to worry either way. Richard Barlow didn't live to see the end of that term.

Captain of the school bullies was Bruiser Williams, the big gorilla who had questioned us when we got back from our talk with the principal. Brian Frederick Williams wasn't the sort of guy who'd return your wallet with the money still in it if he found it on the street. Nor was he the sort who would stop and help a struggling older person change a tyre if he came upon them broken down by the side of the road. Brian Williams was just a thug. He had no redeeming features. None whatsoever.

Bruiser generally left people like Jack and me alone. He got his kicks from picking on kids who dared not answer back. He reckoned it built character, so I pointed out that bullying built character like nuclear waste created superheroes. He looked at me blank. He didn't even understand. Some people don't - the stupid ones.

I once walked in on Bruiser scaring a youngster shitless by making him stand on a chair while he placed a wire noose over his head and around the fluorescent light fitting. If the boy had fallen, the light fitting would probably have crashed down on top of him. But he didn't know that and had just peed in his pants. That was the sort of mean, nasty brainwashing that Bruiser Williams was known for.

And Cockroach Cochrane used to egg him on. Cockroach was the sort of person who would pin a 'kick me' sign on someone's back, and then tell Bruiser how clever it would be if he kicked him. He'd load the gun and tell Bruiser when to pull the trigger.

Bruiser had been expelled the previous term but had returned to college a couple of weeks later after his father, a wealthy stockbroker, had put pressure on the school trustees. He had also made a hefty donation to the appeal for funds to construct a new science block. That was how the public school system worked, and probably still does today. Bruiser knew he was on his final warning, but it didn't change his bad habits. In fact, in some ways, it might have made him even worse. I think he felt he was untouchable.

It didn't come as a huge surprise to Jack or me when, a few days after the Basil Harvey incident, Bruiser barged into our study along with his shadow Toby Cochrane - the sneaky little tosser who would steal the pennies off a dead man's eyes when no-one was looking. Cochrane may have been the loader of the gun, but he was nobody without his over-sized mentor.

"What are you two knob-heads up to?" Bruiser demanded, sidestepping any form of introduction.

I looked up. "What's up, Bruiser?"

"I said, what are you two knob-heads up to?"

"I heard you, but I have no idea what you're talking about. Do you want to give me a clue?"

"You bloody know."

"What do I know? Spell it out for me will you? I have a shit load of English prep to do and it's got to be handed in tomorrow morning."

"That stupid little prick-sucker's school magazine that you two contribute to."

"You mean 'The Farrowvian', named after our eminent founder?"

"Knobhead little rag. What's all that shit about bullying? You wrote it Parsons."

"I did," Jack said, tapping his biro against his lower lip, "and proud of it. I'm sure you'd agree with us, Bruiser, that bullying is bad for the soul. It makes people depressed and demoralised if they are hit by other pupils."

"It turns them into men," Bruiser said. "Doesn't it Toby?"

"Sure does, Bruiser. Turns them into men is what it does."

"What would you know, Cockroach? You're still a child, hanging onto Bruiser's coat tails and giving his arse a regular licking."

"No bugger touches my arse," Bruiser said.

"Metaphorically speaking."

"What's that mean? Stop talking crap and use words we can all understand."

I took a deep breath, like a parent speaking to their child. "A metaphor, Bruiser, is a figure of speech in which a word or phrase is applied to an object or action to which it is not literally applicable." I was the one studying English, so I knew these things.

"See, there you go again. You two talk crap, and it needs to stop."

Every time I spoke to Bruiser, I tried to work in one or two words of more than one syllable, just to piss him off. Worked like a charm. "Yeah well plenty of clever boys at this college have to pretend to be not clever or else they get bullied by the stupid ones."

"I'm telling you, talk fucking sense," Bruiser shouted.

Cochrane chirped up, "He said that—"

"I know what he bloody well said. I just didn't understand it."

I smiled to myself and chalked up another win.

"You're also fucking with the system," Bruiser continued. "I don't know how, but you are. I hear you want Patterson to apologise to everyone that's ever been through Lower School. I also hear you've got Knuckle Dragger Harvey demoted from vice-principal. Is that right?"

"I'm afraid you've called our bluff," I said. "Guilty as accused."

"If it is true, does it bother you?" Jack said. "Don't you want to see Patterson and Harvey pulled down a peg?"

"Suits me just fine, but I want to know how you did it. Or are you just bragging about something you had nothing to do with?"

"I wasn't aware we were bragging about anything," I said. "Why would we brag?"

"Because you're a pair of useless tossers. You may not have said anything but other people have. Word's getting round that you have something on the Prinky. So come on, what is it?"

I glanced at Jack who frowned back at me. "No idea what you're talking about," he said to Bruiser. "Who told you we had something to do with the recent changes?"

"Some of your little bum boys. Those two queers, Loveless and Tanner for example, have told some of my group that they think you're blackmailing Armstrong."

"What group's that?" Jack asked.

"My group. People who like me and know I'm the only one who talks any fucking sense round here."

Jack sniggered. "And you reckon we're blackmailing Armstrong? That's ridiculous. How would we blackmail the principal?"

"That's what we want to know, don't we Toby?"

Cochrane stepped out from behind Bruiser's bulk. He had a burbling, uneven voice, as if he were always speaking through a throat full of packed phlegm. He wasn't fat, but his flesh had a loose, pale look, like the undersides of some mushrooms. "Yeah, that's what we want to know," he repeated. "How are you blackmailing the principal?"

"Shut up, Cockroach, you tedious little shit," I hissed. "We're talking to the organ grinder, not his monkey."

"You can't talk to me like that."

"I think you'll find he can," Bruiser said, seemingly content that we considered him to be the organ grinder. It was our first hint that Bruiser's mind had travelled beyond the caveman system it normally inhabited. But he soon went back to his cave. He turned his attention back to Jack and me. "I'm going to smack some heads together till I find out what the fuck is going on. You get that? If there's a scam going on with Armstrong, I want in on it."

"If I find out what it is, I'll let you know," Jack said, trying to look serious.

"Make sure you bloody do," Bruiser said. He turned, pushed Cochrane out of his way and stormed off up the corridor, his feet sounding like the beat of an angry bass drum. Toby Cochrane scuttled after him, leaving our study door wide open.

I stood up to close it. "What do you reckon, Jack? Are we getting into deep shit?"

"I'm not too bothered," Jack said. "Only you, me and Pete know the truth. So long as we keep it to ourselves we'll be fine. The others can speculate as much as they want, but it will be nothing more than educated guesswork. And in Bruiser's case, you can even take away the word 'educated'. He's digging in the dark because there's a situation that he neither controls nor is part of. As you know, that's not his style. Well tough shit, he'll just have to put up with it."

"Do you reckon he means what he said about banging heads together?"

"Phil and Rick are big enough to look after themselves. Bruiser only picks on easy targets. So whose head is he going to bang? Nobody knows anything, so nobody can say anything. If that pisses Bruiser off, so much the better."

CHAPTER SEVEN

Life after the outbreak of the Coviman-12 Virus on the island was never going to be easy. We were all scared. In fact, we were shitting ourselves, but none of us were ever going to admit it. Night-time was worst, when I was alone with my thoughts. I would lie awake and the only thoughts that would swim into my head were about this damned virus. It felt like I was being injected with darkness. Like cold, black water settling into my body where my blood and marrow used to be, pushing every other feeling and thought out as it filled me from my feet to my scalp. It left me with nothing but a body filled with shadows.

But we went on. We had no choice. Big brave men, all of us, at the age of eighteen. We were immortal. It was the us-versus-them attitude that we used to hide behind to cover up how terrified we were of falling foul to the virus. We knew that if it ever hit College, it would sweep through us like treading on a dog turd and walking it through onto the lounge carpet. It would end up stinking out the whole house.

And it wasn't just the thought of catching Coviman-12 that changed our lives that Spring term at College. When the island-wide quarantine had been sanctioned on the Isle of Man it was sudden and non-negotiable. It was enforced by thousands of storm troopers from the mainland - soldiers, policemen and the like, all in protective clothing. It would last exactly as long as the virus kept on killing people. So we suddenly found ourselves not only confined to the school and its grounds, but when the gates were metaphorically locked shut, only ten masters and three of their wives were left inside College. The rest were locked out, and many never came back. We assumed that, like thousands of others, their bodies had been burned up in the hills. Jim Lewis, Harry Bird, Stan Collis, Mr Jarman - we never did learn his first name - Tony Peacock, and many others never came back to College. The same was true for a large percentage of the two hundred or so day boys who were confined in their homes. Many were our friends. Most were lost to Coviman.

So we found ourselves with just ten masters and 317 boys inside the boundaries of College. From a situation of fifty-two teaching staff and average class sizes of about ten or twelve, we had to somehow work with only ten masters. In reality it was nine, since Gordon Maxwell taught only music and Chaucer. Not everybody's chosen topics. But Gordon Maxwell's wife, Angela, had a degree in modern languages so she helped out with French and German. Arthur Bannister, however, was a dead loss. Arthur was like a stray dog that had been adopted by the school. He had suffered as a submariner during the war and it had affected him in more ways than one. So those pupils taking maths at A level found themselves being instructed by a master who had never taught anyone older than thirteen.

Arthur's stock phrase, which he wheeled out daily like an ageing relative in a wheel chair was, "Algebra is the same as arithmetic, only different." Well we sort of know that, Arthur. Even us English students. What about telling us how to calculate the area under a curve, or teach us some differential calculus - the application of the derivative of a function? Nope. Best Arthur could do was, "Algebra is the same as arithmetic, only different," so pretty soon people stopped turning up to his classes. Andy Pemberton and Phil Loveless kept going, otherwise it would look bad on Arthur, but they just sat quietly at the back and played chess on a little portable chess set. Arthur droned on at the front like it was a normal day. Another of his regular expressions, "Change side, change sign. That's what you do in algebra, boys," was regurgitated when he felt like a change of pace.

But everybody loved poor old Arthur despite his waffle and bumble. We all adopted him and treated him kindly. He once beat me for smoking. "Can you please be in my study after lunch?" he asked in a sad voice reminiscent of the Tex Avery cartoon character 'Droopy'. Like Droopy, Arthur's movements were slow and lethargic, and he spoke in a jowly monotone voice. I knew why Arthur wanted to see me so I girded my loins accordingly. It was a Tuesday, the day we spent the afternoon marching round the parade ground dressed as soldiers. Our combined cadet force was meant to instil character and nurture leadership qualities. Didn't work for me. But it did give me a reason to wear thick khaki army trousers over my normal trousers, with underwear and swimming trunks beneath. First of all, Arthur apologised for having to beat me, then he patted my bottom and said, "Good padding boy, good padding." And then he promised it wouldn't hurt. And it didn't, bless him. I hope he's in a better place.

One of the consequences of the Coviman-12 outbreak was that the ten masters and three wives were housed on the campus. The main school buildings comprised a massive grey stone edifice. Lower School stood on its own 150 yards away. It wasn't a school as such, just a cold, draughty, soulless building of uncertain age that housed junior pupils when they weren't attending lessons. Unlike the main buildings, which were constructed from large limestone blocks, Lower School was rendered with cement that had simply turned grey with age. It suited its character.

Upon the island being quarantined, the fifty or so pupils who were housed in Lower School were wedged closer together to make room for the masters. There were four large dormitories in Lower School, with about fifteen boys in each. Beds had been rearranged to squeeze the same number of boys into three dormitories. In addition to the dormitories, Lower School had three living spaces, occupied by Cedric Patterson and his wife, plus the two assistant house masters. There was one further living accommodation for masters at College, and that was in the main school buildings. It was occupied by Mr Bond, who taught history. He too had a wife. So in Lower School there were six masters and one master's wife to share the empty dormitory.

One of the Lower School assistant housemasters - my old friend Smoothie Jones - vacated his small apartment and offered it to Gordon Maxwell and his wife Angela. It left six men sharing a dormitory and washroom facilities designed to house about fifteen pupils. It seemed somewhat extravagant for an emergency situation, but who said that life in a public school in the late sixties should be fair or reasonable? Particularly when there were few other options. There were a few small empty rooms that had been used by kitchen and maintenance staff in the main buildings but, with no cleaners available, these were considered to be unsuitable. In any case, they were spread about the school and out of touch with other locations. The masters felt that life would be more convivial if they were all together.

Angela Maxwell, wife of the music teacher, was in her mid-forties. She was not your picture postcard pin-up. She was a little large round the waist, a little large round the chest, a little large round the hips and thighs. Well, okay, Angela was well padded and a little on the plump side. But when you're a hormonal eighteen-year-old, little things like that don't matter. She had tits and a bum. When she walked, her breasts bounced and her backside featured a seductive sway with the rhythm of her steps. She smiled a lot, she smelt good, and she wore bright red lipstick which sort of drew you in. I'm not sure if she meant to flaunt her hard-boiled sexuality, but it worked anyway.

Mrs Maxwell's vocal range was masculine, like someone straining to lift a barbell in a gym. But it sounded to us for all the world like Eartha Kitt singing, 'Just An Old Fashioned Girl'. My God, Eartha, you were sexy. Yet there was something about Angela Maxwell. She had an intelligent face, with steady enquiring eyes and an expression that made you think she was just on the verge of asking you something.

Because of Angela Maxwell, Jack and I developed a new interest in studying French but we were already in our final year of A level classes which had nothing to do with other languages. I was studying English Language, English Literature, and History. Jack was taking Physics, Chemistry and Biology.

Pete Scott, on the other hand, had been studying French, German and Art for his A levels, so he now scored a double dose of Angela Maxwell every week. Pete being a horny so-and-so, took it upon himself to educate Angela in the fine art of satisfying a concupiscent eighteen-year-old. From what he later told us, she had almost certainly had some considerable education in that department over the years because she already possessed certain skills that weren't even in Pete's repertoire. And Pete had a broad repertoire. She was what today's generation would call a MILF. (Look it up if you don't know.)

When Pete came into our study with a triumphant look on his face, Jack and I just glanced at each other and shrugged. Pete Scott was never going to change and good luck to him. This time next week we could all be dead, so you might as well grab what you could, while you could. Our only question was where he had done the dirty deed.

Pete chuckled. "Angela had a word with Matron. She let her use the storage room where they keep the clean bed linen."

"What? Just like that?" I asked.

"Almost," Pete replied. "Apparently she said 'no' to start with, but then Angela told Matron she knew about her and Jaap van Anrooy, and might be inclined to spread the word if she didn't feel able to help."

Jaap van Anrooy was the head boy and, once a week while the rest of us were dressed in army uniform marching up and down - in order to improve our characters and build up our leadership qualities, remember? - he and Matron were hard at it in her little flat at the top of the building. I'm pretty sure that they didn't restrict their horizontal pleasures to just Tuesday afternoons either.

"Matron thought it was their big secret," Pete continued, "and was quite shocked that Angela knew. But she soon relented and gave Angela the spare key to the linen store."

"And did Mrs Maxwell meet your requirements?" I asked, grinning from ear to ear.

"She was lush," Pete said. "She was there in abundance, but the body, despite the extra padding, was well sensuous. Unlike Cordelia Armstrong, whose arse cheeks are firm and sculpted, Angela's were a bit saggy and squashy like a soft meringue. Same for her tits. If you didn't have a torch and a compass, you could get lost between her tits. But she was wholly delightful nonetheless. A truly voluptuous feast of womanhood."

"A few extra wobbly bits though?" Jack asked.

"Oh, you savage, Jack Parsons. One of Auguste Renoir's last paintings was called 'The Bathers'. The two fleshy nymphs are considered beautiful and graceful by all the art critics, yet they carry quite a lot of extra flesh. Same for 'Seated Bather Drying her Leg'. A little extra weight doesn't necessarily mean ugly."

"You're the one studying art," Jack said, "So I guess you should know."

"I'll admit there was a lot of her to explore," Pete said, "so we've chalked up another rendezvous next week. Same time, same place."

"And you'll take a torch and a compass next time, so you can find your way out?"

Pete shook his head in mock sympathy.

"You are a horny sod," I said.

"Jealousy, my boy, will get you exactly nowhere. You want more than a quick wank, you need to go looking for it. And then ask - nicely."

I laughed. "Pete, there are just six females in College

at the moment. Untouched by your over-used dick are Mrs Patterson, Mrs Bond, Matron, and the repugnant Miss Partridge. I wouldn't touch any of them with yours, never mind with mine."

"Beggars can't be choosers," Pete laughed.

"Then there's Angela Maxwell and Lesley Parkes, both of whom you already seem to have bagged for yourself."

"You're forgetting the maids in Farrow Hall." Pete said. "There's only two of them now, but they look quite tasty. Anyway, nothing is exclusive. You're aware that Lesley and I have a fairly broad outlook on these things."

"You mean I could talk your Lesley into a bit of nookie?"

"Of course you could. I've already explained that we have an open relationship. She'd quite enjoy deflowering you pair. She's always going on about having more people about my age instead of her extra-curricular activities being limited to George Armstrong."

"And what makes you think we haven't already been deflowered?" Jack said.

Pete smiled to himself, but neither Jack nor I missed it. Eighteen years old and I'd never even come close to having sex. Neither had Jack. This was 1967 when stuff like that didn't happen till you were married. Nowadays, young people have moved away from feeling guilty about sleeping with somebody to feeling guilty if they are not sleeping with someone. I don't see why people at that time made such a heavy guilt trip out of sex, but they did. A left-over from Victorian ideals I guess, where stuff like that only happened behind closed doors. Having wallowed in sexual liaisons all through my adulthood, I now realise it isn't anything complex. It is simply the best thing in life, even better than food. But when Pete suggested that his girlfriend take us in charge and plunder our innocence, neither Jack nor I knew that. We still had some growing up to do.

It was a different world then. Sure, I'd groped a few breasts and fumbled around in a couple of girls' knickers. But the enigmatic clitoris was still a mystery. Nobody except its owner was sure precisely where to find it or what it did. Lots of things were mysteries, but that doesn't mean there isn't an answer to them. It's just that at the age of eighteen, we hadn't found the answer to the clitoris - yet. Just give us time and aim us in the right direction.

Some of the girls from the Lady Burnside School for Girls, just a mile away, were up for it. But they only ever went so far. In any case, they were mostly socialites with an IQ lower than their bra size, which didn't make them much fun to be around. The contraceptive pill had only been available in UK for six years. Health Minister Enoch Powell announced that women who wished to have oral contraception would be able to receive it through the NHS and the family planning association. What he didn't mention was that women under the age of eighteen would need their parents' permission.

Since nobody trusted the London Rubber Company to produce a safe condom, groping and fondling was as far as it went with the Burnside girls. In any case, in those far off days, using a condom was like washing your feet with your socks on. They've become a bit more refined and sensitive since then, but at the time, you could make wellington boots or diving suits out of them.

So a bit of fumbling with bra catches and floundering around trying to get past industrial strength knicker elastic was where my life experiences started and ended. Neither Jack nor I ever admitted it to anyone at school. But teenagers can sniff out weakness and lies the same way pigs can sniff out truffles. And, somehow, everyone knew. They also knew that they were in exactly the same boat, so the subject was never really discussed - except by the lucky few who had gone all the way, and they made sure everybody knew.

When Jack asked what made Pete think we hadn't already been deflowered, Pete didn't respond directly. What he did say was going to profoundly change Jack and me forever. "You want me to ask Lesley if she's interested?" he asked.

Jack and I looked at each other and discovered we were both blushing. We both wanted to blurt out a loud 'yes' but we both wondered whether we would be up to the job. It was an unspoken fear.

Jack Parsons and I were night and day, yin and yang, fire and ice – totally different but near inseparable. We brought out the best and worst in each other, always striving to outdo ourselves for outrageous stupidity and daring each other to take the next ill-advised death-defying step. We never acknowledged the reasons why we behaved the way we did, we just knew that we understood each other and that we had each other's backs. I recall Jack as always charging at the world head on with a full head of steam and a gleam in his eye that said, 'Here, take this, world'. Right at the moment, Jack was as reserved as me.

"First one to say 'yes' goes first," Pete said.

No further hesitation, I said, "Sure, Pete, that would be nice. But maybe one at a time?"

Pete laughed. "I wasn't suggesting a twos-up for your first time. I'll have a word with Lesley. I'm sure she'll be more than willing." He turned and left Jack and me looking at each other. Both of us were blushing, but we'd learnt more about each other in those two minutes than we had in seven years at College together.

I liked to think I was smart, but Jack was the emotionally intelligent one and could always see through my bullshit. He'd call me out on it and make me face up to who I was and what I could be. No-one else did that; they just thought I was either bad, sad, mad or a combination of all three. But now, we saw through each other's bullshit and ended up howling with laughter. Two days later, I was no longer a virgin. The following day, neither was Jack Parsons. We never discussed the subject. It was private and very personal. But we both knew we had become different people thanks to some specialised private tuition that wasn't on the official timetable.

Lesley Parkes was accommodating and gentle with us. As I believe I may have already mentioned, she was lush and smooth and silky and…. well you get the picture. I can't imagine a nicer person to have taken away my unwanted innocence. I take my hat off to you my dear - and the rest of my clothes if it's still on offer.

CHAPTER EIGHT

Sport was a significant part of life at College, particularly the two big beasts, rugby and cricket. In athletics, Jack was a runner. I was more the muscle man, good at javelin, discus and shot put. Both of us were okay at rugby, but neither of us excelled at cricket. On the other hand, what we had both mastered was hockey. Jack on the right wing and me as the fullback that nobody ever got past. Both of us were on the 1st XI for three years running, which meant we'd first been selected to represent the school when we were only fifteen. My ideal life would have been to play hockey every day and getting laid every night. One out of two would have been an improvement on my current situation.

The best game of the season was always the boys versus the masters. Usually it took place towards the end of the Spring term. It was a friendly and I particularly enjoyed it because Steven Smoothie Jones was the masters' right winger and I was the boys' left fullback, so we would clash - in a goodhearted manner. Field hockey strikers have to be adept at shooting goals, possess quick stick skills, and have explosive speed and athleticism. Smoothie had all of that. He ran like a cheetah - well, like a cheetah that smoked too much. So I needed to have a strong tackle and be able to channel him into a weaker striking position. That had always been my strength.

During the match against the masters, with a polite smile on his face, Mr Jones would hook my hockey stick with his to stop me clearing the ball, and I would stand on the blade of his stick to block him from striking the ball. Lots of fouls called, and plenty of free hits given, but it was all in the spirit of fun and extremely bad sportsmanship. While the ball was at the other end of the pitch, we would spend time throwing easy banter at each other. When it was obvious the masters were getting thrashed, as they always did, Smoothie would say stuff like, "It's not whether you win or lose, Nick, but how you play the game."

"In that case," I'd quip, "why bother keeping score? I think it's about 27-0 at the moment."

So he would trip me up and push my face into the mud while the referee wasn't looking.

"Learn to lose with class," I would mutter, picking myself up.

"Class, my ass," he'd say, charging off to try and pick up a loose ball.

It was always a fun game, and hockey between Steven Jones and me was not for pussies. Technically, it was defined as a sport. Words like play and game got thrown around liberally to shield its true nature. But hockey against the masters was warfare with a polite smile.

Despite the virus and the quarantine, College made an effort to stick to the accepted routines and demonstrate some form of normality. As far as possible, sports were continued as before. Cross-country was out, which annoyed Jack, but pleased me. At least sport offered a diversion from the ever-present threat of death by an invisible enemy. And for sure, that played on all our minds inside our protective cocoon. It was an all-enveloping life-sucking drain on our moods and morale. The

Students v. Masters game had been brought forward from mid-March to mid-February. It was difficult to drum up enthusiasm for anything, so a clash with the masters was just what everybody needed to lift our spirits and divert our thoughts from the death plague that was just beyond the granite boundary wall. Any day, it could climb that low wall and kill us all. The British will play field hockey in any weather. Thunder, lightening, plague of locusts. Nothing can stop the hockey - except possibly Coviman-12, but it hadn't yet climbed the wall into College grounds.

Give it time.

One thing that almost stopped the game against the masters was that there weren't anywhere near enough masters to make a team. Ruling out the old and unfit, only Smoothie Jones, Jim Turnbull, and Jeremy Foister were young enough and fit enough to take part. Vlad Kelsey, Cedric Patterson, and Arthur Bannister were well past it. Gordon Maxwell, the music master, had no idea what hockey was all about, and probably couldn't tell the difference between one end of a hockey stick and the other. Dicky Bond was a rugby man. He thought hockey was for girls, so didn't want to know. David Cash was game, but was well overweight, so they used him to block the goalmouth. To help make up the numbers, our principal, George Armstrong, stepped into the breach. He may have been in his early fifties, but he was not a man who spurned a challenge. Give him a problem to get his teeth into and you would notice a glint appear in his eyes. He was not designed to give up. It just wasn't in his DNA.

To facilitate the annual clash, the masters' team was supplemented by six boys. To this day, I don't know how or by whom the decision was made, but somehow Bruiser Williams ended up playing for the masters - like myself, in fullback position. Maybe the principal thought it might help Bruiser to integrate a little better into College life. Maybe they thought that somebody with his bulk would intimidate the opposition. But Bruiser was too slow of foot and of thought to be much of an obstacle. In fact, I don't think he even understood the rules. After about ten minutes, when it was obvious just how bad he was, it became a game to dribble the ball close to him, but just out of reach. He would swing wildly with his hockey stick, hoping to connect with the ball, but it was never going to happen while there were good players who were fleet of foot on the opposing side.

Bruiser tried to shoulder charge Jack several times, but Jack ran circles round him. At one point, Jack sent the ball between Bruiser's feet, and ran round him to pick the ball up again on the other side. Bruiser was getting more and more frustrated and irritated. He was warned more than once for bad language and then the inevitable happened and Bruiser lost the plot.

The midfield positions in field hockey are the inside-left, the inside-right, and the centre half. They will roam the field and are used to link the defence with the offence. They are often required and expected to do a lot of running to make this happen. Our best mid-fielder by a long way was Andy Pemberton. He seemed to have an inexhaustible supply of energy. He was determined to be on the winning side, even in a friendly match. So when, for the tenth time, he ran straight past Bruiser like he wasn't there, Bruiser blew a fuse. As Andy trotted back to position after scoring another goal, Bruiser swung his hockey stick and smashed it into Andy's leg.

To this day, I don't know whether the crack that resounded round the field was the hockey stick hitting Andy's shin, or the sound of Andy's bone breaking. The result was the same. Neither Andy Pemberton nor Bruiser Williams ever played hockey again. Mind you, neither did any of us. We heard later, via Lesley, that the principal had told Bruiser that, as soon as the restrictions were lifted, he would be required to leave college and never return. There would be no more chances. Meanwhile, Andy was trapped in a bubble of quarantine that had no hospital facilities, no way to set a broken leg, in fact nothing that would help him heal. Matron gave him Paracetamol. In her paucity of any medical training, she thought it would keep him out of pain. Andy needed something with a bit more punch than Paracetamol. So that his groans of pain wouldn't disturb other students at night, he was placed in one of the gloomy, unused employee rooms just off the stairs that led up the tower. He never walked properly again.

The game against the masters was intended to reduce tensions and raise morale. It succeeded in doing exactly the opposite. Bruiser Williams had become a loose cannon, and it was best to avoid him. But that wasn't always possible.

Public school was like prison. I don't know if they've improved over the years, but back in 1967 there was no privacy. Dormitories were Spartan and were shared by many boys. They held narrow steel beds with hard, horse-hair mattresses. In the communal washroom next to the dormitories that Jack and I shared with about thirty others was a range of hand basins, and three baths. Bath nights were allocated on a rota. You had 15 minutes, and then the next person on the list got a chance. There was one toilet with no door. It's a very strange experience to be soaking in your bath while another boy is using the toilet about three feet away from you, in open view.

Showers after sports were different again. Apart from School House, everybody shared the same showers. There were no waist-height modesty walls or shower curtains - just a load of shower heads and taps sticking out of the walls. The changing area, too, was completely open and it wasn't possible to dress or undress with any privacy. The only people of authority were the praepositors. They would usually overlook any minor altercations, as long as the contestants didn't make too much noise. But in the heat and noise and steam of the showers scores were settled and deals were done.

As most of us showered in silence, stunned by the savagery of Bruiser's attack, he strode into the showers like nothing was wrong. He caught us all staring at him, so picked on the smallest boy there - Bill McCormick. "What you staring at, you little tosser?"

Bill was small, but not one to be cowed by Bruiser's size. "I'm staring at you, you stupid lummox. What the hell got into you?"

Bruiser took two steps in his direction, but stopped when he saw every one of us move towards him. He was brave against a single small boy, but not against a united hockey team "It was just an accident," he said. "There are injuries all the time in sport."

"No way," Jack said, from behind him. "No way was that an accident. You hacked down Andy Pemberton on purpose because he was a far better player than you."

Bruiser wheeled round. "What the fuck's it got to do with you, Parsons? You're talking crap as usual."

"It's got everything to do with all of us, you scrotum. You just smashed Andy's leg, and we can't even get him to a hospital. What the bloody hell were you thinking?"

"He wasn't thinking anything," I said. "Bruiser has problems thinking when his little Cockroach isn't about, don't you, Bruiser?"

"Brain-dead cretin," someone called out from behind me.

"Bloody buffoon," someone else shouted.

Like a cobra surrounded by a hoard of mongooses, Bruiser turned in a full circle, then spun back again. After a moment's silence during which we expected all hell to break loose, he turned and pushed his way past Jack and me. "I'll square with you two shit-stirrers later," he muttered.

CHAPTER NINE

After another encounter with the principal, Jack came back from his meeting with the news that Cedric Patterson had finally agreed to make his apologies, but wanted time to negotiate the when and the how. "I suppose it's better than nothing," Jack said, slumping into his chair. "I would have liked to have seen him make a bloody spectacle of himself in front of the whole school, but it seems that that's out of the question. To balance the equation, the Prinky has agreed to ban any and all beatings immediately. He is going to tell the masters who are still here straight away, and then advise whoever is left of the rest when they are able to come back to College."

"It's a good result, Jack. No more poor little buggers getting their arses whipped by that sadistic bastard."

"Beating boys was bloody archaic," Jack said, "And it was going to stop anyway if what the Prinky said was true. I'm more concerned that Patterson is humbled. He deserves a lot worse, but at least he'll have a problem holding his head up afterwards."

As I was speaking, the door burst open and Bruiser Smith once again blocked the doorway. I sensed he wasn't alone and my instinct was proved correct when Toby Cochrane peered round Bruiser's arm. There had always been a strict dress code at College. Grey shirt, black tie, grey trousers, College blazer. On Sundays, today, the shirt reverted to white and the trousers and blazer became a grey suit. Bruiser had his tie undone, no jacket, and his shirt cuffs rolled back to show his hairy wrists. He didn't look very happy. Bruiser never looked happy.

"What's up?" I asked.

Bruiser stood there huffing heavy breaths out of his nostrils, looking like a stick of dynamite about to explode. "You fuckers, stirring everyone up against me in the showers yesterday. I should break your fucking arms for that."

"You already broke Pemberton's leg," Jack said. "Settle for that, Bruiser."

"Yeah, well don't do it again, or it will be all the worse for both of you."

Jack and I waited for more.

"What did you want?" I asked. "Was that it?"

Bruiser looked like the oven light had just come on. "Oh yeah. You heard about Knuckle Dragger Harvey?"

"No. What have I not heard?"

"He's dead. Shot by the street marshals."

I dropped my pen on the desk. Jack's chair scraped back on the wooden floor. "You what?" he said.

Bruiser grinned at him, but it wasn't a pleasant grin. It was a grin that said, 'You've fucked up and I'm here to tell you about it'. What he actually said was, "Pantin and Crossley - you know, those two holier-than-thou little creeps - they were knocking a tennis ball about, up on the top playing field when their ball landed a bit close to the wall. When they went to fetch it, one of the street marshals spotted them and warned them off. Eventually he let them get the ball, but covered them with his rifle all the way. He told them that one of their masters had been shot dead a couple of nights ago. Walked straight out onto the main road and didn't stop when warned."

I reached to my neck, my collar feeling more like a noose than anything else. I tugged and fumbled the buttons until they popped open, then I gasped for air. My mouth was unhinged so I couldn't speak, but Jack could. "How do they know it was Harvey?"

"The bloke described him. Looked like a walking skeleton, he said. Was staggering around the place. Anyway, they found identification on him. It was The Knuckle Dragger alright."

"Bloody hell," Jack muttered.

Bruiser laughed in a grunting Bruiser fashion. "I thought that would amuse you. No more fucking Latin lessons at College from now on. The street marshal told Pantin and Crossley that they had a lot of people commit suicide by walking out in the street and not stopping when told to. Seems that it's the best thing to do when you get the virus. Quick and painless. Get it over and done with."

Jack and I sat with mouths open. My stomach squeezed and I was sure I was going to give myself a headache if I didn't relax my face from the building tension. "So do you think Harvey had contacted the virus?" I asked, thinking aloud.

"I can't imagine so," Jack replied. "If it happened a couple of nights ago, and he was contaminated, we would have known by now. College would be under the same restrictions as the rest of the island."

"I don't give a shit about all that," Bruiser snarled. "I still want to know what you have on the Prinky to get all this to happen. It's got to be something juicy."

"I keep telling you Bruiser, I don't have a fucking

clue what you're on about," Jack said.

"No? Then how is it you're selling fags at ten bob a packet? Where are they coming from Parsons? Nowadays, everything that comes into this school comes via the principal's office. He wouldn't be ordering smokes for you if you didn't have him over a barrel."

He had us there. We hadn't thought that one through. Or at least I thought so until Jack said, "You're wrong, Bruiser. It's Miss Partridge that's getting them for us."

Bruiser thought about that. Thinking was a slow process for Brian Williams.

"Why would that old bag Partridge get cigarettes for you?" Toby Cochrane asked. "She looks like a fucking dead bird."

"Because she's a friend of my great-aunt," Jack said, quick as a flash. "Jessica Partridge and my great-aunt went to school together."

Bruiser never thought to ask how Jack had contacted his aunt, all contact with the outside world being cut. But Toby Cochrane did. He might have been a creep but he had a few more brain cells than Bruiser. Mind you, a tadpole had a few more brain cells than Bruiser. "That's rubbish," Cochrane said. "How would your old aunt know you needed cigarettes?"

Jack laughed. "Because she's a smart cookie, Cochrane. Not like you. She might be a bit ancient, but she's wicked as hell. Great sense of humour too. As soon as the news got out that the Isle of Man was in lock-down, she knew we wouldn't be able to get smokes. She taught me how to smoke when I was ten. So she rang Jessica Partridge and asked her to help out for old time's sake."

"There are no phones in or out of the island since quarantine," Cochrane said.

He had us there.

"Wrong again," Jack said. "Aunt Lucy got hold of Jessica Partridge the day that quarantine was announced. Initially, there was some confusion with the telephone operators. They thought it was only outgoing calls that weren't allowed. All calls were cut the next day."

"What, and that crabby old cow agreed to smuggle cigarettes for you?"

"As a favour to my aunt and for old time's sake, she agreed to turn a blind eye. But she didn't want her name to be associated with it, so it was all done through Lesley Parkes. Lesley deals with a lot of the administration, including ordering food and other supplies from the people administering the quarantine."

Cochrane looked suspicious and Bruiser Williams looked puzzled. But he was still a threatening figure, blocking the doorway as he did.

My knee bounced under the desk as I murmured, "It's the truth, Bruiser. To start with it was just a couple of hundred ciggies a week to see us through, but Lesley upped the quantities because it wasn't just Jack and me that needed a smoke. Miss Partridge has no idea whether a smoker smokes ten a day or a hundred a day. She just sniffed and went along with it apparently."

After a pregnant pause, Bruiser said, "So how come you got Knuckle Dragger Harvey sacked from the vice-principal's job?"

"We didn't get him sacked," Jack said. "I went to see the principal because I was angry. I thought that

Harvey trashing Phil Loveless' radio was just a step too far. The Prinky agreed with me. In fact he said that he'd been considering how to deal with Mister Harvey's rigid authoritarianism for a long time. I guess the radio incident gave him the excuse he needed to demote Harvey and reduce his powers. Looks like poor old Knuckle Dragger was more affected by it than we thought if he went out and got himself shot."

"You don't suppose he was drunk do you?" I said. "You know he liked a little tipple on the side?"

"Who? Harvey?"

"Christ yes. The man's insides must have been pickled considering his age. He was what they call a functioning alcoholic."

"You're being fucking ridiculous," Bruiser hissed.

"I don't think they are, Bruiser," Cochrane said. "The Knuckle Dragger always came into classes stinking of that Old Spice deodorant. But you could small the alcohol through the splash-on. He smelt like a walking brothel."

"Of course he did. It was to cover the smell of booze," I said, agreeing with Cochrane for the first time in my life.

"No worse than smoking," he said. "Smoking can kill you."

"Sounds better than being bored to death by an obnoxious little fart like you. Anyway, you have your answers, so now maybe you'd like to go away and annoy somebody else."

I glanced at Bruiser, sensing his suspicion as it billowed across the room. Neither he nor Cochrane looked totally convinced with our story but between them they couldn't think up any rebuttals that would make sense. They stood in silence. Cochrane tucked his chin into his neck and flashed me a questioning look. I've always been leery of silence. It doesn't necessarily mean you've won the argument. Often, people are just busy reloading their guns. But soon, Bruiser turned, swiped Cochrane out of the way and strode into the corridor. Then he turned round again, stepped back into the study and overturned my desk with me trapped behind it. His second departure was more permanent, though about as graceful as an axe murderer.

Jack came to my aid. We righted the desk and picked my papers and books off the floor. Jack slammed the door shut. "He's fucking unstable, Nick. He's getting worse every day. I heard that, yesterday, he grabbed some small kid who had dared to tell Bruiser he didn't want to join his little gang. So Bruiser smashed his nose to pulp. What an arsehole."

As I finished straightening my papers, I said, "When someone picks on me, Jack, it's always a comfort to know that someone else thinks they are arseholes too. It helps a great deal. I think that's some kind of rule for the universe, don't you? But what can we do about him? He's getting more and more unpredictable."

"Don't know mate, but we need to think of something."

"We could begin by swapping desks," I said. "Just coz I'm nearest the door, he decides to give me the good news instead of you."

Jack wasn't taking any notice, but he laughed anyway. In fact, he began to laugh like a loon. "Bloody priceless," he said. "You and your Basil Harvey excuse. Other than maybe a glass of cider, I doubt that The Knuckle Dragger has ever had an alcoholic drink in his life. How did you dream that one up?"

"I didn't, Jack. Harvey really was a piss-head. You being in the science stream didn't see as much of him as I did. He arrived for lessons sometimes with a far-away look in his eyes. Could hardly focus. Speech a bit slurred. I didn't make up what I told Bruiser and Cockroach. I reckon Knuckle Dragger Harvey got himself well and truly hammered then went for a walk. The street marshal said he was staggering, so that tends to confirm it. Anyway, don't look at me Jack Parsons. What's all that crap about Jessica Partridge being a friend of your great-aunt? I didn't even know her name was Jessica."

"Nor did I," Jack chortled. "I've no idea what the old crow's name is. And I don't have a great-aunt either. In fact, I don't even have an aunt. But a bit of bullshit seemed to work."

I laughed. "You reckon you want to be a doctor when you've finished your studies? I think you could make a better living as a bloody salesman. You can come up with any old shit and make it sound half convincing."

Jack turned his palms up to the ceiling and fell back into his chair with his smile crinkling the corners of his eyes. "It's just my natural brilliance and charm," he said.

I raised one eyebrow and grinned.

Jack continued, "Bruiser fell for it, coz Bruiser's thick. But I don't think that little worm, Cochrane did." Jack's face took on an unusually stern look. "Seriously though, Nick, this virus is getting everybody down. Everyone is nervous and getting short tempered over little things."

"Can you blame them? Any moment now, just one person could fall ill and, next thing we know, they'll be burning our bodies up on the hills."

Jack nodded. "I know, but there's nothing we can do about that. There is something we can do about Bruiser, and that's to work out some form of defence. Have you noticed that, more and more, he has a band of acolytes following him round, doing his bidding? And I don't just mean his head honcho, Cochrane."

"Yeah, I did notice. But did you spot a similarity about his disciples?"

"What? Like they've all got big noses or something?"

I laughed. "There's a commonality, Jack. Take a look next time you see them swarming in Bruiser's wake."

"Come on, tell me. You know I don't like suspense."

"Well for a start, they're all from Dickens House."

College had long had a house system - useful for battles where the combatants were rugby players, or athletes. There were four houses at that time, Colman House, Dickens House, Walkers House and School House. School House pupils always saw themselves as superior to any of the others. But the real king of the jungle was Colman House that Jack and I belonged to. Last year, we had bagged every single house shield except one - music. Walkers House was welcome to that one. Though the houses were different, they were nothing more than abstract concepts separated in the real world only by open corridors. The intermingling of students had never been a problem.

"His little followers are all from Dickens House," Jack said, "because Bruiser himself is from Dickens House, I suppose."

"More than that, Jack. Look again, and you'll find that, with the exception of Cockroach, none of Bruiser's entourage are sixth-formers. Take a look next time he's swanning round the place with his zombie acolytes behind him. I can't see anyone who's not fifth form or below. Fourteen-, fifteen-, sixteen-year-olds, all of them."

Jack thought for a moment. "It could just be coincidence. But on the other hand, they are more easily swayed by Bruiser's bully-boy tactics. Sixth-formers are more inclined to just ignore him."

"It could be. But I don't like the amount of influence he seems to have over them whether it comes from simple bullying or something more malevolent."

"Malevolent like what?"

"Like maybe Cockroach acting as Bruiser's spokesman. Do you know the 'Friends, Romans, countrymen' speech?"

"Not verbatim," Jack said. "Julius Caesar in Shakespeare, wasn't it?"

"Mark Antony delivered a eulogy in honour of the recently murdered Julius Caesar. Friends, Romans, countrymen, lend me your ears; I come to bury Caesar, not to praise him. The evil that men do lives after them, blah, blah, blah ... In a clever speech, Antony turned the mob against Brutus and the other assassins."

"So what's that got to do with Cockroach?"

"I'm wondering if the combination of Cochrane's mouth and Bruiser's muscles is turning gullible young minds into little Bruiser zombies. I have the feeling he's up to something and is using his threats and Cockroach's rhetoric as an incubator for recruitment."

"What would he be up to?"

"Don't know. But we have a situation where there are over 300 pupils locked down here, and just ten masters."

"Nine, if The Knuckle Dragger is dead."

"Okay, nine masters who, frankly, now have very little authority over pupils. Bruiser looks like he's building up to take over the place or something."

"If that's true, there's nothing we can do about it, Nick. Anyway his little followers are nothing more than a swarm of flies gathering round a large piece of walking dog shit."

"Also Bruiser is reading a lot into our secret source, don't you think?"

Jack chuckled. "And so he should. But we're never going to admit to it."

There was a quick tap on the door and Pete Scott came in looking curious. "What was all the noise?" he asked.

"Just Bruiser Williams getting a bit anxious," I replied. "He wanted to know where the cigarettes were coming from, and Jack spun him a yarn about Miss Partridge - Jessica Partridge, would you believe - getting them as a favour for Jack's great-aunt, who she knew at school."

Pete laughed. "You've got to be kidding. If Miss Partridge - and she's Edith, by the way - knew what the Prinky had sanctioned Lesley to do for you, she'd blow a fuse. Anyway, I just popped in with a bit of news about Basil Harvey."

"We heard," Jack said. "Stepped out of the gates and got himself shot."

Pete nodded. "I never liked him, but it still comes as a bit of a shock. Bit sad really."

Jack and I nodded. Unpleasant though the man was, his death was not at all what we had foreseen. Seeing the fires on the hills every night when it turned dark, we thought we were immune to death, but discovered that, when it was close to home, we were still as shocked as we would have been before the outbreak of Coviman-12.

Pete brightened a little. "Anyway, talking to Lesley, it seems that the virus could be stabilising a bit. As you know, Manx Radio broadcasts the official government line, which means nothing at all. You might as well listen to the weather forecast to get the football results. But Lesley's dad is something in the government over here and she's been chatting to him on the phone from the Prinky's office. Seems that the number of known new cases has gone down a little in the last few days. It's still very severe, and it's by no means under control. But thanks to the rigid quarantine measures, the virus may be finding it harder to spread through the population."

"Does anyone yet know how it started?" I asked.

"The fact that they've brought in Britain's foremost bio-weapons experts raises the question of whether Coviman-12 is the result of naturally emergent mutations against the possibility that it may be a bio-engineered strain meant for defensive immunotherapy protocols. It may have been released into the public by accident. Lesley's dad says that the bio lab opposite the airport has been taken over by the military, so that might give a clue as to what these so-called experts are thinking."

"Jeez. Thousands dead because somebody took the lid off a jar of bacteria or something."

Pete shook his head. "According to Lesley's dad, they're still shipping in food and supplies for over 45,000 people, but that figure includes all the storm troopers out on the streets and other British government agents and scientists over here at the moment. A quick check of the maths, and it seems well over 10,000 people have probably already died."

"Time to make a will, I think," Jack said. "I hereby leave my stash of mucky mags and my spare cigarettes to Nick Quine. Can you witness that for me Pete?"

Pete laughed, but it lacked any real humour. When he left, I just sat looking around at my surroundings. - the grimy cream walls that had last had a coat of paint before I was born - the badly-fitting sash window held together by coats of paint applied over many years. Questions rolled around my head like dice, but above all, I wondered if this was going to be my final resting place. I hoped not. I had a life I wanted to live.

CHAPTER TEN

The next day, just after lunch, Jack marched into the study looking rather pleased with himself. Jack always looked rather pleased with himself when he was planning some new adventure. He reached behind him, between his blazer and his shirt, and pulled out two long kitchen knives. He offered one to me. "Defence if Bruiser becomes really aggressive," he said. "Just try not to kill him though."

I took the proffered knife and turned it over in my hand. "Where did this come from?"

"The kitchens. I stayed behind after lunch and had a word with one of those two red-haired maids. You know, the ones who look like sisters."

"The ones Pete mentioned last week?"

Jack nodded, with a smile playing in the corners of his mouth. "I told her we were planning a science project but that we weren't allowed to take anything sharp out of the lab."

"So she gave you two knives?"

"Yeah, sort of."

"What do you mean, sort of?"

"Well, no, actually. She said they were needed in the kitchens. But while we were chatting, I leaned up against the worktop and slid these down my belt."

"You must have been talking quite some while for her not to notice you doing that."

Jack's face took on the appearance of a child who'd ended up with just what he wanted from Santa. "I got more than the knives, Nick. A lot more."

"What do you mean?"

Jack laughed. He said, "According to a book I was reading the other day, he who is satisfied with what he has, is a rich man. But I don't buy that bollocks. I think you've always got to go looking for more. So I started chatting to Rhonda - that's the maid's name - and I asked her what she thought about being incarcerated with over 300 horny adolescents. She thought it was funny. But she also said that the idea of catching Coviman-12 scared the living daylights out of her. She said that she and her sister —"

"The other one really is her sister then?"

"So it seems. Anyway, Rhonda said that she and her sister wanted to live a bit longer before dying."

"I can sympathise with that point of view, Jack. That about sums us all up. Everybody's nerves are shredded. If just one person in this place gets infected, we're all up shit creek without a paddle."

"Which is what I told her. Anyway, the long and short of our conversation was that recently, Rhonda and her sister - it's Michelle, by the way - have been nipping down to the swimming pool late at night and skinny dipping. Since we were quarantined without notice, they have no swimsuits, so they go naked. She reckoned it was just a silly bit of relaxation that stopped them from dwelling too much on all the shit that's going on outside College grounds. Said it was like injecting a little bit of innocent excitement in their lives. Stopped them from going stir crazy."

"A sentiment we all share."

Jack paused while he examined my expectant face. "She and her sister are hot and horny, Nick. I ended up having a good snog with her before I came back down here. Her hand was stroking my dick over my trousers before we heard someone coming. As we parted, she said she'd like to take it a bit further so she's invited us to join them tonight. Midnight at the swimming pool. Take just a towel."

The knife I'd been holding fell from my fingers. "You're kidding, aren't you?"

"I wouldn't kid you about something as serious as this, my friend. Rhonda reckoned it's dead easy. The masters are all shut away in Lower School, except for Dicky Bond who's way over the other side of the main buildings, tucked up cosy with his wife. Rhonda said they don't even try and hide; they just walk across the quad, out through the archway, and alongside the Bursar's office."

"And she definitely said skinny dipping?"

"On my life, Nick. She had that glint in her eye."

Every student at College knew about skinny dipping, but not with the innuendo that now laced the conversation. In the summer term, students were roused out of bed by a bell at seven o'clock. We had to walk the fifty yards to the swimming pool and take a naked dip. It was called 'Early Morning Dip' - very original name, that. The rule was that the water had to go above your shoulders. It was supervised each morning by the same Dicky Bond who lived in his married quarters at the other end of the school. Dicky had eagle eyes and if you tried to get out without the water reaching your neck, you had to go back in and get your head under water.

"Christ, you reckon we could be in for more than just a swim?"

"I'm dead certain of it, old son. Rhonda made that very clear in fact. I tell you, Nick, she's hot."

"Bloody hell. So, not satisfied with having sex with Lesley, we're now going to take on a maid a piece?"

Some sort of divine grace, swathed in a broad smile, took up residence on Jack's face. "The question 'at what point am I finally satisfied?' begs the answer 'at no point'. And that, my old friend, is the whole point. Maybe we should be grateful to that bloody virus, because for sure, if life at College had carried on as normal, that pair would not be talking about going skinny dipping with us. Nor whatever follows after that."

"You're right there, Jack. The maids are usually not too talkative. They bring out the food, they clear away the dirty dishes, and that's all we see of them. I guess it's what they've been instructed to do. Those two must be pretty pushed at meal times at the moment because none of the others were here when they quarantined us."

"There's that third one - that older woman - but she's now helping the cook. They're the only ones who live on the premises for the moment."

"How old do you reckon Rhonda and Michelle are?"

"Rhonda is the older of the two. She's thirty-four. Michelle's thirty-two."

"About fifteen years older than us then."

"And fifteen years more experienced. If I had to choose between Angela Maxwell or Michelle and Rhonda, I know who I'd choose. I mean, Pete's a jammy bugger keep scoring with the women, but I think we may have struck lucky here. To be honest, Nick, I can't bloody wait."

I wriggled my shoulders and bounced a foot. "Nor me. Roll on midnight."

Jack chuckled. "And you know what else I learnt from Rhonda?"

"Go on."

"Well her room overlooks the airport it seems. She said that a group of students were risking their lives at night going for a walk down the main runway of the airport."

"What?"

"That's what I said. Rhonda said she'd thought about it and realised that the street marshals treat the airport and College as one entity and consider them 'clean'. The airport has been closed ever since quarantine was announced. Nobody lives there or goes there. We're also considered 'clean' so they guard the perimeter of the airport and College but not the shared boundary. There would be no point. Rhonda reckoned these boys only go there at night when nobody will see them, and they go no further than the nearest runway. They don't go near the terminal or other buildings, just in case."

"That's bloody mental, Jack."

"It's also very logical. Though I can't see much point in doing it except just to kick against authority."

"Which is probably why they do it. Did she say how many of them there were?"

"She thought about thirty. But she did say they were led by a big bloke. The way she described him, it could easily be Bruiser. He's mental and he has his band of younger acolytes following him everywhere."

"But why would they do that?" I asked.

Jack laughed. "I have no bloody idea. Sounds like Bruiser 'training' his troops. Make them feel important. You can ask Michelle about it yourself tonight when we go swimming. See if she knows more than Rhonda."

"This isn't a Jack Parson's piss-take is it? This swimming thing?"

"Deadly serious, Nick. Skinny dipping with a couple of hot and horny women is not something I would joke about."

CHAPTER ELEVEN

The day passed slowly. Like a snail crawling through treacle. Thoughts of those two women inhabited my head like welcome squatters. I pushed my studies to one side. There was so much to do - cigarettes to smoke, thinking about having sex, thinking even more about having sex, having another smoke. I'd have plenty of time for reading when I was a boring old fart.

My adventure with Lesley had, I now realised, been uncertain and fumbling. A bit tense, even. Lesley had been kind about it, but I knew she had experienced more sophisticated lovers than me. For me, our evening together had removed much of my adolescent angst. I would not now die ignorant of what it was like to have proper sex. Sex with a woman, not my right hand. In our private conversations, Jack had admitted to having exactly the same feelings. We knew we could trust each other even with our deepest secrets. But after Leslie, I was sure that I could relax and enjoy the experience more. I could be more adventurous and more at ease. It's just that I had never expected the opportunity to arise so soon.

When they turned out the lights that evening at ten o'clock, I lay in the dark clutching my dick, stiff with anticipation. I wanted to do what I'd done many nights and relieve the pressure in my balls, but knew that if I did, I would spoil the enjoyment later. It was like holding an unexploded bomb in the palm of my hand.

I must have dozed off because the next thing I was aware of was Jack shaking my shoulder. "Come on," he whispered, "time to go skinny dipping."

I was instantly hard again. I couldn't help myself. The anticipation was killing me. I slid out of bed and into my slippers. I pulled on my dressing gown and followed Jack out of the dormitory. We grabbed our towels as we passed the washroom. As we crossed the quad, the clock on the tower struck midnight. I wondered if Rhonda and Michelle would be there, or whether Rhonda had just been winding Jack up. We were about to find out.

They were there, and it was no wind-up. As we walked into the changing area on a wide balcony above the pool they were both stepping out of their jeans. My heart rate ticked up a notch as excitement flushed through my body. We couldn't turn the lights on of course, but there was plenty of ambient moonlight from the high atrium glazed roof. Along with the green glow from the emergency lighting bulbs, we had no difficulty seeing what we were doing. The one who I assumed was Rhonda came forward and began snogging Jack, even before he'd let his dressing gown drop. The other lady, wearing only bra and pants, came towards me and held me round the waist. "I'm Michelle," she said, taking my hand and guiding it to her breast.

"And I'm Nick."

She said nothing more, just latched onto my lips and began to probe my mouth with her tongue. I was still carrying round an erection, so Michelle reached in and grabbed hold of it. "Seems like you're pleased to see me," she said, chuckling to herself.

I was.

Michelle lost no time pushing my dressing gown off

my shoulders and pulling down my pyjama bottoms. I never wore the tops. She took me in her hands with infinite care and began a slow massage. I heard somebody moan, and realised it was me.

A few feet away, Rhonda broke away from Jack. "Come on you two, let's go skinny dipping."

Michelle made no move to oblige. As the others threw off what was left of their clothes and took the steps down to the pool, wearing only their birthday suits, she knelt on the hard tiled floor and took me in her mouth. It was a sensation I cannot describe. I've never had any difficulty manipulating and mastering words, but trying to describe the exquisite sensations that overwhelmed my senses, is beyond my mastery of the English language. I was a budding wordsmith with no way of describing what I was feeling. A Shakespeare without a quill, or pen, or whatever the hell Shakespeare used to write with. He may well be regarded as the greatest writer in the English language and the world's greatest dramatist, but there was no way he could put into words the sensation that I was experiencing with Michelle's lips wrapped round my shaft. I'm damn sure that unrhymed iambic pentameter was not what was going through my mind at the time.

I have no idea how long it took, I just know that I held onto Michelle's head as she imbibed every drop of my ejaculation. She stayed glued to my shaft for a while and purred like a cat. As I shuddered and shook, she stood, licked her lips, and grinned at me. "That's how it's done, young man. Let's go and join the others and cool you down. Then we can go back to my room and you can work your magic on me. You owe me after that."

And indeed I did. After ten minutes in the pool, Michelle and I left Jack and Rhonda to do whatever they were going to do, and we went back to Michelle's small room in the attic above Farrow Hall, the huge dining room. Michelle glided up the service stairway and I followed like a little chick following the mother hen. I was aware of the lack of experience that surrounded me, but I needn't have worried. Once we were in Michelle's room, she said, "Just to be clear, Nick, I'm slot B, and you're tab A. I can draw you a diagram if you want, but I'd rather show you. First of all though, there's a ritual to go through using our mouths and our tongues. You ready?"

I was.

She giggled and dragged me towards the bed. With a grin that lit her face from ear to ear, she said, "During the course of the next hour or so, I plan to use my hands, my mouth, and my pussy to fuck that schoolboy ignorance right out of you."

So she did. She really did.

Michelle spent some considerable time tutoring me in the fine art of giving a lady good oral sex. I've never puzzled out who enjoyed it the most, but I am grateful for the lesson. At last I now knew where a clitoris was located and, having found it, what to do with it. The most important education I received from Michelle that night was that giving could be just as pleasurable as receiving. It's a lesson that has stood me in good stead right through my adult life. After pleasing her orally, we moved on to various penetration techniques and positions. It wasn't coaching or training, just us romping round the bed wherever our fancy took us. But I realise now that Michelle gave me many subtle clues with squeezes and sounds. A sigh here, a moan there, a touch and a gentle push in the right direction from time to time. I soon discovered the things that pleased her most. It was quite a while before we finished up with her riding me to a mind-shattering climax. I wished that all education could be as enjoyable. The hours I spent in Michelle's room that night have remained with me always.

Grateful as I was for expelling the hormonal urges that rule an eighteen-year-old's thoughts, I have remained indebted throughout my life for the lessons Michelle and her sister taught me in the following weeks. By the time Coviman-12 had been eliminated, Jack Parsons and I had developed a certain expertise when it came to all matters of a sexual nature. I had entered carnal adulthood and still hadn't finished my academic studies. But then, who gives a damn about whether it's who or whom, or how to avoid ambiguous pronouns, when there's a willing lady waiting for you in her bedroom? Got to get your priorities right.

I have endeavoured over the years to perfect the fine art of pleasing a woman. But my starting point was, and will always be with Michelle and Rhonda Owen during those dreadful, dark days at College in the spring of 1967. While Lesley Parkes helped me over the first hurdle, the Owen sisters turned Jack and me into sexually experienced young men with an understanding of how to please a woman and how to accept pleasure from a woman. Bless them. They are almost certainly both dead by now, but I know damn well they would have led full and interesting lives.

Even now, when I think of them, I think of Hunter S Thompson's 'The Proud Highway'. In his book, Thompson vividly caught the tenor of the times in 1960s America. He channelled it all through his own razor-sharp perspective. He was a writer of great passion. He was also merciless in his scorn, and never anything less than fascinating. 'The Proud Highway' - recommended reading by Mister Jones - offered an unprecedented and penetrating gaze into the evolution of the most outrageous raconteur-provocateur ever to assault a typewriter. The quote that has always stuck in my mind, and which I shall have printed on the side of my coffin, is, 'Life is not a journey to the grave with the intention of arriving safely in a well preserved body, but rather to skid in broadside, thoroughly used up, totally worn out, and loudly proclaiming, "Wow what a ride!"'.

Having lived for months with the threat of imminent death, and having been just moments away from death myself, it's a sentiment I have tried to live by. I have lived my life and enjoyed every damn minute. Including my many mistakes. Being close to death as we were makes you appreciate the simple pleasures in life even more. But while receiving my sexual enlightenment, I was always aware that not all of us would have lives to lead if the virus ever hit College.

I crawled into my bed that morning just as the first light was beginning to soften the night sky. The junior dormitories held about twenty boys, the senior ones about ten. Jack and I had hit lucky and shared a dormitory with just six beds. A long bank of windows looked out over the adjacent airport and across the bay. On summer mornings, the sea gleamed like burnished gold in the rising sun. On winter mornings, we perished because none of the windows fit the frames. College was ageing, and not too gracefully. As I entered the dorm, I heard a cough. I was instantly alert. Coughing was one of the first signs of the Coviman-12 Virus. We were all wary of anyone who coughed. But it was only Jack, who had arrived back from Rhonda's bed half-an-hour earlier. He was all hyped up and couldn't sleep.

Not that either of us was going to catch much sleep before the bell rang to wake us up.

He raised a 'thumbs-up'. "Turned out well, didn't it?" he whispered.

"Turned out fuckin' marvellous. Michelle reckons we should swap partners next time."

"Rhonda said the same. You game?"

"Damn right I am."

The boy in the next bed to Jack turned over. I tip-toed to my bed and thought about what had just happened. Time enough to swap notes with Jack during the day.

CHAPTER TWELVE

In the end, neither Jack nor I caught very much sleep, yet I was up and out and getting washed and dressed, perky as a rat in a bag of discarded carrion. Jack and I were dog tired, but happy little campers as we tucked into bacon, tomato and scrambled egg, washed down with several cups of tea. As Michelle leaned over me to reach for an empty plate, she pressed her breast into my shoulder and squeezed my arm, but showed no other signs of what had happened. All four of us made out it was just another day. But it turned out to be far from that.

As breakfast finished and Jack and I descended the wide stairs from Farrow Hall, a shout erupted from the quadrangle below. More shouts and some screams followed. Then there was a wet thud that sounded like an exploding water balloon, and then silence. Utter silence. But only for a few seconds, before somebody started to cry.

We ran down the stairs, pushing juniors aside like handfuls of straw, and charged out into the quadrangle. Directly in front of us lay a spread-eagled body. Vibrant streaks of red surrounded him like glistening jets of paint. The brown check jacket belonged to Cedric Patterson, housemaster of Lower School and, as we soon discovered, so did the body. He had landed almost at the bottom of the four wide stone steps leading from the entrance where we stood down into the quad. Bloody rivulets seeped across the paving slabs from his front, back and sides. The streams of gore contained entrails that had exploded from his body.

Younger students pressed against each other, staring down at the man split apart on the ground. They ignored desperate pleas from the older boys for them to make their way to their house-rooms. It reminded me of the Roman Coliseum - of a bloodthirsty crowd fascinated by the sight of a gladiator being torn apart by lions. And then the first of many younger pupils vomited. It was contagious and spread to others, but at least it thinned out the ogling horde.

As we later learnt from Phil Loveless and Rick Tanner, who did most things together, they had been walking across the quad when somebody pointed up at the massive square tower that overlooked the whole school. I never discovered how high the tower was, but it had to be 100 feet if it was an inch. Phil and Rick turned round to see Cedric Patterson balanced on top of the crenellations. Just moments later, he launched himself outwards in an arc.

On his downward journey, Patterson's head hit the edge of a parapet that jutted out about 40 feet above ground level. It was, I realised, right next to the window of the bedroom in which I had spent most of the night. Patterson's head had already split open before his body burst on final impact. Seeing the final result was bad enough, but it must have been an appalling and gruesome experience watching it happen. I recall later looking up to the top of the tower and trying to picture Patterson's fall. All I remember is that the air was fresh and the sky was clear with just a few small clouds. I somehow closed my mind to everything else. I didn't want to hear the wet thud as his body hit the concrete slabs in the quad. And I didn't want to see him fall. I'd seen the results and that was more than enough for me.

Years later, while on holiday, I went to see the high cliff divers diving one hundred feet from La Quebrada cliffs in Acapulco. After the first one, I couldn't watch. My mind went straight to Cedric Patterson, splattered on the concrete slabs of the quadrangle.

I'd never seen a dead body before. I'd always imagined that, when I did, it would be some ageing relative lying in a pristine lined coffin. What I saw was blood and bowels spread over a wide area, accompanied by a dense, cloying smell. Halfway between decaying fruit and rotting meat. I am no wise man. Every day of my life has shown me how little I know about life, and how wrong I can be. But there are things I know to be true. I know I will die. And I hope to God that when I do, I will be that ageing relative in his lined coffin, and not a Cedric Patterson spread over dozens of cold concrete slabs having my insides ogled by shocked but curious onlookers.

Within minutes, the principal arrived. Since the outbreak of the virus, he had taken to eating his meals with us plebs in the main dining hall. We suspected that it had nothing to do with solidarity, and quite a lot to do with the fact that his wife wasn't at home to cook for him. For a moment, he stood and stared, then he snapped into action and ordered a complete lock-down. Nobody except the praepositors were to leave their studies or their house-rooms.

Jack and I made our way back to our study but couldn't help staring out through the window at the mess of gore that was once a physics master, a housemaster, a sexual deviant, and a sadist. It was the second week in February. A blustery day, but those few slate and silver clouds marbled the powder-blue sky, misting the weak sunlight but taking none of its warmth. Yet out in the quad lay the cold, cold remains of a man we both knew and detested. After a long silence, Jack said, "We did that. We caused Patterson to do that."

I nodded. But then I thought about it and said, "No, Jack. He did it to himself. For as long as he has been at this college, he has beaten little boys without mercy, just to satisfy his own perverted lust. Don't ever forget that."

"I haven't forgotten it, Nick, but all we wanted was a public apology. I never expected a public suicide."

"That's as good an apology as any." I glanced at Jack. "Screw him. He could have landed on someone and killed them. Did you see poor young Montgomery? He was head to foot in blood. Patterson must have landed right next to him. And how do you think the youngsters will react to this? This is the stuff of nightmares. As if this fucking virus wasn't enough to live with, the poor little buggers will be scarred for life. Dammit, I'm feeling pretty chewed up myself."

"I get that," Jack said, "but it just seems an awful waste. It's like Knuckle Dragger Harvey. I doubt he would have gone staggering up the road pissed as a parrot if he hadn't been demoted."

"We didn't demote him, Jack. Like you said to Bruiser and Cockroach the other day, the Prinky had been considering how to deal with Harvey's rigid authoritarianism for a long time. Unless, of course it was one of your inventions to put Bruiser and his lap dog off the track."

"No, that was right enough, Nick. I wouldn't mind betting the Prinky knew of his drinking habits too."

The pair of us sat for a long time, just staring at the

walls, wrapped in our thoughts. Up on the rooftops, a scattering of seagulls had collected like scrounging vultures, waiting for a chance to swoop down and grab a tasty morsel of offal. Their hunched postures emphasised their resentment of the praes patrolling what the seagulls saw as their feeding ground.

Later a group of men dressed in green hazmat suits, full face masks, and breather filters came and cleared away what remained of Cedric Patterson. Much of his remains had to be scraped up and bagged. After they had left, the college fire engine wheeled into the quad, through the large archway at the western end. It was an old Merryweather engine dating back to the 1930s. It was probably incapable of dousing a Boy Scouts' camp fire, but it was good enough to sluice down the whole quadrangle and remove the worst of the blood splatter.

Meanwhile, the seagulls grabbed their last chance to plummet down for an appetising tit-bit. What remained days later, and almost certainly still to this day, was a pale brown stain in the shape of a multi-pointed star. That was all that was left of Mister Cedric Patterson. It seemed so shocking it had happened here, right in the heart of the school. It felt like a much-loved family dog that you trusted, turning on you without warning.

The news of Basil Harvey's demise had shaken us up, but to witness for ourselves the latest result of our quest for justice, was beyond horrific.

Like most pupils, we skipped lunch. Difficult to eat braised beef and carrots when you've been looking at a man's intestines a few hours earlier. I don't know how surgeons do it. The evening meal was a subdued affair. Dozens of places on the hard wooden benches were empty. Normally, strident voices called out above the clatter of plates and cutlery. That evening, what few conversations that could be heard were whispered and restricted to requests to pass the salt or pepper.

As the meal finished and we stood to leave, George Armstrong approached us. "Quine, Parsons, my study in five minutes, please." Jack and I glanced at each other and made our way to the principal's study. We waited by the door for his arrival. He led us in and pointed to the two chairs on the other side of his desk. He set a few things down and began sifting through stacks of papers. The place was a mess and lacked the organisation I would have expected from someone in his position. But then, with the chaos of dealing with the current situation, it should have come as no surprise.

When we were all sitting, the principal took a deep breath and said, "I could make you two sweat. I could make you punish yourselves for the rest of your lives, and I am tempted to do so. I have been weighing up whether to have this conversation with you or not. But I think it's right and fair that I do. Just at this moment, you don't need any additional weight on your shoulders."

I had a bad feeling about what was about to pass.

CHAPTER THIRTEEN

The principal paused and eyed up first Jack and then me. "You caught me at an indiscreet moment and you have used that knowledge to line your pockets by selling cigarettes at twice their price. You also used that knowledge to try and have Mister Patterson apologise in public. And you approached me regarding Mister Harvey's dated attitudes and actions."

"Sir, that was—"

"Shut up and listen, Parsons. It's my turn to speak." He kept his gaze locked with Jack's, refusing to look away.

Jack glared at the school principal from under his brow before nodding.

"And I want your absolute discretion," the principal added, drumming his fingers on his desk. "This conversation goes no further than these four walls. Am I clear?"

This time, we both nodded.

Armstrong continued, "I'm prepared to let your cigarette trade carry on until the quarantine is lifted. This isn't a favour to you but I smoked myself when I was your age and I know what it's like to be without. There's enough pressure on the students with this god-awful virus, without the added frustration of not having their secret smokes. However, you will stop profiteering. You will sell them for the going rate which, I am assured, is five shillings and tuppence a packet and you will pay for the cigarettes you get. They will no longer be free. I can hardly distribute the damn things myself, but I'm not going to tolerate you two profiteering. Is that understood?"

We both of us nodded again.

"Right, concerning Mister Harvey first of all. I would like to make you two feel guilty for his death, but I can't. I meant what I said to you some days ago, Parsons. Mister Harvey was indeed a dinosaur. His antiquated methods no longer suited a modernising educational establishment. And, yes, he had a problem with alcohol. I don't believe that me relieving him of the post of vice-principal had any bearing on his walking out of College. In fact, when I did so, we discussed it quite amicably. He seemed relieved, as though a weight of responsibility had been lifted from his shoulders. So don't hold yourselves guilty for Mister Harvey's actions. He was in the habit of taking late evening perambulations, often heading up to the airport and back. I genuinely believe he was so inebriated he forgot all about being quarantined. His death is very regrettable because, no matter what we may have thought of his rather old-fashioned views, he had given twenty-eight years of his life to educating students in this college, and that should not be forgotten."

Jack and I mumbled our assent. The Prinky was right. Poor old Basil Harvey was just someone who should have retired years earlier.

"And now," the principal said, sitting up, "we come to Cedric Patterson, rest his soul."

He said no more and just looked from Jack to me and back again. "Like I said, I've been tempted to let you stew and think you were responsible for his actions this morning. But in clear conscience, I can't dump that weight of guilt on your heads. So I'm going to tell you the truth. But once again, I remind you that this conversation goes no further than this study. I am putting you both on your sacred trust."

"Yes, Sir," we answered in unison.

"Mr Patterson may well have been guilty of everything you claim. In fact, I believe you have told me the truth in that respect and I deeply regret that I wasn't aware of his failings sooner. But I never did approach him with a view to him apologising."

"Why not, Sir?" I asked.

"Because Cedric was a very sick man and, thanks to Coviman-12, was doomed to an extremely painful death."

"You mean he had the virus?" Jack cut in.

"No, but he had something which, for him, was just as bad. In early November last year, as the winter term progressed, Mister Patterson suffered health problems. He became tired quickly. Had trouble sleeping. You may even have noticed, Parsons, in your physics lessons that he had to leave the room two or three times during each lesson."

Jack nodded. "We did wonder."

"It was because he needed to urinate more often. And when he did urinate, there was blood in his urine. He had problems walking because his ankles and feet were swollen and painful. He lost his appetite and suffered from severe muscle cramps."

The principal looked again at Jack. "You're planning to join the medical profession I gather. Any idea what might have been the problem?"

Jack considered for a moment. "It sounds like

toxins and impurities in the blood. Probably a kidney disease of some sort."

The principal smiled. "You'll make a good doctor if you can focus more on your studies instead of trying to beat the system. It was indeed kidney failure. He'd already seen specialists during last term but, over the Christmas break it was determined that he had end stage kidney failure. He had lost about 85% of his kidney function and had a glomerular filtration rate of less than 15%. Mister Patterson was destined for his first dialysis session when this damn virus struck and we were quarantined. So he was stuck like the rest of us and confined to College grounds. Without regular dialysis, he was dying an excruciatingly painful death. He has tolerated his situation for many weeks but, this morning, since there is no sign of the virus being beaten, he chose to end it all. The pain had become too much to bear. Sometimes even to live is an act of courage, as the Roman philosopher Seneca once wrote."

Jack and I looked at each other aghast. After a pause, I asked, "But why kill himself like that from the top of the tower?"

"As you can imagine, Quine, Mrs Patterson is distraught. But she shared with me his final letter to her, which he left by her bed some time in the early hours of this morning. He wanted to be certain of his death. He didn't want to make a suicide attempt that failed. That would have made things even worse for him. So he headed to the highest place in College - the tower. In his letter, he said he planned to jump while students were still asleep. That way, nobody would see him do it. My best guess is that the walk from Lower School and then the climb up the tower was more painful and energy-sapping than he had imagined and that he arrived at the top of the tower much later than planned. He had become very weak in recent days and may have had to rest several times as he climbed to the top. But he went through with it anyway."

"And fortunately didn't land on anybody," Jack added.

The principal nodded. "That thought had crossed my mind, Parsons. I suspect that he may not have thought clearly about what the impact from over 100 feet would have on his body. Or maybe, in despair, he didn't care anymore. Cedric Patterson killed himself because he was going to die a painful death anyway. He just chose to end his life in seconds rather than suffer debilitating pain until it was too late. This damn virus is like quicksand, boys. The day they confined us to the buildings and grounds, it crept over our toes. Now, weeks later, it has covered our mouths and is tickling our nostrils. I don't know how much longer we can hold things together. Thanks to the pressure we are all feeling, College is becoming like a ticking time bomb. I'm sure you must have sensed it already."

A shiver ran through me and my mind jumped to Bruiser Williams. He had always been unpredictable, but now he was on the verge of exploding. For most of us the virus was terrifying, but we managed to hold it in. We were all running out of hope, like someone holding us underwater, and there was nothing we could do about it.

"No sign of the virus burning itself out?" Jack asked, as if reading my mind.

"You know the answer to that as well as I do, Parsons. I'm sure you are in touch with Miss Parkes, whose father's head of the island's Department of Health. Coviman-12 is still spreading, but the rate of spread has reduced somewhat. Even if there were no more new cases this week, it would still be weeks or even months before the quarantines were lifted. They would need to make sure that the incubation period had passed with no new cases before they lifted the restrictions."

"And there's no sign of a vaccine?"

"Far too soon," the principal said. "Nothing seems to work once someone has the virus. They live or they die. Either way, it's not pleasant. Antibiotics have no effect whatsoever on viruses. The moment a person becomes infected, the virus will run its course, either killing its host, or being overcome by the body's own defences. More often than not, it kills its host. It is monstrous in its single-mindedness."

After that, we chatted. Like three old buddies at the bar, Jack, myself and George Godfrey Armstrong held forth on the weather, the news that Apollo 1 had been destroyed by fire at Cape Kennedy, killing all three of the American astronauts on board and, of course, Coviman-12. Everything was about Coviman-12. It ruled our lives. All three of us had realised weeks ago that unless a person has experienced true fear, there is nothing you can do to make them understand how utterly debilitating it can be. Or how your safe, ordinary life can disappear in the space of a heartbeat.

Looking back now, I'm sure that George Armstrong found some relief in having someone to talk to, even if it was only two sixth-formers who had tried to blackmail him. During the conversation, the principal told us that College was the single largest community on the island that hadn't been infected. It seemed that Noble's Hospital had fallen foul of the virus a few days earlier. The hospital had almost 200 beds, most of them occupied when Coviman struck. There had been no new admissions since quarantine, but neither had anybody been allowed to leave. What few patients were left now were already dead or rapidly dying and the doctors and nurses were falling ill too. So it seemed as though Bishop's College was now standing alone as an intact community.

The three of us ended our meeting by agreeing to try and support the younger boys. They would be suffering more than us. And, like us, they couldn't even contact their parents.

As Jack and I made our way up to the dormitory that night, we had no inkling that things were about to change. What we had thought of as a bad situation was about to get a lot worse.

CHAPTER FOURTEEN

The following morning, Jack and I felt more human, having caught up on our missed sleep from the night before. As we ate breakfast, notices were circulated to all pupils, laying out changes effective immediately. First of all, there would be no more sixth form lessons due to the shortage of teaching staff. For the foreseeable future, sixth formers would be trusted to move their educations forward for themselves. The remaining eight masters would work together to try and help younger pupils, particularly those around the age of sixteen, who were in their 'O' level year.

Students were instructed that, to help administer the school with minimum staff, they should, as far as possible, stay in their house-rooms or studies while not actually attending lessons. We couldn't puzzle out the thinking behind this edict but it would soon become a critical factor. As far as we were concerned, the houses served only for purposes of competition, allowing every pupil in the School the opportunity to participate in team activity across all year groups.

During our open conversation with the principal the previous evening, Mr Armstrong had brought us right up-to-date with as much as he knew about what was happening beyond the walls of College. While Lesley Parkes was able to contact her father, Armstrong had an approved line from his study and his house to the emergency control room in Douglas, the capital town some ten miles away. He told us that the war against the virus was only being won because it was no longer a town-by-town or village-by-village lock-down, it was now a building-by-building lock-down.

Basic food and hygiene supplies were left outside each door on a regular basis by people in protective clothing. They would knock on the door, or ring the bell, and await an answer. If no answer came, they would try a second time. Then, if there was still no response, they would remove the supplies and move on to the next house. It was a huge logistical operation, and it was a long way from perfect, but at least it was showing signs of reducing the spread of the virus that threatened everybody's lives. If a house didn't respond for a whole week, the street marshals went in, dressed in their protective clothing, removed any bodies, and set about disinfecting the empty building or apartment. In a rather Biblical touch, they would then mark the front door to show that the house was empty and had been disinfected.

The principal told us that, at the beginning, people had been tempted to break the tough quarantine restrictions and dodge from one house to another. They thought they were doing their neighbours a favour by checking up on them. In fact, they were just spreading the virus. To begin with, the miscreants had been told to return to their houses. But they only ever got one warning. After that the army made an example of them by shooting them dead, and letting it be known that they had done so. Now, the vast majority showed more respect for the draconian rules. They began to realise the rules had been imposed for a reason. A few had been tempted to loot empty houses, but they, too, had been dealt with without mercy. Savage though it was, it was the only way the Coviman-12 virus was going to be beaten. Normal rules of engagement had been well and truly dumped for the time being.

Some young hot-headed teenagers thought that joy-riding the empty roads would be fun. They, too, were dealt with in the harshest possible way. Included amongst them, I later discovered, had been one of my friends. John Baker had forsaken the idea of using a car and had mounted his Triumph TR6C Trophy, a 650cc high performance motorbike. I guess he thought that the extra speed and acceleration would allow him to dodge the bullets. He was right there, but it didn't help him when he misjudged a bend and smashed into a granite wall. If the virus didn't get you one way, it would get you another.

I think it was Lenin, who argued that 'you cannot make a revolution in white gloves'. Well you couldn't stamp out Coviman-12 in white gloves either. When I think back on it now, all that stuff fills me with a curdling discomfort that can last for days. But back in 1967 we just accepted how things were. We had no choice. We were schoolboys encased in a gilded cage surrounded by sharks. It would take only one small breach of the cage and the sharks would be in, ripping us apart. Whatever radical rules were being applied outside the school grounds were for our protection. If you are going to stand in a shark cage, you wanted the bars to be toughened steel, and the oppressive enforcement of tough quarantine was our only protection.

The island's residents were no more than feathers blown around in a storm that lasted for days, and that bled into weeks, and now months. Only the hope that we'd somehow get through it held us down, stopping us from drifting into oblivion. I wondered what my parents were making of it all.

They probably put their trust in God, like they did everything else. My father had been vicar of a church on the island when I won my scholarship to College. Two years earlier, my parents had moved back to England, so I knew they were safe. They, of course, had no news of me. As, indeed did none of the other students' parents.

At the foot of the directive that Jack and I were reading during that breakfast was an apparent afterthought. 'Mealtimes will, in future, be staggered. Sixth form will now eat immediately after the rest of school. This is to help the kitchen staff cope with limited resources'.

Jack looked at me as he finished his buttered toast. "You read that last paragraph yet?"

I nodded.

"How many boarders do you reckon there are in the sixth forms?" he asked.

I did a bit of quick mental arithmetic. "No more than one hundred here at the moment. Why, what are you thinking?"

"I'm just trying to puzzle out what the advantage is to having us all eating separately."

"Dunno. You done?"

Jack nodded and slurped his last drop of tea. We made our way down the wide stone stairs and out into the quad where Cedric Patterson had landed the previous morning. As we walked towards our study, I nudged Jack and nodded towards Angela Maxwell, the wife of the music teacher, wearing a black dress that clung like a limpet to her generous rear end. She strolled across the quad in the other direction, no doubt leaving a trail of perfume behind. And, for those of us in the know, the thought of her unarticulated promise of slippery sex in the big linen cupboard next to matron's quarters. "You reckon Pete's going to be busy again, I asked?"

Jack checked his watch. "Bit early for rumpty-pumpty isn't it? We've not even had time to let our breakfast settle yet."

"Never too early," I laughed.

Jack followed my look. "Jesus Christ, Nick, that's mutton dressed as lamb if ever I saw it."

"Yes, but a decent slice of mutton can be quite tasty when you're hungry. She's the sort of woman my dad would refer to in his strong Lancashire accent as 'proper breeding material'. Good child-bearing hips on her, but a little bit past her prime."

He laughed. "You still hungry for sex after the other night?"

I was always hungry for sex, but I shook my head. My eyes were still glued to Angela Maxwell's well-padded rear end as it made its way through the door on the other side of the quad. Pete had described it to us and I just couldn't help myself mentally undressing the lady in question. A bit saggy and squashy like a soft meringue had been Pete's description. It actually didn't look too bad from where I was. I could easily imagine clasping those generous buttocks as Angela Maxwell rode me to euphoria and back.

"Well?" Jack asked as we crossed the quad. "Are you still hungry for sex?"

I laughed and nodded. "I thought all my teenage needs had been satisfied in the last week or so, what with Lesley and then Michelle. But the sight of another female, albeit a well-padded female, has made me change my mind."

Jack chuckled. He knew what I'd been thinking all along. He'd been thinking the same thing. As we crossed the quad, Jack said, "You know what, Nick, I think I get my sex-hungry genes from my mother."

"Why's that?" I asked.

"Because she's been a naughty lady. As you know, my father is a barrister – a QC actually. He's a decent enough guy, but he's somewhat old fashioned, and he can be a bit pompous and aloof. Anyway, he's out in chambers all day. He's never liked the idea of my mother working. He thinks she should amuse herself flower arranging or knitting, so she's at home all the time getting bored. I can remember the young legal clerk who lived just round the corner and how he would come over when my father wasn't home. I can almost hear the squeaking bedsprings and some rather naughty words that came from the bedroom mixed in with my mother's cries. Cries which, to me, sounded both happy and hurt all at the same time. "Our secret," my mother used to say afterwards, giving me a hug. "He's just a friend and your daddy doesn't need to know anything about it, right?" It seemed natural to agree. My mother seemed happiest when my father wasn't around. And besides, young boys always agree with their mums."

I chuckled. "And does that still go on?"

"I think the bed has been changed so there are no squeaking springs. And the legal clerk has been changed for a newer version. But basically, yes. It's my mother's and my secret. We just smile and nod when the doorbell rings, and I slope off to my room, or go outside for a walk. Anyway, I'm fairly sure my father's had a few affairs in his time."

We stepped into our study and Jack slumped behind his desk. "So do you want to come for a second helping tonight then?" he asked. "Rhonda said to give the swimming pool a miss and just go straight up to their rooms. She also reminded me that we could swap partners tonight. You go with her and I'll go with Michelle. How does that sound, or are you not interested?"

I diverted my gaze to my friend. "Not interested, Jack? Not fucking interested?" I howled. "What the—"

Just then the door burst open. Bruiser battered me aside and overturned my desk without even the courtesy of an introduction. I bounced off the wall and tripped over a pile of books. I was getting fed up with this and, as I picked myself up off the floor, I noticed Jack slide open the drawer of his desk where he had hidden his knife. His spine was curled in the chair and he had an angry teenage look on his face. I made eye contact. My brows shot up and I gave him a slight shake of the head. If you're angry at stupid people, you're tempted to join them in their stupidity. Jack nodded, folding his arms tight over his belly before lowering himself back into the chair. I brushed myself down and turned my attention back to Bruiser. "What's your problem today, Bruiser? Has Cockroach not bent over for you this morning?"

Toby Cochrane peered round Bruiser's bulk. "Don't be bloody crude, you faggot."

"Or what, you little scroat? Or you'll tell your big buddy and he'll come and tip my desk over again? You know what you remind me of, Cochrane? You remind me of a slimy little grub inside a cocoon that will be reborn as an even uglier grub. Or maybe reborn as a moth with broken wings, fluttering like a spastic into the mouth of a hungry predator."

Bruiser looked round at Cochrane. "Did you get all that Toby? What does he mean?"

Jack whispered, "Bloody hell, Nick, it lives and breathes, and will one day get a vote."

"What did you say, Parsons?"

"I said, you get my vote, Bruiser. You know, for showing restraint and all that."

I hoped Jack would stop there. Even Bruiser could work out sarcasm if it wasn't too well concealed.

Bruiser stared at us both. "You've been selling fags at normal price since yesterday evening. Five and tuppence, I gather."

"It's a special offer for people we like," Jack said. "We felt a pang of guilt after you last came in and told us how what we were doing was wrong. We've learnt our lesson, and we'll never do it again."

Bruiser's brain tried to work on that one. It took a long time. "Is he taking the piss?" he asked Cochrane.

"Are you taking the piss?" Cochrane asked.

"There's an echo in here," I said.

Cochrane looked up at Bruiser. "They can't be taking the piss if they've actually been selling ciggies at the right price."

Bruiser looked puzzled. Bruiser often looked puzzled. He turned, stumbled over Cochrane's feet and stormed off along the passage. I brushed myself down and closed the door.

"I wouldn't have been as patient as you," Jack said helping me sort out my desk.

"I noticed. I think it's a bit early yet to go threatening Bruiser with knives. I'm a patient man, Jack, until I'm not. Then I go ballistic." I glanced at my friend. "You know he's quite insane, don't you?"

"I know, Nick. Mad as a sack of ferrets. But I guess you're right. We need to humour him as far as we can. An angry ferret can rip your balls off if you put it down your trousers."

"You're strange, Jack Parsons. Why ever would you think of sticking a ferret, or Bruiser Williams, down your trousers? And anyway, talking of things down your trousers, I think you were suggesting that we go see Rhonda and Michelle tonight. You've spoken to them, I take it?"

Jack nodded. "Midnight in their rooms. But like I say, they fancy a swap. What about you? I'm game for it. Rhonda was fantastic, but Michelle looked hot as well."

"Michelle was bloody amazing, but a change of partners suits me just fine. Let the good times roll."

As we had been talking, I detected a dull metallic sound from just outside the door. I whispered to Jack, "I think someone's listening in." I put my fingers to my lips, eased from behind my desk as quietly as I could, and then made a grab for the door knob. It was one of the old brass knobs. Most of the doors around the school were fitted with them. The knob turned, but the door remained closed. I tried again, but to no effect. Then I heard a giggle from the passageway beyond. "Got you now, you peasants," a voice shouted. "Cost you a packet of smokes to get your door knob back."

It dawned on us both what had happened. Someone had unscrewed the knob from the outside and removed it, along with the metal spindle that passed through the opener. Without that, we were unable to action the latch. Jack and I both knew who it was. Mike Taggart was famous for his practical jokes. "Come on, Maggot, stop arsing about."

A face appeared at the window. It was another joker called Roy Barr. Roy's sense of humour had no limits. One of his classics was that, in normal times, we had a blind master at school, nicknamed Chud. He had been blinded during the war. He taught scripture and French, sometimes helped by an assistant, but mostly on his own just using braille. When Chud was alone in the classroom, Roy would get us all in silent hysterics with his outrageous actions. He sat near the front of the room, and he would undo his shirt and squeeze his nipples towards Chud. He had quite a repertoire of stupidities. The game was to make us laugh so we would get into trouble. Inevitably, somebody would end up having a coughing fit and have to leave the room. On one occasion, Roy took out his dick and waved it at Chud as we were discussing the virgin birth. Roy got in big trouble over that because some creepy little git sneaked on him. Could have been Cockroach now I come to think about it.

Anyway, Roy Barr was a lifelong joker. Sadly, his life was to be curtailed by Coviman-12 and he would die in agony, riddled with the virus. Mike Taggart lived through it. None of us who survived were left without the mental scars.

Roy tapped on the glass and Jack hauled up the sash.

"Mike said he'll settle for one pack of cigarettes."

"Mike doesn't even smoke," Jack said.

"No, but I do," Roy said, "and Mike's my agent. He said that for one pack, he'll give you the spindle back, and for two packs you can have both the knob and the spindle."

"You do realise, don't you, Roy, that if we give in to your blackmail attempt, every bugger in the school will be unscrewing our door knob and demanding payment in kind."

"Not if we don't tell anyone."

Jack smiled. "You and old Maggot not telling anyone when you've scored one over Nick and me? Don't make me laugh. It'll be all round the school like the bloody virus."

Roy looked to one side as Mike Taggart arrived at the window. "They won't haggle, Mike."

Mike shrugged. "How boring. You're no bloody fun nowadays, Jack Parsons." He offered Jack the doorknob with the spindle attached.

Jack looked surprised, but reached out and took the knob. "Oh, you fucking twat," he screamed, letting it go. He nursed his hand in his armpit.

Mike and Roy ran off giggling like school girls.

"What happened?" I asked.

"The knob was bloody hot. I guess Mike must have put it over one of the gas rings in the boiler room. He didn't feel it because he was holding it by the spindle." He shook his hand trying to cool the burning. "Bugger, that hurts."

"Best you go get a bit of ointment or something before it blisters," I said. I took a small screwdriver set from one of my desk drawers, jumped out of the window into the quad, picked up the cooling door knob, and marched round to the outside to screw it back in place.

Jack nodded his thanks. "Back in ten," he said. "I'll

see what Matron's got." Since the school had been placed in quarantine we'd had no daily surgeries as was the usual practice. The appointed doctor and the school nurse, a rather sexy number whose name now escapes me, were both quarantined outside the school. So Matron had taken a supply of simple drugs and ointments up to her quarters high up in the rafters, and she was now the go-to person for any minor mishaps. Poor old Andy Pemberton's smashed leg was bad enough, but God knows what would happen if there was a really serious injury. Like a master jumping off the top of the tower, for example. No amount of balm was going to make that one better.

Jack was back quicker than I thought. I could smell some sort of ointment, so guessed they'd found something suitable. "Guess what I just saw?" he said, his voice excited like a kid on Christmas morning.

"What did you just saw, Jack Parsons?"

"I just saw Angela Maxwell sliding into the linen store. And guess who she had with her?"

"I suppose you are going to say Pete?"

"Nope. Not Pete."

"Go on then. Who was with Mrs Maxwell?"

"Braxton Bloody Boddington, that's who."

"What, that sneaky little tosser from School House? You're kidding aren't you? I thought he was retarded."

"Why?"

"Well with a name like Braxton Boddington, there's got to be something wrong with you. And you reckon he's in there with the over-ripe Mrs

Maxwell?"

"Straight up, Nick. Angela Maxwell is getting her horizontal pleasures this morning from Braxton Boddington."

"But it's only nine o'clock and the guy's a nonentity."

"That's obviously just our opinion. I know he's a bit of a dick, but he keeps himself to himself. The dirty little bugger is getting his end away right as we speak. I don't think he's taking much notice what time it is, to be honest." Jack stayed silent and stared at the screwdriver I'd used to replace the door knob.

After a moment, I asked, "How's your hand? Still sore?" Jack continued staring straight ahead. "Jack Parsons, hello! Anyone in?" I waved a hand in front of his face.

"Sorry. What?" Jack blinked.

"Your hand. How is it?"

"Er yeah. I just had a thought, Nick."

I could see by the look on Jack's face it was a thought that involved us both doing something outrageous. And so it was.

CHAPTER FIFTEEN

That evening, Lance Clooney burst into our study waving a thick leather-bound volume in the air. "You guys into witchcraft?" he asked.

Lance was a praepositor - a prae, as we called them. Like a prefect in state schools but posher. Nice guy who'd set his mind on becoming a dentist, so was following the A level subjects that would gain him entry into London's University College Dental Hospital. He'd already gained a very credible seven O levels - and these were in the days when an O level was worth having. Lance would do just fine in life - if he lived through the virus.

Jack and I both looked up. "You okay Lance?" Jack asked. "Today's half-an-hour of sunlight hasn't got to you has it? All you praes are like vampires and sunlight can turn a vampire into dust in minutes."

"I bet your school file says you could have made prae had it not been for your irritatingly smug attitude." Lance said.

"What irritatingly smug attitude?"

No facial reaction from Lance at all. "Do you find yourself funny, Mr Parsons?"

"I did, but you've convinced me otherwise."

Lance laughed. "You talk bollocks, Jack."

"I know. So why have you come charging in here waving a library book around the place? You know we're allergic to them, just like you vampires are allergic to garlic and sharpened wooden stakes."

"I got bored, Jack. No lessons, I'm all up-to-date with my revision, so I went kicking my heels round the library, see if there was anything interesting there."

"And you found an old moth-eaten book on witchcraft."

"I was reading some stuff on local history and was curious about the plaque in the market place in Castletown."

"What plaque?"

"The one about burning a witch in 1617."

"I know it," I said. "It's fixed to the base of the Smelt Memorial - the one that never got finished coz they ran out of money. So what about it?"

"Well the plaque commemorates the death of Margaret IneQuaine. And that led me to read up about her, which is where I found this book on Bishop John Farrow, the founder of our esteemed educational establishment." Lance waved the book at us and parked his tail bone on the corner of my desk.

"Sounds riveting," I said, trying not to smile.

"You'll like this," Lance said. "I read a couple of paragraphs and was about to shut the book and pick up something else, when this sentence caught my eye." Lance opened the book, flicked a couple of pages and read, "Bishop Farrow had a reputation of twisting arms to elicit donations to the church."

"Nothing unusual so far," I said. "The church always wants your cash. Seems that God can't manage money. I should know, my parents are always planning the next fund-raiser."

Lance ignored me and continued, "But he appeared to have hit a blank wall when, in 1617, he officiated over the burning of Margaret IneQuaine and her son Robert, who was just a baby."

"The bastard burnt a baby?" I said with genuine horror. "I knew the church was bloody barbaric, but burning babies—"

"She refused to pay Bishop Farrow's redemption money."

"What the hell is redemption money?" Jack asked.

"It was Farrow's version of forgiveness," Lance said. "He was a young, fat bully of a man with the overpowering authority of the church behind him. He discovered it was easy to elicit donations by threat."

I smiled. "As Thomas Paine said in The Age of Reason, 'It is from the Bible that man has learned cruelty, rapine, and murder; for the belief of a cruel God makes a cruel man'."

"The fuck is rapine?" Jack asked.

"The violent seizure of somebody else's property."

"Good job it's you taking English A level and not me, then."

I laughed. "You'd have liked Paine. He also said, 'One good schoolmaster is of more use than a hundred priests'."

Jack nodded wisely. "I'm with him on that one, whoever he was."

Lance ignored us and continued, "As was usual in the day, it was his parents' money that had bought Farrow his bishopric. And right from the start he was renowned for building up his own treasure chest. Anyway, some strange and damning accusations had been made against Margaret IneQuaine by various members of the community. The accusations revolved around her being a witch, although the record of her death in this book suggests it was because she and her husband had avoided being touched by a sickness that had swept across the island the previous year. Goes without saying, you couldn't avoid a sickness sent by God unless you were in league with the devil. They said they saw her dancing naked in a field, casting spells to protect her and her family."

"So Bishop Farrow had her burned?"

"Farrow presided as a judge over Margaret IneQuaine's witchcraft trial. Though there was no evidence whatsoever of the poor woman being a witch, the suggestion is that he guided the jury - which included several clergy under his control - to a verdict of guilty. In fact, the Bishop himself gave testimony that he had seen her dancing naked, singing and chanting in a strange dialect. The Bishop's position in the church prevented him from direct involvement in the legal shedding of blood, so he left the room before they sentenced Margaret IneQuaine to death. But it's clear he had instructed his clergy beforehand."

"So they burned her. But what about the child?" I asked.

"I'm coming to that," Lance said. "Bishop Farrow tried again to extract money from the woman, offering God's forgiveness if she gave half of her lands to God - in other words, gave them to him. He phrased it as, 'Your gift of land to the church will help greatly your passage to heaven'. But she was a stubborn woman and refused. It's possible she didn't think that Farrow would go through with the sentence since nobody had ever been burned on the isle of Man."

"Or more likely that he would take her lands and still burn her." I said.

Lance nodded. "That's also well possible."

"But he did go ahead, didn't he?" Jack asked.

"In the end, when she gave him no choice, yes. It had gone too far and neither of them was prepared to back down. According to the report, a great fire of faggots was prepared in the market place next to Castle Rushen and Margaret IneQuaine was tied to a stake. Farrow asked her over and again to repent her witchcraft and pay the church for her redemption. She repeated over and over that she was not a witch so had nothing to repent."

"So they lit the fire?"

"Before that, Farrow took Margaret IneQuaine's baby boy and laid him on the wood, ready to burn. The guard charged with setting fire to the pyre refused to do it, so Farrow lit it himself. It stunned the crowd into silence. They were so horrified at watching the bishop burn a woman and her baby son that women accused of crimes against the church were thereafter always acquitted. In fact, Margaret IneQuaine was the only person ever executed for witchcraft in the Isle of Man."

"But what about Slieau Whallian, near Peel?" I asked. "Isn't that famous for executing witches?"

Lance chuckled. He reopened the book where he had left a slip of paper sticking out between the pages. "I was curious about that too," he said, "but those witch deaths were not considered executions."

"Hang on you two," Jack said. "I haven't the faintest idea what you're talking about. I got lost when you said Slieau Whallian."

"Slieau Whallian is a hill near Peel," I said. "It's known as Witches Hill. It has a grisly reputation due to the reputed punishment of witches in past centuries. Any woman accused of witchcraft would be put into a barrel with sharp iron spikes inserted round the interior, pointing inwards. Then the barrel would be allowed to roll from the top of the hill to the bottom. It's very steep and it's a long way down. Even without the iron spikes, you probably wouldn't stand a chance. Anyway, it was said that if the woman survived, she was indeed a witch, and should be drowned. If she died, she was innocent and would receive God's forgiveness. As you might guess, everybody who was rolled down the hill died."

"So there were no witches," Lance concluded.

Jack roared laughing. "Manx justice at its finest."

Lance said, "Practices like that were common throughout Britain at the time. At Slieau Whallian it wasn't just witches who got the spiked barrel treatment. Men did too. So it's fair to say that Margaret IneQuaine was the only person ever to be actually executed for witchcraft."

"The others who were accused were judged innocent by God," I said.

Jack asked, "That's all very interesting, Lance, but why did you think Nick and I would like the story particularly?"

"Because, in her dying breaths, Margaret IneQuaine cursed Bishop Farrow and his ghastly church to one thousand generations. 'A curse on you and all that you touch', she said. It seems the bishop just smiled and cursed her back."

"And?"

"Well according to this account, a generation in those days was thought to be about twenty-five years. Remember, she was burnt in 1617." Lance tugged a piece of notepaper from the book and read, "Twenty-five years later, in 1642, the Bishop gets married and his wife chokes on their wedding night with a fish bone stuck in her throat. That was generation one. In 1667 the house of Bishop Farrow burns to the ground. The bishop narrowly escapes with his life, but his second wife and his two sons are burnt alive. That's generation two. The bishop decided at that point that enough was enough so he created the Bishop Farrow Trust, to provide education for clergy and their sons on the Isle of Man. He signed the document and immediately died. Probably today, we'd say it was a heart attack."

"Pure coincidence, surely?"

"You reckon?" Lance said, with a glint in his eye. "They buried the bishop in the cathedral in Peel Castle. In 1692 the cathedral roof collapsed and crushed the Bishop's tomb. That was generation three. The building was never rebuilt and fell into ruins during the years that followed. I could go on because every 25 years something weird and catastrophic happened to Bishop Farrow's legacy." He looked down and moved his finger down the page. "Here's another example. Do you know St Trinian's Church at Greeba?"

I nodded. Jack shook his head.

"It's the roofless ruin of a small chapel at the foot of Greeba Mountain, right next to the main Douglas to Peel Road. In Manx gaelic, it's called a Keeil Brisht - a broken church. Anyway, at the time of Bishop Farrow, it was nothing more than the ruin of a 14th century church on an ancient site. Bishop

Farrow wanted a new church to be built on the site as a legacy to himself. He left money aplenty in his will to rebuild St Trinian's."

"But it never got finished, did it?" I said.

"There's a lot of folklore attached to it concerning the Buggane, a huge mythical ogre who lived on Greeba Mountain and who vowed that the church should never be completed," Lance said. "But the actual facts are that, every time the workmen put a roof on the building, it would collapse overnight. The church of St Trinian has remained to this day without a roof."

"It's all myth and legend," Jack said.

I frowned at him. "If you were Manx, you wouldn't say that. We're quite proud of our little people over here. And I'm not talking midgets; I'm talking THE little people."

Jack chuckled, but Lance cut in. "There's a lot more relating to the Margaret IneQuaine curse, guys. The really interesting bit starts after the College buildings as we know them today were built. The Bishop Farrow Trust did indeed educate boys for the clergy on the island. He placed the farm of Ballagilley in the hands of the trustees, and the rents - then about £20 a year - were used to pay for the boys' training. Within 150 years the value of the real estate increased more than thirty-fold. So in 1830, the trustees decided to use the surplus funds to construct the college as we know it today. The original building was commenced in 1830 but today's Bishop's College really started life in 1843.

In 1867, the chapel roof collapsed killing the school chaplain. That was another generational milestone. They rebuilt. Then, in 1892, the next generation, as they were raising the roof of what we now know to be Colman, Dickens, and Walkers Houses to create five new dormitories, the scaffolding collapsed, crushing several workmen and a student. And so it goes on."

"Just coincidence." I said.

"Could be, but that brings us to 1967 and what have we got?"

"Fucking Coviman-12 Virus," Jack said.

"Yeah, but that's the whole island," I said. "It's not specific to College. In fact, so far, we've been spared."

"That could soon change," Lance said, "because the one final fact, which is bloody scary, is that all of these events took place on the anniversary of Margaret IneQuaine's death - 16th February - which is?"

"Tomorrow," Jack and I said in unison.

"Bingo!" from Lance. "If my research turns out to be true, the shit will hit the fan tomorrow." He stood up and opened the door. "Sleep well, chaps, and don't play with matches."

"Blood-sucking vampire," Jack shouted after him.

CHAPTER SIXTEEN

Jack and I were still chuckling as we crept up the back stairs close to midnight. First of all, we'd decided that Lance Clooney joining the dots was just a string of coincidences, and that if one looked closer, there would almost certainly be other intervening events just as serious. For instance, on 27 Jan 1844, just one year after it opened its doors, the school buildings were more or less totally destroyed by a massive fire. That was not one of the generational anniversaries. So Margaret IneQuaine's curse was an interesting theory, but that was all it was.

What was really making us smile was that we'd done to Braxton Boddington and Angela Maxwell what Mike Taggart and Roy Barr had done to us. We'd tiptoed up to the linen store and unscrewed the handle. This one was a proper handle with a lock plate, but we knew as long as we took the spindle, the effect would be the same. We left the handle on the floor near the door.

Apparently, it had taken Boddington and Mrs Maxwell some time and a lot of noise to draw attention to their plight. Matron was having an 'early siesta' - possibly involving Jaap van Anrooy - and heard nothing. It was Vlad Kelsey, the maths master, who had rescued them. Vlad was, of course, his nickname, being short for Dracula. I don't think I ever knew his real name. He was a coarse individual. As eccentric as a transvestite squirrel, except that Vlad's interests lay in young boys. Him being boarded in Lower School for the duration was a move born out of necessity. But it was probably not a wise move if the rumours about little Charlie McDonald's rear entrance being defiled were true. Jack and I had spent the day giggling about Boddington and Mrs Maxwell's discovery, like naughty school children. Which, indeed, we were.

Now, as we approached midnight, and reached the top of the service stairs that led to the staff quarters, we were no longer naughty school children. We were sex-hungry teenagers on a promise. A door opened to our left and Mrs Maxwell stepped out of one of the other small staff bedsits. She was dressed only in a see-through nightdress. Her hair clung to her pale cheeks in tight Little Orphan Annie curls. She looked like a waif with no friends - except maybe for an extra helping of Cheddar cheese from time-to-time. When she spotted us, she froze, stared at us, then turned and shut herself back in the room without saying a word.

"Bugger, she gets about doesn't she?" Jack whispered.

"Do you reckon she'll drop us in the shit?" I asked.

"I doubt it. I mean, what's she doing here herself. She's supposed to be tucked up in bed with our esteemed music master. Or Pete Scott."

"Or Braxton Boddington," I chuckled.

"Come on, let's see what Michelle and Rhonda have in store for us."

I can only guess what Michelle had in store for Jack, but what Rhonda had in store for me was a mad romp that lasted almost two hours. She was, as Jack had commented to me the other day, a very athletic lady. When we kissed, she tasted sweet, like dark chocolate in my mouth. Our tongues played together in liquid sunshine. Missionary position was out: every other known position was in. Rhonda wasn't a teacher like Michelle; she was the examiner making sure I had learnt my lessons well. She was insatiable - almost. Just after quarter to two, she gave me a small nod followed by a cheeky wink as if to tell me I had achieved some sort of pass mark on her shag-o-meter. "Shall we grab a bit of sleep now?" she said. "I have work to do in a few hours."

"Like serving food to a load of hungry school boys."

She laughed. "We've been told we have to place all the serving dishes out on the tables before you lot arrive, and only take them back to the kitchen when Farrow Hall is empty."

"Who said that?"

"Orders from the principal. I think he's trying to make our lives a bit easier. He's right, because it's quite tough with just the two of us in the hall and two in the kitchen."

I kissed her one last time, pulled the sheet over her, and exited the room, pulling on my dressing gown. I half expected to bump into Angela Maxwell, but it didn't happen. I stepped into our study for a smoke on the way back to the dorm. For the first half of my life, one of the joys of good sex was the cigarette after. Then I grew enough balls to quit smoking and discovered it made no difference. So I became addicted to sex instead of nicotine. I was back in my own bed before the tower clock chimed two. Jack still hadn't arrived. Guess he and Michelle had hit it off.

The following morning, I found myself looking at Braxton Boddington's body, slumped against the sundial in the middle of the quad. His head looked like a soft-boiled egg with the top removed. The principal arrived, vomited, then staggered off to report a second death to the authorities.

As Jack and I stood in our study staring out of the window and the gaggle of gawping students, he said, "Don't fancy much for breakfast this morning. You?"

My brows pinched as I stubbed out my cigarette and the smoke drifted into my eyes. "Actually, Jack, I'm bloody ravenous. Rhonda was everything you said she was and more. What about Michelle?"

He grinned. "Words fail me."

"So have you got your appetite back then?"

He nodded. "Maybe I have, Nick, but something is bugging me. Well two things actually. Why was Boddington killed, just the day after shagging Angela Maxwell? And why was Angela Maxwell up in the kitchen staff quarters last night? Seems to me the two may well be connected. I just don't know how."

"Nor me, but it's not our concern." I checked my watch. "New rules, we have to wait half an hour now for the younger boys to eat." Out of the open window I saw the praepositors, including Lance Clooney, herding everybody away from the body and towards the dining hall. Lance glanced our way and shrugged his shoulders. It was like he was asking if this was the next generation of Margaret IneQuaine's curse to strike Bishop Farrow's Trust. When I saw the full extent of the mess that used to be a student's head, I took a step back into the study. I wasn't sure too many fellow pupils would be wolfing down bacon and egg this morning."

As the younger pupils were eating, or poking food round their plates, we watched a group of men in their regulation green hazmat suits, face masks, and breather filters clear away Boddington's remains. If it was the same group who had turned up last time for Mr Patterson, they must be wondering what the hell was going on at College. Or maybe, because of the harsh quarantine conditions outside, they had seen more than enough death not to worry too much anymore. I guessed that there would be an enquiry of some sort when the virus had passed.

As we came out of breakfast, the Merryweather fire engine turned up again through the Western arch. It was driven and operated by senior boys who presumably had been put off their breakfasts by the gore. They hosed down the quad with a certain efficiency. Must have been all the practice they were getting.

Jack and I smoked another cigarette in our study. It seemed futile now to try and hide the fact. Nobody took any notice anymore. Noticeable too was the fact that boys slouched around with their hands in their pockets. Many had given up wearing ties. It seemed that nobody polished their shoes any more. Knuckle Dragger Harvey would have had an absolute field day. And Cedric Patterson's child-beating arm would have needed frequent resuscitation. A feeling of malaise had settled over the whole school. Five weeks of being confined to the grounds was taking its toll. Five weeks living in fear of an outbreak of Coviman-12 was taking an even bigger toll. So was the fact that there were now only eight masters in charge.

Later, Jack and I stepped outside for a mid-morning smoke. It was a new experience just strolling around the place with cigarettes in our hands. We saw no sign of any masters, and I don't think we would have bothered if we had. Smoking was a serious business when I was eighteen. We didn't realise until years later that those tubes of tobacco were killing us just as surely as the virus would if it reached us. It was only a question of speed.

Since giving up, I have analysed the ritual of smoking, how a large part of the satisfaction is the look and feel of the box, pulling off the foil wrapper inside, and taking out a cigarette. The slightly woody smell of the fresh tobacco. Smokers love the gestures - lighting, flicking the ash, holding something between their fingers. And then the actual smoking of it. Pull with your lips on that filter and feel the smoke drift across your tongue, down your throat, and deep into your lungs. It may sound weird to a non-smoker, but it's first class transport to nirvana for the committed addict. I still remember how it felt after inhaling, as the nicotine hit the bloodstream. A few seconds of both serenity and attentiveness, together, in exactly the right amounts. Then the slow exhale - forceful enough so that the smoke didn't merely seep from my mouth but not so energetic that it disturbed the moment.

Smoke over, Jack and I strolled back into the quadrangle and through to our study. As we entered, I swore. "Oh, for God's sake. This has gone too bloody far."

Jack pushed into the room behind me. Everything had been trashed. The desks were overturned, books and papers scattered everywhere. "Fucking Bruiser," he cursed. "This is just too much, Nick. We have to go and take him on."

Lance Clooney arrived and looked over Jack's shoulder. "Is this Bruiser's doing?"

We nodded. "Nobody else is this unstable," I said.

"Well you'll have to have a clear up later, chaps. I've

been trying to find you. The principal has asked me to get you to his office pronto. He said it was urgent. Top priority were his actual words."

Jack and I cast a glance at each other, closed the door on the carnage, and headed towards George Armstrong's office.

CHAPTER SEVENTEEN

As we made our way to the principal's office, Bruiser and his shadow stepped out from behind a recess in the corridor. The first thing that struck me was that Bruiser had his tie round his head, like a bandana. The second thing that struck me was that he had our two long kitchen knives tucked down his belt like cutlasses. He looked like a poor imitation of a pirate captain. If he fell over with the knives like that, he might well end up as a pirate captain with a high-pitched voice. "You going to a fancy dress?" I asked.

"Don't try and be fucking clever, Quine. I confiscated these knives from your study earlier. I warned you there would be a payback, and now it's going to happen."

"You're the wanker who wrecked our study then," Jack said, as if he didn't already know.

Cochrane spoke up. He was brandishing a sports javelin in one hand, like a spear. "Yes, and we confiscated your stash of cigarettes too. We'll take over the cigarette supply from now on."

"You cheeky fuckers," Jack snarled. "You have no right going into another pupil's study unless invited. And you had no reason to wreck it like you did."

"We invited ourselves," Cochrane said.

I tapped my watch. "We have to meet with the principal. We'll sort this out later."

Bruiser grinned. "I will sort it out, that's for sure."

He pulled one of the knives from his belt and waved it under my nose with his big clumsy hand. I stood my ground and held my body upright, but the skin was crawling beneath my shirt, sweat prickling from my pores. Anyone as unstable as Bruiser Williams was a danger at the best of times, but armed with a long, sharp knife… "You pair of faggots are going to get your come-uppance," he grunted.

"Wrong, you brain-dead tosser," Jack snarled. "You and your arse-wipe are going to be the ones that will get sorted out. Have no bloody fear of that."

Cockroach made a mock pistol with his hand and mimed shooting himself in the temple. Bruiser laughed as Jack and I moved away feeling shocked at the turn of events. We were about to feel a lot more shocked.

George Armstrong was still looking pale when we knocked on his study door. I realised that, after our conversation with him the other evening, both Jack and I had stopped referring to him as the Prinky, which we had always done. We were now using either his name or 'the principal'. Sigmund Freud would no doubt be able to make something out of that.

Before we sat down, he asked, "A question to you both first. Have either of you been in touch with any juniors - that's anyone not in the sixth form - or any masters yesterday or this morning?"

"After a moment's reflection Jack and I both replied in the negative.

The principal nodded and pointed to the two chairs facing the desk. "Okay, I have some grave news," he said, tapping a letter-opener on his blotter.

"Braxton Boddington," I said. "We saw him

earlier."

"It goes far beyond that, boys." He looked up. "For the moment, what I am going to tell you stays within these four walls." He allowed himself a grim smile. "I'm getting used to saying that to you two."

We both nodded. Jack said, "You have our assurance, Sir, that whatever is discussed will remain confidential."

The principal glanced from one of us to the other as if assessing our ability to accept bad news. We thought we were prepared but we were not.

He said, "There's a very good chance that the Coviman-12 virus has now entered College. In fact, it's pretty much a certainty."

Jack and I gasped. Someone had opened the cage door, and the sharks were circling. Nothing stirred in his office except for the tick of a clock somewhere on his shelves. "Can you say that again, please?" I asked in a trembling voice.

"Yes, Quine. Almost certainly Coviman-12 is here, and we have to take immediate steps to salvage what we can."

"How do you know? Can you explain further?" Jack asked, his voice almost as weak as mine.

The principal nodded his head. "It began with Cedric Patterson's suicide the day before yesterday. As you might imagine, Mrs Patterson was distraught. In her grief, she did something rather silly. And before you are tempted to make a judgement on her, when people kill themselves, they think they're ending the pain, but all they're doing is passing it on to the people they leave behind. And try not to blame Mister Patterson either. A man devoid of hope has no future, and he knew that.

Anyway, Mrs Patterson was feeling the pain of her husband's death. She felt that she had no-one close who she could confide in so went to see her brother. He lives on Fuschia Green."

Fuschia Green was a small estate of houses that bordered the college to the South-West. Nowadays, they call it 'social housing'. Back then, they were always referred to as 'council houses'. A low granite wall was all that defined the boundary.

I said, "But that's outside—"

"I am well aware, Quine, where Fuschia Green is. I am also well aware that it should be impossible to walk the streets without drawing the attention of the street marshals. But Mrs Patterson's brother's house is one of the ones that back onto the school playing fields. She only had to climb the wall which, it seems, she has done many times in the past with the aid of some folding kitchen steps, and she was straight into her brother's back garden, and thus his house."

"And her brother was infected?" Jack asked.

The principal looked grim. "This virus is a lot smarter than the ones you see in zombie films based on Haitian folklore. It doesn't make its victims stagger around wide-eyed and moaning so anyone in their right mind would run the other way. It gets you cosying up to people so you cough and sneeze it right into their faces. Mrs Patterson's brother was already dead, his body riddled with the virus. Judging from what Mrs Patterson has just told me, he may have been dead for a day or more."

"She's been here in your study?"

"No, Parsons. As I'm sure you're aware, there's an internal telephone system at college that links all the independent buildings like Lower School, the woodworking school, the art school, Matron's quarters, and similar locations. Mrs Patterson telephoned me and updated me. The masters have been advised of the risk and have decided to self-quarantine. If you look up towards Lower School on your way back to your study, you will see that street marshals are already sectioning off Lower School with metal road pins and yellow tape. It has now become part of the island's general quarantine zone."

"Ye Gods," I muttered. "Can I ask when this happened? Her going over the wall?"

"The evening of Mr Patterson's death. So 36 hours ago. There's a high likelihood that she is infected. It seems that, on finding her dead brother, she held his hand and stroked his head. It's a natural reaction, but an extremely unwise one in present circumstances."

"And then she went back to Lower School and mingled with the masters and the junior boarders?"

The principal nodded. "They are all at very severe risk. Judging from what I have been told of Coviman-12, the likelihood is that the whole of Lower School has fallen."

"And what of the rest of College?" I asked.

"Also at risk, and that's why I need to enlist your help. If Mrs Patterson did indeed pass the virus on to the other masters or the junior boys, then they may have also passed it on to the rest of the school."

"Oh shit," came from Jack.

I found myself feeling queasy with Lance's warning. "Jinny the witch," I mumbled.

Jack and the principal looked at me strangely.

I said, "It's a Manx children's song for Hop-tu-Naa - that's Halloween to you non-Manx people, Jack. Jinny the Witch went over the house. To get the stick to lather the mouse. Hop-tu-Naa, my mother's gone away. And she won't be back until the morning."

Jack pulled a strange face. "So what's Halloween got to do with— Oh, God, the witch theory?"

"You two are obviously talking about the Margaret IneQuaine curse," the principal said.

"You're aware of it?"

"Of course. It's not something we talk about though, particularly as we approach 16th February on an anniversary year."

"So it's true then?"

"It's just a series of coincidences."

"Which has conveniently struck again today," Jack said.

"Chaps, much though I would love to chat about the so-called curse of Margaret IneQuaine, there are things we need to get done straight away. So put thoughts of witches away and pin back your ears. Here's my logic. Only sixth formers have been free from contact with younger students or masters."

"Is that the reason for yesterday's notice about staying within the houses and sixth-formers eating separately?"

"No, Parsons, that was fortuitous, but I can't claim to have been blessed with some sort of divine foresight. I was trying to deal with the shortage of teaching and supervisory staff, and the pressure the kitchen staff are under. It does, however, give us an opportunity to do something, as long as we act quickly." Again he eyed us both. "Quickly means straight away. I'm going to ask you to enlist the help of a small handful of boys and prepare for the worst."

"Why us?" I asked. "Why not the praes?"

"I knew you would ask, Quine. It's because the praepositors were chosen for their good sense, their willingness to abide by the rules, and their understanding of the community that is Bishop's College. Right now, I need people who can get past the idea of always living by a set of written rules. I'm looking for risk-takers and original thinkers. People who are willing to adapt at a moment's notice."

"And the praes don't fit that bill?"

"Some but not all."

"And we do?" Jack asked, smiling for the first time. "What makes you think that?"

"You're impetuous and tend to act spontaneously, John Parsons. And you, Nick Quine, are cocky and acerbic."

I took issue with him labelling me as cocky and acerbic. I preferred to think I was charming. And if he didn't like it, then he could kiss my hairy arse. What was cocky or acerbic about that?

The principal continued, "But both of you have qualities which, God willing, will help you through your adult lives. Everything that has gone on between you and me over the past couple of weeks shows that you don't care too much about the rules. In fact, the pair of you sneaking round the kitchen staff quarters late last night displays your willingness to take risks and break every rule in the book."

I looked at Jack. He looked at me. We both said, "Mrs Maxwell?"

The principal chortled. "Mrs Maxwell has some issues with her marital relationship at the moment. I'll tell you about it in a moment. She has now taken up temporary residence in one of the empty kitchen staff apartments. But don't look so surprised. Over the years, a small handful of other boys have trodden those stairs and held secret liaisons with the serving staff. For those rare few, it has become a rite of passage from adolescence into manhood. While it has remained discreet I have turned a blind eye to it."

Jack and I looked at each other. "Bloody hell" Jack whispered.

The principal chuckled. "We were all young once, lads. Don't forget that. There's nothing new about teenagers hankering after the opposite sex. I sowed my own share of wild oats when I was young during the war."

George Armstrong just went up another notch in my esteem. He blushed a little as he added, "And as you'll no doubt discover for yourselves in time, there's nothing new about adults having extra-marital affairs either. It doesn't mean they no longer love their partners." He hurried on without pausing. "Now, let's talk about this bloody virus. You do realise what a virus is, don't you?"

We thought we did, but stayed silent.

"Most people think of viruses as parasites, but they aren't parasites at all. An organism has to be considered alive to be classified as a parasite. Viruses don't do any of the things living organisms do. They don't grow, they can't move on their own, and they don't metabolise. They don't even have cells. But the one thing a virus is very good at is reproducing. When it finds a suitable host cell, it attaches itself and injects its DNA through the cell's plasma wall. The virus' genes are transcribed into the host cell's DNA, and the host cell's genetic code is rewritten. Whatever its job was before, its new job is to do nothing but produce copies of the original virus, usually until it's created so many that the cell bursts open and spreads the infection. At secret labs in Porton Down, which I'm sure you are aware are the Ministry of Defence's most secretive and controversial research facilities, domestic animals collected from the Isle of Man have shown signs of carrying the Coviman-12 virus. But it has not affected them the same it has us humans. So we humans are the definitive target."

"Understood," Jack said. "But what do we do now to stop it spreading throughout the whole school?"

"We separate those who are at higher risk from those who are at lower risk."

We waited for the explanation which arrived after a short pause while the principal again tapped his letter-opener on his blotter.

"Let's look at how this thing could spread," he said. "First of all, contact with Mrs Patterson was made by the masters in Lower School who tried to comfort her when she told them that, like her husband, her brother was dead. They only thought to ask the next day - yesterday evening in fact - how she knew of her brother's death. That's when she admitted that she had climbed over the wall and made the discovery herself. By that time, it was too late. The masters have been teaching in enclosed classrooms. They have mingled together in the master's common room. They have supervised recreation time and more."

"So we're all at risk then?" I asked.

"Maybe not. For a start, the sixth forms have not

attended any classes due to the shortage of masters. With the exception of School House, sixth-formers stand the best chance of having avoided contact with a carrier."

"Why do you exclude School House?" Jack asked.

"Because Mr Bond, as you know, lives on the premises and often tours School House studies and house-room. But he has also been in contact with the other masters. So all School House students are at risk. That leaves sixth-formers from Colman House, Dickens House and Walkers House. But now we have to eliminate any of those who may have made contact with juniors or with masters."

"Which is why you asked us if we had, when we arrived?" I said.

The principal nodded.

"Sir, what's the end game?" Jack asked.

"The end game, Parsons is to try and immediately segregate low risk students and get them into the chapel."

"The chapel? Are we all going to pray for redemption before being eaten by Coviman-12?"

"Wait and I will give you the whole picture. We've always had a contingency plan in case of an incident such as this."

I had a sudden deep dread that Bruiser Williams with his knives down his belt and his army of cohorts was the very least of our worries.

CHAPTER EIGHTEEN

The principal took a deep breath before explaining his plan. "As you know gentlemen, Reverend and Mrs Cain were at home in Castletown when we were quarantined. Without a chaplain, there have been no services, so the chapel hasn't been used. Right at this moment, it's the only place in College that is one hundred percent free of risk. We need to move 'safe' pupils into the chapel. In fact, we've been using it to store emergency supplies ever since we were quarantined, and I also have supplies in the garage of my home and in the small cricket pavilion nearby. If we get safe students into the chapel now, any outbreak of the virus in the main school can be contained there."

"And how's that going to wash with the other boys? The ones who are left behind?"

"We're going to announce exactly the opposite. We'll erect tape and posts round my house, the pavilion, and the chapel and tell them that it is us who are being quarantined. Only if the virus breaks out in the main school will they realise that the opposite is true."

Jack and I understood and affirmed. "How do we select 'safe' pupils?

"It has to be done straight away," the principal said. "And by that, I mean as soon as you leave this study. I want you to choose two trusted boys from each house except School House. They must talk to sixth-formers in their own houses and find out if they have been in touch with any juniors or masters yesterday or this morning. Just as I did for you earlier. If they have, move on and ask somebody else. Same if there's any doubt, move on. We must err on the side of caution. Boys who have definitely not contacted masters or younger boys in the last twenty-four hours should be told discreetly to make their way immediately to the chapel, bringing their wash bags and towels with them. Immediately means right away. They shouldn't talk to anybody or make physical contact with anybody. I shall be in the chapel to explain to them."

"How do these trusted students find out if other boys were in touch with any juniors or masters?"

"Pretend it's some sort of simple questionnaire devised by me. No need to go at it like a bull in a china shop. They can be a bit subtle like, 'The principal is trying to work out how to staff College during the lock-down. He needs to understand boys' movements. Did you remain in your study yesterday as required, or did you mix with other boys or masters?'."

"Okay, I see what you mean," Jack said. "Presumably we have to ask the same questions first of our chosen interviewers?"

"Yes. And if they pass muster, you need to advise them to avoid getting too close to other boys. You can tell them that it's another precaution that I am considering."

"Got it. Excluding School House, I guess there are only about 75 sixth-form boarders."

The principal nodded. "Seventy-eight, to be precise. But don't include the praes, so that reduces it by fourteen to sixty-four."

"Why not the praes?"

"Because, with the exception of Lance Clooney and Jonathan Davis, they are all teaching this morning. I had a difficult decision to make. To try and keep some semblance of normality, with the masters self-quarantining in Lower School, I assigned the praes to simple teaching tasks. And yes, before you ask, I do realise that I am exposing them to risk. Sometimes in life, one has to make difficult choices and then live with them. That decision may well remain on my conscience, but it's my decision to live with."

"Jon Davis is in School House," I said, "so he's a no-go anyway. But Lance Clooney is in Walkers House, so we could ask him."

The principal nodded. "It would be nice to spare at least one of them," he mumbled.

"And while these guys are asking questions, what do we do?" Jack asked.

Armstrong drew a deep breath and sighed. "Here's the hardest part. Harder even than selecting those who are given a chance and those who aren't." He reached into his desk drawer and took out a worn green leather wallet, the size of a large envelope. "As you know, Mr Flanagan has not been here since quarantine."

Charlie Flanagan was a former soldier who had served in the war. He liked to assure us that he had been Regimental Sergeant Major, but we all doubted that. He may have made it to sergeant, but corporal was more likely. Charlie was a solid man who was good at marching, at shouting instructions, and at being the school gofer. I think his hours were limited to two or three each morning when he went round each classroom checking that all students were present and correct, and circulating notices from the principal. Charlie was also in attendance every Tuesday afternoon when he would scream and shout at us in the combined cadet force, trying to keep us in step, or teaching us how to blow a bugle. For the last few weeks, since quarantine, there had been no Tuesday cadets.

Charlie's other task was as the school armourer. Behind the swimming baths was a squat stone building. External stairs led to three classrooms on the first floor where poor old Arthur Bannister and two other masters taught the youngsters. Below, on the ground floor, was the school armoury and cadet stores. You needed a new pair of boots? You went to see Charlie Flanagan and he would issue them on receipt of a chitty signed by your housemaster. From what I had been told, there was a good trade in stolen army boots at the port in Douglas. Ten shillings a time - that's 50p in today's money. Sounds cheap now, doesn't it? But that trade had dried up since quarantine.

Also on the ground floor of the armoury were two locked rooms. One was Charlie Flanagan's little office and the other was the armoury itself. Over one hundred Lee-Enfield bolt-action, magazine-fed, repeating rifles that served as the main firearm for the British during the war were chained to wooden racks fixed to the walls. One lad was appointed armourer and every Tuesday he spent the afternoon pulling pieces of oiled four-by-two through the barrels with a pull-through, and keeping the stocks oiled. The .303 packed a hell of a punch. A .303-inch or 7.7 mm calibre rimmed rifle cartridge was as effective a deterrent as you would find, even today. And, old as they were, those rifles had been maintained in top condition.

The principal pulled open the green leather wallet. Inside was a selection of keys. "Only Mister

Flanagan and myself hold keys to the armoury," he said. He began to separate a small handful of keys. "I want you to take these and go to the armoury. I assume you both drive since you have an old Morris Eight stashed away in the station car park?"

Jack and I both laughed. "Caught red-handed," I said. "We only use it for—"

"I know what you use it for," Armstrong said with a twisted smile. "Anyone who can get away with sliding out most Saturday nights for over a year without getting caught gets my deepest respect."

"And you never did anything to stop us?" I asked, astonished.

"Poor Mr Harvey was the school policeman. I only draw lines in the sand when I feel it necessary. You can't enforce rigid rules and at the same time encourage individual thinking. Anyway, assuming at least one of you knows how to drive, I want you to take my car to the armoury. Reverse up to the doors and take as many rifles as you can fit in the boot. Try not to get seen. If you go into Mr Flanagan's office, you'll find a locked, steel cabinet. Inside is ammunition for the .303s. Most of them are blanks for shooting on exercise, but there should be a couple of big boxes of live rounds. You know how to tell the difference?"

We nodded. Live rounds were about three inches long with pointed bullets. Blanks were slightly shorter, snub-nosed cartridges, crimped at the end. They were filled with wadding and were harmless unless you shot yourself in the foot at close range as one student did. He didn't think it would hurt. It did, and he had to have his toe removed.

"So load all the live rounds and as many rifles as you can get into the boot of my car. Then bring the car back to the chapel. Again, reverse up to the doors so nobody sees what's being unloaded."

"Do you really think it will come to shooting?" Jack asked.

"I hope not but, as the Boy Scouts say, we have to be prepared. As I told you, what we'll do is erect a post and tape perimeter boundary and patrol it day and night. It will seem that we are doing exactly the same as the street marshals, except we'll have no biological hazard suits. It doesn't matter. We wouldn't need any if we were already infected. Any questions?"

Jack and I looked at each other. "It's a hell of a thing isn't it," I said.

"It is, indeed, a hell of a thing," the principal replied. "But it's a hell of a necessary thing."

"I have one question," Jack said. "We've spoken about getting students into the chapel, but what about staff?"

"I'll deal with that. Mrs Maxwell is clear because she has slept in the staff quarters for the last two nights. She has not been in physical contact with her husband, and has done no teaching. Lesley Parkes and Miss Partridge will be invited to join us as long as they've not contacted the wrong people. And before you ask, the two young ladies who have been keeping you amused will also be invited. I issued instructions for them to avoid contact with pupils this morning, just in case. Good job I did. Mr Tobias, the chef and Miss Margerson will be asked the checking questions too."

"Who's Miss Margerson?"

"She used to be a maid, like your young friends, but she was needed to help with the food preparation."

"Got it. Middle-aged lady? Dark hair?"

The principal nodded. He clapped his hands. "If you've no more questions, get moving. This has to be done now."

"You forgot Matron," Jack said.

"I didn't. She spent last night with Jaap van Anrooy. As Head Boy, he mixes with boys from all houses and all years. If he's infected, she's infected. Here are my car keys. Now go."

As Jack and I left his office, Jack said, "The old bugger knows everything, doesn't he?"

"It seems that way. He's been very good at focusing on what matters and letting little indiscretions slip by."

"Little indiscretions like owning an old car to get us into Douglas on Saturday nights?"

"And illicit sex with the maids," I added.

Jack said, "Life's full of surprises, isn't it? I feel mean as hell now. I couldn't let his little lapse with Lesley just slip, could I? I had to charge in there with threats and demands."

"Well he did say you were impetuous, Jack."

"He's right. It seems like a bloody miserable thing to do now."

"Don't beat yourself up over it, just apologise to Armstrong in private if you get the chance. Life deals us some strange hands at times. None more so than right now. Let's get things moving."

Three hours later, just as we were feeling hungry, the last of the selected sixth-formers made it to the chapel with puzzled looks on their faces. In honesty, I felt like running away and hiding in a small, dark place. But that wasn't going to happen, and we had to face whatever developed head-on. Inside, I felt weighed down, as if something had sucked out all of my energy. We were now trapped in limbo, where only the chapel existed, surrounded by the same blackness from which the universe was made.

Including the adults, there were a total of forty-seven of us. Forty-two pupils, the principal, Lesley, Michelle, Rhonda, and Angela Maxwell, who was looking far from happy. The principal later told us that he had excluded Miss Partridge, Miss Margerson, and the school cook, because they had all been in close contact with some of the masters yesterday. He was gambling that they hadn't passed on any infection at breakfast this morning. He said that the whole thing was a gamble, because it would only take one infected person, and we would be right back where we started.

When asking their questions of the sixth-formers, Lance Clooney had teamed up with a tall lad who we all called Lucky. Lucky's real name was Sameer Lukuvi and he was from Zanzibar. Black as the coal face with a smile that would light up any room. Together they'd canvassed Walkers House sixth form pupils. Bruiser's big supporter, Toby Cochrane, had seen them asking questions. He had become obstreperous and waved his javelin at them. He demanded to know what they were doing and why all the questions. They couldn't tell him because they didn't know the details themselves. They were about to leave Cochrane alone when Bruiser arrived on the scene, throwing his weight around for no reason. He was still sporting his home-made bandana and carrying both knives in his belt.

"What do you and the nigger want?" he had shouted at Lance. While the rest of us were growing out of outdated stereotyping, Bruiser was the sort who regarded homosexuality as a laughable affliction. He also believed most blacks were thieving, lazy niggers.

"Leave it out, Bruiser," Lance had retorted.

"Or what? What will you and the sambo do?"

Lance and Lucky decided by a mutual nod of the head to leave them alone, and left the pair brandishing their weapons, and swearing and cursing at them because they didn't know what was going on. Not a bad decision as far as the rest of us were concerned, particularly since Bruiser's loyal little followers were mostly fourth and fifth form students. I suspect though, that even if Bruiser and Cockroach had been considered 'clean', Lance and Lucky would still have left them to stew after an outburst like that.

When Lance told me about it, I replied, "You're bound to get racists and anti- homophiles in deprived areas. You always will until people are educated differently."

Lance laughed. "Bishop's College is hardly a deprived area, Nick. And Bruiser's father is a wealthy stockbroker. The racists are more likely to live on country estates rather than housing estates. Those living at the top of the pile, not the bottom. The aristocracy, the establishment, the elite, whatever you want to call it."

I had to agree. Change was coming, but was slow to take a foothold. I pictured the huddles of judges and politicians. Old, white, married and male. The sort of people who'd had the best educations money could buy. It was people like that who were most against change. The system suited them just fine. After all, it was created by them, their fathers and their fathers' fathers.

The one person whom the principal raised his eyebrows at when he was carried into the chapel was Andy Pemberton, the boy who Bruiser Williams had smashed with his hockey stick. Andy had been carried to the chapel from the tower stairs where he had been kept in a small bedsit usually occupied by one of the cleaning staff. Apparently despite the pain of being moved, he ground his teeth, clenched his jaw like a vice, and didn't murmur a sound. "It's okay," I told Armstrong. "Nobody has been to see him for twenty-four hours, other than Bill McCormick, who took him his meals. McCormick is amongst the clear pupils."

We didn't tell the principal straight away, but Jack and I had broken into the school surgery. Matron was looking after basic cuts and bruises but, with Andy in such pain, he needed as many painkillers as we could get. Ibuprofen had been discovered in 1961 but wasn't marketed until 1969 in the United Kingdom. Had it been available, I'm sure it would have helped Andy enormously. However, there seemed to be a plentiful stock of Codeine, an opiate that was synthesised to replace raw opium for medical purposes. There was also a decent supply of Paracetamol, so we took armfuls of both. A combination of the two kept Andy reasonably comfortable until his leg could be dealt with by professionals. As long as the virus didn't get him first.

While there, we discovered a large box of disposable surgical masks and took it with us. We spent a moment debating whether to wear a mask each, but decided it would do nothing except draw attention to us. In any case, as far as we knew, the virus was only transmitted by touch.

As far as we knew.

And then we realised how little we actually did know about Coviman-12 so decided to wear masks anyway, and to hell if anyone saw us. Better safe than dead.

Avoiding as many people as we could, we made our way to our study and salvaged the bulk of the cigarettes. Bruiser and Cockroach had only taken the ones that they found in our desk drawers. Our bulk supply was in a cupboard which they had overturned, but not examined.

After Jack and I had transferred the eighteen rifles from the boot of his car, the principal asked Lance and me to close the big double doors of the chapel. He then took to the pulpit and addressed everybody. In carefully chosen words, he explained that Lower School was now confirmed to be contaminated. Smoothie Jones, my English teacher, had contacted him on the internal line and advised him that Mrs Patterson was now displaying flu-like symptoms and abdominal cramps - the classic first signs of the Coviman-12 virus. He'd told the principal that the youngsters were all very upset and many were crying. They were relying on the adults for support - a natural reaction for eleven- and twelve-year-olds. Good job Cedric Patterson was dead or he would probably have beaten them all for crying.

Then the principal outlined how and why those of us in the chapel had been chosen. A few murmured voices moved around the pews from time-to-time but, in general, he was heard out in silence. There were louder rumblings when he said that, this afternoon, we were going to erect post and tape markers around the chapel, the cricket pavilion, and his house, indicating a quarantined zone. There were some fairly blunt questions when he said that we would be taking it in turns to patrol the area and that we would be armed, exactly as the street marshals were armed.

"What do we do if someone tries to cross the tape?" Phil Loveless asked.

"You make every effort to dissuade them by pointing out that the chapel and surrounding area is infected."

"But that's not going to work if the rest of the school becomes infected, is it?"

"No it's not," the principal said. "If anybody tries to cross or break the tape, you fire a warming shot. But just one. If that doesn't work, you shoot them."

"We shoot to kill?" Rick Tanner asked.

"You aim for the biggest mass of the body. That's the chest. With a .303 round, the chances are high that the other person will not survive."

There was an explosion of sound that took several minutes to subside.

"Does everybody have to take part in the patrols?" one student asked.

The principal didn't answer directly. "The women will sleep in my house and will not patrol. I have four bedrooms and there are four ladies. I shall sleep on the convertible sofa in my lounge. The ladies won't be asked to patrol, but will contribute by preparing meals. I would hope that some of you boys will volunteer to help fetch and carry for them. We have sufficient dry stores to last many weeks. But I've spoken to the quarantine organising board in Douglas who have agreed to make a separate food drop for us, the same as they will be doing for Lower School. We have no reason to think there will be any shortage of food, water or hot drinks."

"What about bathing facilities?" Lesley asked.

"I'd like you to get everybody's names and draw up a roster please, Lesley," Armstrong replied. "There are two bathrooms and a cloakroom in my house. The heating and hot water is gas and is independent of the school buildings. There is no reason for any of us not to stay clean. If we are here for a long time, I'll have clean clothing and other necessary personal items delivered by the authorities."

"How will you contact them?" somebody asked.

"The phone in my house is an authorised phone. I've removed the one from my study and Lesley has taken the one from the college office."

She nodded to confirm.

"Now, Michelle and Rhonda Owen, who you know as maids in Farrow Hall, have been busy for the last two hours preparing some sandwiches. I suggest we all grab something to eat then get those road pins and tape markers erected. I have already circulated a notice round the school that Lower School and the chapel are strictly out of bounds due to the virus. Students will draw their own conclusions.

CHAPTER NINETEEN

With there being so many of us, it took only a short while to hammer the spikes into the ground and wind the yellow warning tape around them. Most of the perimeter was grass and the rest was tarmac, which was easy to penetrate with the metal spikes. The principal referred to them as road pins. They were about four feet long with a shepherd's crook head for winding the tape round. No matter what he said, we still kept referring to them as spikes. Radical subversives, that's what we were!

The chapel, the principal's house, and the nearby cricket pavilion were now encircled and were forbidden territory for other pupils. We had included the war memorial for some reason that I now forget. The cricket pavilion, it seemed, contained sleeping bags, camp beds and other necessary items for spending our lives in a school chapel. As about ten or twelve of us erected the warning tape, the other students carried the sleeping bags, camp beds and blankets into the chapel. It was clear that the principal had been planning his emergency strategy for a long time. Again, it raised him in my esteem. Jack's too, when I pointed it out to him.

St Thomas' Chapel was long but narrow. Intermittent vaulting helped support the purlins of the steeply-pitched roof. The pews faced in towards the central nave, not forwards towards the chancel. Within church architecture, orientation is an arrangement by which the point of main interest in the interior is towards the east. The east end is where the altar is placed, often within an apse. The façade and main entrance are accordingly at the west end. For some unknown reason, we were different. The altar was at the southern end and the entrance at the north, nearest to the main school buildings.

When we stepped back into the gloom of the building, we were surprised to see that many of the long oak pews and stalls had been removed and heaped roughly on top of each other in the chancel. The principal had, indeed, been planning his strategy and had provided enough spanners for some of the boys to unbolt every other pew. Without that, there would be insufficient room for camp beds. The stalls that remained acted a little like privacy screens between the different tiers of camp beds.

As we looked around at the frenetic activity, George Armstrong strode up to us. "Glad I caught you. I need a word. Be at the back of my house in five minutes if you would, and bring young Master Scott with you."

We nodded. I glanced at Jack. "What do you reckon?"

"Buggered if I know. Just another surprise, I guess. Let's go find Pete."

When we stepped round the corner of the principal's house, onto the paved patio, the principal was already there, smoking a slim cigar. "I didn't realise you smoked, Sir," I said.

"Lot of things you don't know, Nick. I ration myself to one a day, usually in the evening."

It struck me he had used my first name. Those pleasantries were usually reserved for the praes, not the hoi polloi.

"Right, you three - once again, this conversation is strictly between the three of us." He paused until all three of us had confirmed our understanding. He continued, "Being in close confined quarters with over forty other boys, we need to draw up some clear rules, otherwise the strain, which is already pretty intolerable, is going get a lot worse. I am well aware of your liaisons with Miss Parkes and the Owen sisters - Michelle and Rhonda, I believe. They will be accommodated in my house, and you will be staying in the chapel with everybody else. I expect that, from time to time, you will want to undertake one of your night-time excursions. There need to be clear rules, or at least a clear understanding. Under no circumstances will you visit any of those ladies while you are on duty patrolling the quarantine area. All our lives are at risk if anybody steps through the tape. Is that perfectly clear?"

We all nodded. "Yes, Sir."

"Also, so as not to arouse jealousies or have other boys feeling that you have some sort of privileges that they don't, you must use your utmost discretion at all times. The front door of my house will remain unlocked for people to use the bathroom facilities. If you bump into boys patrolling and need an excuse for being out, you should use that as your reason." He smiled at us. "Or step out for a cigarette if you prefer."

"Then they'll expect to see us come back a few minutes later."

"Not necessarily. It's about two hundred yards round the zone's perimeter. If they are patrolling properly, there will be moments when you could have returned to the chapel without them seeing you. I want six boys, in three pairs, patrolling at all times. I'm going to specify that boys are relieved every two hours. If one pair of boys sees you enter my house, they would not necessarily expect to see you leave again."

I raised my hand as if asking permission to speak. "Sir, this conversation is rather remarkable to say the least. I don't think any of us expected you to tell us how to sneak into your house."

The principal laughed. "Have you not yet learnt, Nick, that I know an awful lot more about what goes on at College than you think? I'm nowhere near as naïve as you seem to think. We're all living on a knife edge at the moment, so no point making things harder than they already are. There's a balance to be drawn between discipline, discretion, and common sense. I see no point in trying to restrict you to the chapel, knowing full well that you will ignore the stipulation. You're young men now, so I ask and expect you to behave like gentlemen. Also, you might be tempted to see your ladies when you should be patrolling the zone. That's the last thing I want, so better that I tolerate some harmless mischief than put us all at risk. Just don't abuse the situation. And if we are still here next term, don't expect me to be so lax, eh?"

I grinned. "Understood." Then I paused before asking, "Do you think there will be a next term, Sir?"

The principal shook his head. "I'm hopeful that the forty-seven of us in this exclusion zone will get through this evil virus. Whether College will ever open again is a moot point. When the virus has been defeated, the true scale and ferocity of this virus will become known. The Isle of Man is going to be a no-go zone for the rest of the world. Fear will keep people away, so it will be generations before it's back on its feet."

That was a sobering thought, and one I had not considered. The island relied heavily on the tourist industry. For sure, that had already been destroyed.

"While I think about it," the principal added, "there are two more things. First, Mrs Maxwell is a trained nurse. She hasn't practised nursing for years, but at least she has more knowledge than the rest of us put together. If anybody feels even in the slightest bit ill, they are to tell her immediately. Can you pass that message round?"

We nodded.

"Matron and Jaap van Anrooy will do whatever they can for the boys still in the main buildings."

Jack and I smiled at each other with raised eyebrows.

The principal smiled too. "It is common knowledge amongst the masters that Matron and our Head Boy are often together. If you think about it, relationships like that with the staff are not so unusual, are they?"

We got the point.

He looked round at all three of us. "Look chaps, here we are in a boy's school with, in normal times, over five hundred adolescent pupils and an almost all male staff. It's obvious that sexual urges play a large part in dictating your feelings. Testosterone is a motivator for everyone who has gone through puberty. So it's obvious that any sort of female encouragement can quickly raise hopes and expectations."

We shuffled a little but nodded. For myself, I felt a certain embarrassment at our principal discussing the masters and their wives the same way he would with his other members of staff. But it was the new reality, and we soon got used to it. "And what was the second thing, Sir?"

"Second thing? Oh yes. Smoking. Now that you can't sneak around the place looking for somewhere to hide, I'm going to lift the smoking ban completely. My reckoning is that there are about twelve other boys in the chapel who smoke, so Lesley is going to provide whatever cigarettes you need at no cost. I don't know what tricks you used to get up to in order to finance your habit, but they're not going to work any longer. So pass the word round. One rule - no smoking inside. You want to smoke, you go outside to do it. If it's raining, you can sit on the verandah of the pavilion. Is that one clear?"

"As day," Jack and I replied.

Before we split up again and went to work helping prepare the chapel as living accommodation, the principal added one more fact. "Mr Jones in Lower School has been in touch again. Mr Kelsey and two boys are now showing the typical symptoms of the Coviman-12 virus. We've always known that it has a short incubation period, but this is quicker than I could have imagined. Mr Bond has quarantined School House and Jaap van Anrooy is now in charge of the remainder of the senior school buildings. He is using Matron's internal phone to keep in touch. He knows the situation and knows the risks. He's told the school that we have self-quarantined here in the chapel to try and save them from exposure to the virus. He said that the atmosphere in the school is very tense, but that they are trying to act as near as they can to normal. I don't believe that normality will last for long. As soon as boys start falling victim to Coviman-12, it will be like a boiling pot in there. That is why we must all be on guard. That is why you brought rifles and ammunition from the armoury."

"Do the authorities in Douglas know what we are doing?" Pete asked.

"They are in full agreement. It was they who, when the virus first broke out and quarantine was enforced, came up with the idea to make use of the chapel as a contingency plan. As they have delivered food and supplies to the school in the last few weeks, so they have also delivered the camp beds, blankets and so on that we are now moving from the old cricket pavilion. Talking of which - time you three got going and helped with the preparation. Did you put the rifles and ammunition where I said?"

"We did," Jack said. "Eighteen rifles and two metal boxes of ammunition. The ammo boxes are marked on the sides as having 400 rounds. That's all the rifles we could get in your boot. They're stacked in the chaplain's vestry." The chaplain's vestry was a small enclosed enrobing space in the main entrance to the chapel. There were two heavy wooden outer doors that led into the entrance, which included the vestry. Then there was an internal double door that led onto the nave of the chapel. It was all very 1879 when the chapel had been consecrated. Nothing much had changed in the meantime, except the addition of brass plaques on the walls, paid for by old boys hoping to buy their way past the pearly gates.

Deep inside of me, there was a real part that wished I could go back a couple of years. The times in my early teens seemed easier, less real, and without the stress of knowing a single mistake could wipe us all out. There was something about being young that gave you a sense of invincibility. Sadly, that same fearlessness was about to get a lot of people killed.

Jack and I wandered off and lit up our Embassy Filters on the grass beyond the cricket pavilion. For some reason mine tasted like a plumber's handkerchief. Small things like that can stick in your mind and the memory can be triggered by the smallest thing. I remember, it was late afternoon, the sky was still bright, but the sun was getting low, stretching shadows to near ridiculous lengths. If I close my eyes now, I can almost hear the seagulls, the way their distant screeches fractured the damp, salty air. The feel of a light breeze in my hair and the sound of the mellow waves as they broke gently against the shoreline on the other side of the school wall. The memories of that time are so vivid that they sometimes catch me by surprise - in much the same way that meeting an old friend in a crowd of strangers does. Other memories fade and eventually disappear altogether. That's what happens when you get old and useless, like a rusting old tanker being pulled by a tugboat.

CHAPTER TWENTY

That first night, nobody caught much sleep. The chapel was cold, but we were all used to that. Conditions in the dormitories were fairly Spartan anyway. It was the feeling that we were riding a tidal wave and that any moment it would come crashing down on us and crush us. In my latter years, since the arrival of the Internet and sites like YouTube and Facebook, I have witnessed some amazing things that I would never have seen years ago. One that sticks in my mind is a short but stunning video of a young man called Sebastian Steudtner, a German pro surfer, riding a wave over 115 feet tall at Nazare in Portugal. The wave is just immense, dwarfing the surfer. Thousands of tons of water come crashing down as the wave breaks. Steudtner managed to avoid what was certain death, but my heart stopped when I first watched that video. And that's how I was feeling back in 1967. I was sure that the wave was about to break and kill us all. And my heart came close to stopping.

The wave did break, but some of us survived.

As the evening had drawn to a close, Rick Tanner had turned on a small portable radio he had brought with him. We all listened to the news on the BBC, but there was no mention of the Isle of Man. The island was an independent British protectorate but the government in mainland UK had taken control, as well they might. The island didn't have the resources to deal with something as devastating as Coviman-12. Everybody was agreed that they should keep it under wraps as far as possible. They were playing down the threat from this monstrous virus. We knew how threatened we were, but there was no-one to tell. As I looked round the chapel, I wondered what our various fates might be. I had no idea that evening that not all of us would make it through to the end.

It was February 1967 and already this year we had seen racing driver and motorboat racer Donald Campbell killed in a crash on Coniston Water in the Lake District while attempting to break his own world speed record.

The United Kingdom had just entered the first round of negotiations for European Economic Community membership. That particular political cartel would eventually become the European Union and Britain's membership would end in tears and protracted negotiations to unravel the umbilical cord.

Jeremy Thorpe had just become Leader of the Liberal Party. He was later to be ensconced in a scandal after he tried to have his homosexual lover killed. Homosexuality was still illegal until later in 1967. It took another thirteen years before Scotland and then Northern Ireland caught up. It took the Isle of Man even longer. Private and consensual acts of male homosexuality on the island weren't decriminalised until 1992.

In 1967, Harold Wilson, a socialist prime minister, nationalised the British steel industry and watched it decline until it lost out to cheap foreign imports. Wilson resigned mid-term. He had begun to drink brandy during the day to cope with the stress of dealing with the demands of the unions who were very much in charge of Britain at the time.

And this morning, police had carried out a drugs

raid on the Sussex home of Rolling Stones musician Keith Richards, following a tip-off from the News of the World. Richards would become the exception that proved the rule. He turned out to be almost indestructible, living his whole life on booze, fags, and drugs.

To put the time line in perspective another way, we were still 32 years away from the impeachment of a bubba from Little Rock, Arkansas who took up residence in The White house and got himself fellated by a young intern in the Oval Office. He went down in history - if you'll excuse the pun - as having a famously wandering eye and a battle-axe wife, the Lady Macbeth of American politics.

So the news reports for the first few weeks of that year had been full of the good, the bad and the indifferent. But there was almost no mention of a virus that was killing thousands on the Isle of Man. A small comment at the end of the radio news that night said that government scientists were working to find a cure for people on the Isle of Man who had contracted severe flu-like symptoms. Meanwhile, the island remained in quarantine. That was all. No mention of the thousands of deaths and bodies being burned on the hills. Flu, my arse.

Before turning in for the night, I stepped outside for a smoke. The air was still and I looked up as my smoke floated skywards. The stone gargoyles which I had never noticed before leered down from their lofty platform, their grimacing faces seeming to change as the clouds floated by, obscuring and then exposing the pearly light of the moon that shone down on them. I caught sight of the odd small, black shape flitting around the memorial to those College boys who had died during two world wars. Bats. All the ingredients of pure horror right there in front of me. Yet the real horror was unseen. The real killer couldn't be beaten with bombs, or sharpened stakes, or silver crucifixes. I shivered and hugged the tops of my arms. I was so, so tired of being afraid. And so was everybody else. But there was no way out. No means of escape. Before going back inside, I looked up again and realised that the stone gargoyles were, in fact, nothing more than stone crosses. My mind, infected by dread for what might be coming, was starting to paint its own pictures.

There are small things in all our lives that have no importance to anyone else, but that keep us breathing - keep us believing. One of my small things was an unshakable belief that I would die an old man, surrounded by my loving family. That belief was now being tested to the limits. I was becoming increasing certain that I would never see old age. And I almost didn't.

Back inside, people were settling down for the night. The next six quarantine marshals were patrolling the exclusion zone as we prepared ourselves for sleep. Nobody had been told to bring pyjamas, so we were all sleeping in our underwear. Some boys chose to sleep naked. Amongst them were Phil Loveless and Rick Tanner who had set up camp beds in a far corner, away from the rest. Good luck to them. Whatever kept them sane in these crazy times.

It took me a long time to get to sleep.

As daylight broke, boys were already moving around in a restless sort of movement. Unplanned coordination like a murmuration of starlings. There was nothing to do and nowhere to go. Later that day we received a delivery of food and supplies, amongst which was a vast pile of new paperback novels. It seemed that the principal had thought of that too. Most of my fellow pupils dived in and grabbed horror stories. They seemed fascinated by terrifying tales or awful deeds that could quite feasibly happen to them in their own ordinary lives. But of course that was because it was a safe fear. They could close the book at any point and keep those emotions in check. Unlike the horror in their real lives.

A large hot water urn had been set up in the chancel so we could make ourselves tea or coffee whenever we wanted. It was up to each boy to keep hold of his own mug and keep it clean. Most of us chose to rinse them out when we took a lavatory visit. I managed to get myself dressed on autopilot. I would grab some time in the bathroom later and freshen up. I discovered that not sleeping was a bit like not eating. You get to a stage where you sort of get past it and just carry on as normal. But the principal had advised us that hot bacon rolls would be available at the house from 7:30am on. By the time 7:30am arrived, we were all awake, and a queue had formed at the kitchen door. Two thick bread rolls each, jammed full of hot, tender back bacon. Just what we all needed to sooth our fears.

As everybody went back to the chapel and chewed and contemplated, I glanced round at the thirty-six boys who ate in silence. Six more were patrolling outside, keeping us safe. They would eat shortly. Meanwhile, inside I frisked the crowd with my eyes. There was Reggie Hare who had a laugh like a gymnasium toilet flushing. And the Larbalestier twins - we could only tell them apart by which one spelt their name which way. There was Frank Johnson who lived through everything and was destined to become a successful novelist. Voller James who survived the Coviman-12 virus, but died the following year in a car crash in Anglesey.

In one corner was Olakunle Onikoyi who became something big in Nigerian politics thanks to all the dead folks who rose up and voted for him. He even made it to a second term, but a faint whiff of sulphur, connected with ballot-rigging on an industrial scale, clouded his re-election to the presidency. He died in a bloody coup and his family burned through his ill-gotten fortune, living the high life for a few years until the money ran out.

Pale and delicate, Thomas Arnold didn't smoke. His preferred habits came with hangovers. He wore thick glasses, which made his eyes look like little black fish swimming in twin fishbowls. Thomas held court with anyone who wanted to listen. His audience was quite limited because he seemed to enjoy the comfort of opinion without the discomfort of thought. His chosen path in life was to become a philosopher, which would usually find him in the Rose and Crown arguing politics and literature with the other would-be philosophers who roosted in the back bar. Social Welfare would see them through, thank you. He was the kind of person who would not use ten words to say something if a hundred could be used instead. But for Thomas Arnold, his life would end when he was found lying in a pool of his own vomit in the gutter. He never even reached thirty.

And there was the bespectacled Donald Harvey McIntyre who had found a route through the discarded oak pews and stalls. He knelt in front of the altar gazing up at the bright frescoes of saints and sinners painted on the walls of the chancel. As he raised his hands in supplication, I could see he held a small wooden crucifix - his own private son of God hanging over him. McIntyre knew he wasn't alone in the chapel, so played up to the audience.

Later, he worked the chapel, giving each of us supporting messages straight from Jesus. Words were whispered, sentences short. He was already learning his trade.

When McIntyre approached me, I was in no mood for his holier-than-thou bullshit. He said, "I'm praying for you Nicholas."

To which I replied, "Thank you. If you're praying for me, then I know God's listening."

"Really?" he said, "How is that?"

I gave him a meaningless half smile. "He'd be afraid not to. Anyone as zealous as you could threaten his position as chairman of the board."

After that, Donald McIntyre avoided me the same way that the rest of us were avoiding the virus. He would become a vicar and serve time in jail for inappropriate conduct with young boys. He was ordered to register under the Sex Offenders Act for the rest of his days. God's position as chairman was safe. Life never quite goes as you plan.

When McIntyre moved on to his next victim, I reached for my coffee mug and curled my lips over the rim. Realising I had already finished my second cup for the day, I told myself I didn't need any more. I was already buzzing with energy, but had nothing to do. As I looked around, I could see others who were also deep in thought, as if assessing the same things as me. Without realising it, I bit my cheek till I could taste blood.

We were a very mixed bunch. All of us with hopes and dreams - some would be realised, some not. The fragility of life was brought home to all of us who had confined ourselves to the chapel. It would be like playing darts in a dark room. If fate had enough darts, he would be sure to hit the target every now and then, and then you had to hope it would be somebody else's number that he hit. Those of us who walked out of there many weeks later were very different people to those who sat round that morning, sipping tea or coffee out of mugs and chewing on hot bacon rolls.

Even to this day, most young men don't know what it means to be a real man. There are so many lies about what it means to be a man. Whether that means to have sex with as many girls as will let you, or make a heap of money, or beat up your wife, or don't show your emotions, or become president of your country. But still, nobody is teaching them how to be proper men. In those dark days of February 1967, a bunch of raw teenagers became real men, and one man led us through it all. He stood head and shoulders above the rest - George Godfrey Armstrong.

CHAPTER TWENTY-ONE

Our first full day passed quietly enough. While we were outside, we spotted some faces peering through the windows of School House. They were staring out at us unfortunate few who they thought were going to die. We were staring back at the unfortunate many who were more likely to perish than us. The zoo animals wondering who was inside the cage, and who was out.

At lunch time, we queued again at the principal's kitchen. We were served macaroni cheese on paper plates. It was hot and it was good. The girls were doing a great job feeding almost fifty people three times a day from a normal domestic kitchen. As I walked by, Michelle winked at me and pushed a small folded note in my hand. Seemingly Rhonda and Lesley had done the same to Jack and Pete. We had been summonsed to attend a counselling session any time after ten o'clock, the notes said.

The principal got a couple of lads to take the TV from his own house and set it up in the chancel. He'd added fifty yards of coaxial cable to his shopping list. The cable stretched from his lounge, across the tarmac path and in through the chapel doors. Now we could catch up with whatever kept us amused. The only rules were that it shouldn't be so loud as to disturb others, and that it should be turned on only between the hours of 8:30am and 10:00pm.

To begin with, the small television stole our attention. TVs didn't exit inside the main school.

First up was Coronation Street. It had already been running for seven years and it's still going today all these years later. Nothing to report - just silly rubbish. We all turned to the screen and listened for the news. I leaned forward, propping myself up on my elbows that dug into my knees. "This just in," the news announcer started in a proper BBC accent. "A young boy in Salford in the north of England has beaten the world conker-eating record… blah, blah." Actually, I just made that up, as you might have guessed. But the news was full of drivel. A man killed a snake that attacked his family. A religious sect in the USA had gone for forty days without food - only five people died. A new amusement park had opened in Germany. Not a single mention of a killer virus. Clearly not something worth commenting on. By mutual consent, we soon turned the TV off. We felt like a forgotten tribe in the Amazon rain forest trying to turn back the bulldozers. Nobody was interested in our plight.

Rick Turner flicked through a few channels first. There were just three to choose from - BBC1, BBC2, and ITV. Not like today with almost unlimited choices. As he flicked the channels, Rick's other hand wandered round to his sculpted buttocks, where it began a lazy scratching. I smiled to myself when I spotted Phil Loveless staring with his mouth open. Nothing interesting on TV, so Rick turned on his portable radio and tuned into Radio Caroline, the offshore radio station which operated out of Ramsey Bay, just beyond the quarantine zone. We listened as Mick Jagger hollered out 'Let's Spend The Night Together'. It had hit the number one spot in the charts, though The Spencer Davis Group's 'I'm a Man' had just stolen Mick's crown. I smiled to myself. Both songs had a special meaning to some of us.

The previous day, we had drawn up a rota for perimeter guards. We were to work in pairs; three pairs at a time, for two hours each, walking slowly around the zone. We would all be armed. With six boys outside at any one time, and forty-two boys in total, that meant that we rotated every fourteen hours. Jack and I were scheduled to patrol this evening between 6:00pm and 8:00pm, so our next stint would be between 8:00am and 10:00am tomorrow. Plenty of time for some serious counselling by the ladies. Pete's schedule too, meant that he would be okay to meet Lesley during the late evening and early morning hours.

After our evening stint patrolling the perimeter, our misty clouds of breath billowed in front of us as we exhaled into the wintry air. Jack and I stood alone and had a smoke. A different sort of misty breath - one that we were addicted to. I thought how the school seemed peaceful and fairy-like in the dark, the true horror masked by a sea of study lights that appeared like welcoming lanterns from where we stood. And then I glanced beyond the school buildings to the hills where fires burned the bodies of those who had died. In the evening breeze, a thin plastic supermarket bag lolled on to its side like a dog rolling on to its back to have its stomach rubbed. I went to pick it up and Jack stopped me. "Best not, Nick. You don't know who handled it last." So we watched as it rolled away over the grass and lifted over the wall out across the airport. Even simple, normal tasks now held a hidden threat.

I glanced at our glowing embers in the dark instead. "If this damn virus doesn't get me, Jack, I think I may try and quit smoking."

"I'll stop smoking only if cows stop chewing grass," he replied. "It's a simple pleasure and we pay more to the taxman than any non-smoker, so stop feeling guilty."

"Smoking's going to kill us," I said.

"Sounds better than being bored to death."

I didn't comment, but deep down, I knew I wanted to stop. I'd become a serious smoker at fourteen. I started sneaking down to the bike shed to smoke and I guess I just never got out of the habit. It was that sense of doing something that you shouldn't be doing that appealed to me. Always has. The first time I was beaten for smoking was like a rites of passage. I had become one of the in-crowd. Or so I thought. When I realised I wanted to stop, it was already too late - I was hooked.

As eleven o'clock approached and slumber had overtaken most of the other boys, Jack, Pete and I crept from the chapel. The inner doors had been left open, but the big oak outer doors were closed. We had noticed earlier that the hinges creaked and groaned when the door was opened or closed so we had found some oil in the principal's garage and given them a good seeing-to. They still creaked. Keeping the noise to a minimum, we exited the chapel and waited. A moment later the Larbalestier twins rounded the corner. We chatted for a moment while Jack and I drew on our cigarettes. We didn't particularly want one, but it was our excuse for being out there. When the twins moved on, we followed them from a distance then waited at the chancel end of the chapel - approximately where Jack and I had crouched on that fateful evening when we had witnessed George Armstrong in his lounge with the desirable Lesley Parkes.

The perimeter of the contagion zone was a little over two hundred yards and as soon as the Larbalestiers disappeared behind the pavilion, we made our move and crossed the fifteen yards of tarmac to arrive at the front door of the principal's house. The hall light had been left on to accommodate any boys wishing to use the cloakroom during the night. We tip-toed up the stairs to our allotted bedrooms - carefully detailed on our individual notes.

Michelle was sitting in the chair wearing a white silk blouse and a skirt so short it could have been redefined as an accessory. Mini-skirts were all the fashion, and this was as mini as they came. She stood when I closed the door behind me and motioned with her hand for me to twist the locking latch. She tucked her usual rogue lock of hair back behind her ear. Both Michelle and Rhonda were tall. Michelle had wild rusty-blonde curls falling across a broad Mediterranean face - though both girls hailed from Blackpool on England's North-West coast. Like her sister, Michelle was a tall woman, probably heading towards five feet nine. Not big-boned, not at all fat, but not classically proportioned enough to be labelled statuesque. It was as if God had started out building a scrum-half then decided to throw in some meticulous curves and heavenly contours to keep a young man cross-eyed and guessing. When she stood, my heart began to race. I watched as she stepped out of her shoes. "Your turn now," she said.

"That's cheating," I said, kicking off my slippers, "I've only got my dressing gown and pyjama bottoms on now."

"And what makes you think I'm wearing anything under my blouse and this skirt?" She lifted up the front of her skirt to prove it, then let it fall back and laughed. "I'm waiting."

I shrugged off my dressing gown. She unbuttoned

her blouse and threw it over the back of the chair. I dropped my pyjama trousers. She didn't go any further until later - she didn't need to. There was nothing stopping us doing what we wanted.

"I've missed you, Nick."

"Which part did you miss the most?" I asked

"This bit," Michelle said, grabbing hold of my erection and smiling at my expression which was a healthy combination of surprise and pleasure.

The night started out cool and smooth and ended up hot. Soon, her mini-skirt joined her blouse, and it was non-stop after that. Bodies banging together, sheets tangled, mouths locked together, lots of muffled laughter, lots of bawdy salacious talk, backed up by action that matched the words. Both Michelle's and Rhonda's bedrooms were situated at the back of the house. Pete was probably having to be less noisy with Lesley since hers was at the front of the house and the principal was directly below in his lounge. Whilst having a glorious time with Michelle, I even recalled some of my A level English as we fucked our way to heaven and back. It was John Donne's, 'Licence my roving hands, and let them go. Before, behind, between, above, below'. Wasn't just my hands either.

Okay, sorry, I just used that bad 'fuck' word. But anyone who calls it 'sexual intercourse' can't possibly have ever actually done it right. You might as well announce that you'd like to experience some interesting sensations by probing her vagina with your engorged penis. Intercourse is the worst euphemism for intercourse I've ever heard. Normal people called it fucking or shagging. So we skipped by that bit of sanctimonious crap and just fucked each other's brains out. How can one be expected to be a gentleman when one's penis is pointing at the ceiling, old chap? Now there was a philosophical question for young Thomas Arnold to think about. And while he was thinking about it, I could engage in some serious 'sexual intercourse' to see if there was a practical answer.

I would soon come to learn that sex wasn't good unless it meant something. It didn't necessarily need to mean love, but it did need to mean intimacy and connection. Thus, my 'counselling' session ended with us both holding on to each other tight and just hugging the hell out of each other. The warmth and softness of Michelle's body was like a soothing balm to my troubled soul. We were both scared, not knowing if we were going to see the sunrise or not, but we weren't going to let it spoil our enjoyment of today. So we didn't. 'Live for the moment' would soon become a mantra between Jack, Pete, the ladies, and me.

I crept from the principal's house just after half-past-twelve as quietly as the tooth fairy deposits a coin under a kid's pillow. I flushed the toilet in the cloakroom on my way out, just to create an alibi. Seems Jack and Pete did the same thing. I nodded to two of the guys on patrol duty before heading back into the chapel. Jack was already there, snoring loud enough to rattle the slates on the roof. Somebody nearby said, "Hit him, will you, Nick." So I did and then I fell asleep in a haze of sensual dreams.

I was woken at seven o'clock by Lance Clooney, the only prae in the chapel. "You and Jack are on patrol at eight," he said. "You'll need to get to the kitchen first so you can eat before you start."

I nodded my thanks and roused Jack. The sky was pale blue with shades of pink where the sun was rising. There was a slight chill in the air, which would soon burn off, even with the weak wintry sun. It was shaping up to be a rather nice day. Somewhere, a seagull cackled and laughed. Further away, another one answered.

When we stepped into the kitchen - today, it was hot Cumberland sausages in soft bread rolls with lashings of ketchup - Michelle and Rhonda gave us broad smiles. There were other boys in the room, so we couldn't communicate all we wanted to say, but Michelle whispered a meaningful 'Thank you'. Having had to prepare the breakfasts, she, Rhonda and Lesley certainly hadn't had time for much sleep. Jack and I hung around, eating our rolls standing up in the principal's dining room but at no time did we get an opportunity to talk to the girls alone. That set a routine that would be repeated many times before we walked free from The Zone, as we had begun to call it.

But there was trouble ahead first.

CHAPTER TWENTY-TWO

The following day, Jack and I weren't due to patrol until midday. After breakfast, the principal announced the death of a 12-year-old called Timothy Manning in Lower School, and that news bounced us all back into feelings of hopelessness. He also told us that more than twenty boys in the main school were showing signs of having caught the virus. Matron was taking everybody's temperature two times a day. Any boy with a temperature of over 100°F was immediately segregated to a separate house-room and dormitory. Anyone over 102°F had almost certainly fallen foul of Coviman-12. There was no treatment. All that the matron and Jaap van Anrooy could do was to make sure they drank plenty of water and dose the boys with Paracetamol to try and reduce their temperatures. It must have been like trying to push water uphill with a fork. Once Coviman got you, nothing could stop it.

During the morning, Jack got his own back on Mike Taggart for the door handle incident. He was taking a small glass holding a few inches of Castrol Oil from the principal's garage to the chapel. The big double doors at the chapel entrance were still squeaking and a glass from the kitchen was all Jack could find, rather than bring the whole gallon can. Mike Taggart saw him and asked, "What you got, Jack?"

Jack winked. "Mind your own, you big gobshite."

"No come on, what is it? It looks like cider or beer."

"You don't miss anything do you?" Jack said. "It's scrumpy that I found in the principal's cupboards. Thought I might give it a little try." He offered the glass to Mike. "You want a taste? Just a taste mind you, not a bloody great swallow." Jack knew full well that Mike would throw the whole glass down his throat and go for the swallow, which left him gagging and Jack laughing.

Scores evened. Honour preserved.

But our good humour didn't last long. The principal pulled Jack and me to one side. "I have some news that you may find disturbing," he said.

"What? More disturbing than knowing that Covicon-12 has found its way into the school?" Jack asked.

"That depends on your point of view." He looked at the two of us as if uncertain to continue. He said, "The other day, you pulled a prank on Mrs Maxwell and Braxton Boddington." It was a statement of fact, not a question.

Jack and I glanced at each other and owned up. "It was just a bit of fun," Jack said.

"It may have had unforeseen consequences," the principal replied. "I wasn't sure whether to tell you this or not, but you are both becoming adults far quicker than you might have expected, so you need to deal with what I am about to tell you."

There was a long pause while Jack and I held our collective breaths.

The principal continued, "Mr Jones and I are in constant contact about the state of affairs in Lower School. This morning he broke the news that Mr Maxwell is now suffering the effects of the virus. He's already a very sick man."

"Oh."

"But this clears up the matter of Braxton Boddington. As you know, Boddington had a secret liaison with Mrs Maxwell the other day and had problems getting out of the linen store. It seems that Mister Maxwell got wind of their encounter. Overnight, in a fit of blind rage, he took a hockey stick to Boddington and left him as an example to the rest of the students to stay away from his wife."

"Jeez. That's a bit over the top isn't it?" I said.

"It was a reaction bred by two things, Nick. First of all, it wasn't the first time he had discovered Mrs Maxwell straying from the marital bed, but never before with a student. Whatever discretion she might have shown before, had disappeared as soon as she chose to sleep with a student. Mister Maxwell knew that her actions would almost certainly become known once young Master Boddington told anyone what he had done. There's no such thing as a secret once you tell one person. And Gordon Maxwell knew that he would become a laughingstock - the cuckolded husband, if you like. Secondly the marriage was already under massive strain because of the virus. Mrs Maxwell is used to a somewhat vibrant social life, and being incarcerated in Lower School was too much for her. She had actually taken up residence in the staff quarters above Farrow Hall a few days ago following a spat with her husband."

"How do you know it was him who killed Boddington?" I asked.

"Because he admitted it to other staff members this morning when it was clear he had been struck by Covicon-12. Knowing he didn't have long left, he wanted to clear his conscience. If he lives through the virus, he will have to face charges. That's if he lives through. For the moment, he can't go anywhere of course. He is yet another tragic victim of this damn virus."

"So Jack and I may have caused Mr Maxwell to kill Boddington?"

"You have to consider that possibility," the principal said, concentrating on the tip of his thumb as it probed the tops of his fingers, like a creature checking its brood. "I know it's not at all what you intended with your prank, but it does seem that there may have been unforeseen consequences." He continued quickly. "Braxton Boddington probably wasn't Angela Maxwell's first choice of partner, but she was not in a very good place mentally. The repercussions of her actions were extreme and we need to do whatever we can to help her through. Right now, she is feeling guilty for everything that has gone wrong. Let's try and show her that it's not all her fault."

"One thing I don't get," I said, "is why they chose the linen store if Mrs Maxwell was using a room in the staff quarters. Why didn't they go up there?"

The principal shrugged his shoulders. "Best guess would be that the linen store is way up in the rafters, well away from prying eyes. The room she was using above the dining hall was, as you discovered yourselves, not as private as she may have liked." He paused before adding, "Every action has a consequence, but you did what you did in fun. It backfired. Just for the record, I don't believe it was your fault. That's the end of it."

Jack and I walked away dragging our feet. After a moment, voice as flat as the fens, I said, "Fuck it, Jack. I just got somebody killed."

"It was both of us, Nick. Don't heap all the blame on yourself. It was my idea if you remember."

But I couldn't help the guilt. Even if you profoundly disagreed with Jack Parsons, he had a way of wrapping his narrative round you, until the way of least resistance - his way - seemed the only sensible option. This time, it had been him who had enticed me into action. Not that I had taken much persuading. But the guilt still lay heavy. The rest of the morning passed in a haze of regret.

At 12:00am, we began the slow walk round The Zone. College was only one hundred yards from the beach and a thick sea mist had rolled in, flowing like tufts sucked from a bale of cotton. We were used to it on the island and called it Manannán's Mist or Manannán's Cloak, named after the sea god who was said to protect the island. He was obviously asleep on the job at the moment.

As we moved forwards, the mist seemed to recede at the same pace, never allowing us to see more than about fifteen yards ahead. The stores that had been kept in the cricket pavilion had included wet weather gear. There wasn't enough for everyone, but we had no problem sharing. The low warning moan of a ship's horn sounding somewhere out on the water added to the threatening atmosphere and to the general feeling of edginess. It was almost certainly one of the naval vessels which were patrolling the island.

We had been walking for about half an hour when a shout from the direction of the war memorial told us something was wrong. Jack and I ran through the wet grass until we could see what was happening through the mist. Two of our number were pointing their rifles at the two mindless mutants, Bruiser Williams and Toby Cochrane. Bruiser was still dressed as a pirate and Cockroach was still brandishing his javelin. We could make out the fuzzy silhouettes of a handful of other boys standing behind them a little way away, unmoving like zombies in the mist. Bruiser was screaming obscenities at our two fellow patrol men. When he saw Jack and me, his obscenities doubled in volume and ferocity. "You two fucking wankers planned all this, didn't you?"

"Planned all what?" I asked, as calmly as I could.

"Locking yourselves in the fucking chapel and leaving infected people behind. You're happy to protect yourselves, and leave us to die aren't you, you f—"

"It's Sunday, Bruiser. We're here saying out prayers."

"Fuck off you fucking fuckwit." His voice sounded like he had coughed up a wet sponge. Not very promising when the school was infected.

"Marvellous what a private education will do for you," Jack said, from next to me. "Such control of the English language."

"Get the f—"

"That's enough," boomed the voice of the principal from behind us. "Go back to your study, Williams, and take those other boys with you. You'll be safer there than out here."

"That's bollocks," Bruiser yelled. "Tell him Toby. It's bollocks, isn't it?"

"Yeah, it's bollocks," Cochrane shouted from behind Bruiser. "Why would we be safer back in the school buildings? There are infected people in there, spreading the virus around like the plague."

"Fucking plague," Bruiser corrected,

"Yeah, like the fucking plague."

"We too are at high risk," the principal said.

"That's crap," from Bruiser. "If you lot are at risk, why not come and join the rest of us in the main building? Put the infected ones in the chapel. That would be safer."

We knew the principal had no answer to that.

"Just go back to your studies," he said, calling out to all of them. "Stay quiet and calm until this thing passes."

"Until we're all fucking dead you mean," one of the ghostly zombies shouted from the back.

"You'll be safer in your respective locations."

Bruiser took two steps forward. I slid the bolt on my rifle - up, back, forwards, down - which allowed the spring in the magazine to push a round up and into the barrel ready for a slight pressure on the trigger to release the firing pin. I took aim, prepared to squeeze the trigger if I had to. Bruiser was a bully. Bullies are cowards. You plant your feet and stay calm, they don't know what to do.

Bruiser could see the determination on my face and stopped in his tracks. "You've not heard the end of this," he shouted. "We'll be back." He turned and stormed off, pushing Toby Cochrane aside. Someone amongst the zombies shouted, "Wankers," but they all followed Bruiser and were swallowed up by the mist.

The ruckus had been heard inside the chapel and, as I turned I saw that over twenty of my fellow students were staring at me with eyes wide like dinner plates. I shrugged. "It worked," I said. "He seems to have gone away."

"It might not work a second time," the principal said. "I expected some sort of showdown, but I thought we might get away with another day or two of peace first." He looked around at the other boys and addressed himself to Lance Clooney. "Lance, can you draw up another rota for the perimeter guards? I want to increase the numbers to six teams of two. That will leave only seven hours between shifts, so all of you should make the best of the rest periods."

Rick Tanner called out, "Would you have shot him, Nick?"

I answered "Yes," although I wasn't totally sure. Though I had been prepared to squeeze the trigger, it doesn't follow that I would have actually done so. That final tiny action - that twitch of my forefinger - would have been a huge step that would have changed my life forever. It was the difference between willingness and action. I qualified my answer to Rick and added, "If Bruiser is infected, he would only have to touch one of us and we, too, could become infected. All of us. Our self-inflicted quarantine would mean nothing."

The principal, who was facing me with his back to the other boys, gave me a small nod of the head, like a 'thank you' for saying the right thing. I smiled, tapped Jack on the shoulder and said, "Let's move, partner, we have zombies to scare off."

We moved away as the other boys began to file back into the chapel. When Jack and I rounded the corner of the chancel and headed out towards the mist-shrouded pavilion, Jack asked, "Would you really have pulled the trigger, Nick?"

I shrugged. "Don't know, mate. I know I intended

to, but I don't know if I would. There's only one way to know for sure and I damn well hope that situation will never arise."

"I wonder what makes his little zombie tribe follow him. He's not exactly Mister Charisma, is he?"

"When people are afraid, they became irrational, Jack. They demand action. And Bruiser has no doubt promised it to them."

"So you don't think Bruiser's going to bugger off and leave us alone now?"

I laughed, but it was a hollow laugh. "Do you think the Pope is going to marry a one-legged clairvoyant pygmy next week? My pet goldfish is more intelligent than Bruiser Williams. He'll be back with some trick up his sleeve to impress his minions."

"Didn't know you had a pet goldfish."

"Nor me. But if I had one, it would probably be the most stupid goldfish in the world, yet it would still be more intelligent than Bruiser or Cockroach. Those two don't have a brain cell. They don't even share one." Jack nodded his agreement. I added, "For the moment, all Bruiser has done is to spit out his dummy. He'll soon puzzle out that he has to climb right out of his pram if he wants to make an impression on us or his minions."

As I spoke, there was a crash behind us. Jack and I ran back to find a handful of fellow students staring up at the broken stained glass window of the chancel. A couple of the zombies had sneaked back with stones from the shrubbery and pelted the end of the building. It was the nearest point to the yellow boundary tape. Five minutes later, a couple of boys had found a brush and shovel and were clearing up the broken glass. It sounded like ragged claws scuttling across the ocean floor. George

Armstrong supervised a small group of guys as they extended The Zone further out into the playing field. It felt like we were drawing up battle lines. We were outnumbered, but not outgunned. Or that's what we thought.

CHAPTER TWENTY-THREE

Monday dawned fair and clear. The sea mist had disappeared and the dawn sky was a Wedgewood blue with just the odd white cloud scudding along, trying to keep up with its mates. Because of the increase in the numbers of boys on patrol, Jack and I had found ourselves keeping watch again at five o'clock. At seven, when we changed shift, it seemed pointless trying to sleep since breakfast would be served by our delightful ladies in half-an-hour. I dodged up to the bathroom in the principal's house and grabbed a quick shower while most people still slept. Clean underwear of various sizes had arrived the day before with the delivery of food and other supplies. It crossed my mind that that idiot Bruiser Williams might try and stop us getting deliveries, but I cast the thought aside. The supply lorries were well guarded and they wouldn't hesitate to shoot anyone stupid enough to get too close.

After I was clean again, I descended to the kitchen for whatever delight-in-a-bun was on the menu this morning. As I stepped through the door, I saw that only Rhonda and Lesley were there. "No Michelle this morning?" I asked.

Rhonda looked up. Her reply was whispered in case anybody else heard. "She's not well, Nick. She's hot and has a fierce headache, so we've told her to stay in her room."

I was shocked. She had seemed just fine the night before last. "But what if it's— "

Rhonda threw me a look to tell me to keep my voice down. "If it's what you're thinking, Nick, we're all in the shit. Michelle's been here in the kitchen preparing food with us right up to last night. She put herself to bed with a headache, and this morning she's burning up. If she has something nasty, then all of us will get it. Every single one of us. There's no point getting up tight about it until we know something for sure. Now eat your bacon and egg, and think positive. Everybody knows that bacon makes everything better." Her eyes grew into large coins as she pinched her lips shut with her fingers. It was her way of saying 'shut up and don't tell anyone else'.

I took the paper plate off her with a "Thank you." Any other day, I would have scarfed down the food. Even apocalyptical situations look less dire when viewed over a plate of crispy bacon. But my appetite had disappeared. I leaned against the worktop and picked at the bacon. After a few moments, I moved to the kitchen sink where I filled a glass of water. I chugged it down, then another. Gasping for air, I gripped the edge of the sink and hung my head. I needed a plan, and fast. Except I didn't have one. Stuck between a rock and a hard place, was the best I could come up with.

After a moment, I binned the rest of my breakfast and left the room. As I climbed the stairs, I remember feeling guilty for wasting the food. My parents had drummed that one into me. 'Think of the starving little boys in Africa' was a common chant in our house if you dared leave your Brussels sprouts uneaten. I think the most remarkable thing about my mother was that for all of my eighteen years she had served our family nothing but leftovers. We've still never found the original meal. My father could cut a slice of ham so thin it only had one side. You could actually see through them. Funny how silly memories like that can jump into your head at the most inappropriate moments.

At the top of the stairs, I took a left turn and paused outside Michelle's door. I couldn't allow fear of the virus to seep its way into my thoughts. If Michelle had indeed contracted Coviman-12, then, as Rhonda had said, it was already too late. Deep down, I knew that if I caught the virus, it wouldn't take long before I used one of the rifles that we were protecting the zone with on myself. From everything we knew about Coviman-12, the effects were an excruciating death as your body ate itself up. No way was I going to wait for that. Jack, too, had said the same. We'd even reached a pact to shoot the other if we were unable to end it ourselves. As I approached Michelle's door, little did I know that I would soon be squeezing the trigger on one of those rifles.

I opened the door into Michelle's bedroom. I didn't bother to knock. I was going in anyway, no matter what response she may have given. Michelle lay on top of the bed which was under the open window. Her skin was naturally pale, but what little colour she normally had in her cheeks was gone. "You'll catch your death of cold like that," I said.

She turned her head to see who had spoken. "What are you doing here? I've quarantined myself." She ran a jerky hand through her flaming red hair.

I sat on the bed and took her hand. It was cold and moist. "Yes I know. But it's already too late for that, Michelle. If you have the virus, we all have the virus. You and I have been in pretty close contact. Couldn't have got much closer, could we? And anyway, you, Rhonda, and Lesley have all taken part in the food preparation, so any infection has already been passed around."

She closed her eyes and sighed. "I think I already knew that. Now get the fuck out of my bedroom before I report you for being a pervert."

I raised one eyebrow. "Honest and direct, Michelle. That's something I can always rely on from you."

"Yeah, well, I'm lazy and lying requires too much effort."

I laughed. "At least you still have your sense of humour."

"Maybe it's all I have left." She looked me straight in the eyes. "I feel like shit, Nick. I don't want to die though. I still have a lot of living I want to do."

"Me too, honey. We make a good team, you and me. I'd like to think that could continue a while yet."

She nodded, but I could tell she was struggling to keep her eyes open. I held her hand as she drifted into sleep. Inside my mind, I could see this beautiful woman dancing and twirling around me. I could feel her pulse tick against my fingers as I held her close. I could still see the look in her eye after our first wild encounter in the swimming pool. The scent of her perfume still clung to my dressing gown. Once, not very long ago, I was the awkward gangly teenager who blushed every time a girl looked my way. Now, I had the confidence to make Michelle's cheeks bloom a rosy red when I winked at her, as I often did.

I wiped my clammy palms on my thighs, shuffled my feet, and left to descend the stairs and find my best friend, Jack. We had never kept any secrets from each other, and I needed to put him in the picture. As I closed the front door of the principal's house, I glanced to my left where the sound of raised voices caught my attention. I diverted round the back of the chapel towards the cricket pavilion and found a large group of our zone patrol teams with rifles raised. They were pointing them at two fifth-form boys, Simon Wigglesworth and Adrian Chadwick, who were red in the face with indignation. They waved their fists in our direction and screamed obscenities. The only two remaining boys still patrolling, Phil Loveless and Rick Tanner, approached, again with rifles raised. Now all twelve Zone guardians were there.

I ran to the scene. "What's going on guys?"

"These two clowns tried to breach the zone," Lance Clooney said. "We've warned them that one more step and we fire." I could tell by the look on Lance's face that he meant it. And I knew him well enough to believe he would follow through with his threat.

Chadwick said, "It's bluff," and took a step closer.

Lance squeezed the trigger, a shot rang out, and a clump of turf lifted up, just inches from Chadwick's feet. "Next one will be for real," Lance said, reloading and lifting the barrel of his rifle. He aimed it dead centre of Chadwick's chest. Adrian Chadwick backed off.

"What's the issue?" I demanded.

"You fuckers are the issue," Wigglesworth snarled. "The bloody virus is all round the school and you buggers have isolated yourselves while we are all at risk."

I couldn't deny his logic. "That's just how it is, Simon. We tried to segregate all those who had not been in contact with the virus."

"And left us to bloody die," he shouted.

Just then, a disturbance to our right caught our attention. Boys were shouting warnings. Phil Loveless and Rick Tanner ran back the way they had come. Wigglesworth smiled like the snake he was. "Never heard of a dummy tactic, you pathetic fucks? This was just a feint to draw your attention away." He pointed to where Phil and Rick had gone. "The real action is just about to happen. Goodbye suckers."

Simon Wigglesworth and Adrian Chadwick turned round and walked away smirking.

I shouted, "Lance, keep these two covered and shoot to kill if they make their way back. Rest of you come with me."

We ran like hell down the side of the chapel. As we rounded the corner of the chapel I stopped dead in my tracks. The hairs on the back of my neck stood on end. A tingle rolled down my arm. My heart beat faster and every sense in my body was now on high alert. Approaching from the reading room door, past the shrubbery, and towards the war memorial was a gang of about thirty boys, headed by none other than Bruiser and Cockroach. They were all carrying rifles, and now even Cockroach and the zombie tribe had their College ties round their heads like bandanas. It would have been laughable had it not been so pathetic – and so potentially dangerous.

Phil Loveless and Rick Tanner were standing right next to the war memorial pointing their rifles at the approaching crowd. "They're all armed," Rick called out.

I lowered my chin and ran towards the war memorial with a lengthening stride. "They have rifles," I called, "but that doesn't mean they're armed. Jack and I took the only live ammo we could find. All this lot will have are blanks."

I was wrong. Somewhere along the way, Jack and I must have missed some live shells. A shot rang out and Phil Loveless staggered backwards then fell. I looked down at the gaping hole in his neck and knew it was too late to do anything for him. But I had no time to reflect on his demise. More shots rang out and bullets ricocheted off the chapel walls behind me.

If there is one good thing about an angry mob, it's that they are so focused on being angry and mobbish that they sometimes miss little things. Things like a sixth-former called Nick Quine grabbing Phil's rifle. A surge of adrenaline topped me off with the confidence I so desperately needed. Just as Charlie Flanagan had taught us, I threw myself flat on the ground to make myself a smaller target. I took careful aim, and wiped out Toby Cochrane. I discovered that, when needed, yes I could kill someone. When Cochrane fell, the others, including Bruiser, stopped their advance, hesitated, and a few even began to back slowly away, still firing at us. I took a shot at Bruiser, missed him and hit the boy behind him. His name was David Newbold and he was just fifteen years old. He seemed to react in slow motion, like the world had decelerated. His arms flew up and his rifle dropped onto the tarmac. He fell to the ground against the school wall, his mouth hanging open. For a moment he sat there, a look of surprise on his face, and then his upper body slid sideways onto the ground. It left a trail of red on the wall, like a snail leaves behind a trail of slime.

Then things sped up again. More shots rang out and Rick Tanner, who had stood frozen to the spot with his mouth open, dropped his rifle and held his arm. Blood ran between his fingers.

Pete Scott and Sameer Lukuvi - Lucky - were two of the zone guards who had run back with me. Pete raised his rifle and fired shot after shot at the receding crowd. Past the bubble of hearing my own heart thrashing, there were voices and cries mixed between the screams of terror. The Lee-Enfield had a muzzle velocity of 2,441 feet per second. The mob was less than 50 yards away, so Pete's .303" cartridges hit their targets approximately 1/16th of a second after he squeezed the trigger. Mine too, and every round found an easy target since the pack was all bunched together. Either they had learnt nothing from their Tuesday afternoons in the cadets, or they though that superiority of numbers made them invincible.

Invincible, they were not. The magazine on the Lee-Enfields were designed for just 10 rounds. I used up all 10, so did Pete. I grabbed Rick Tanner's rifle from where he had let it drop when he grabbed his arm. I hammered out another ten rounds. I wasn't even aiming now - just firing at random into the crowd and watching the bodies drop. Lucky used up seven rounds before a bullet struck him in the chest. The other zone guards, having recovered from an initial inertia, began to fire. Shots rang out like a war movie, and echoed round the high stone buildings. And that was where the ground battle began and ended. By the time the other boys and the principal made it to the war memorial, the few remaining zombies still standing had dropped their weapons and fled, fighting and scrambling to get past each other into the main building through the open door of the reading room. One was too slow and was picked off as he made to run through the door. His rifle clattered to the ground, his body twitched, and then lay still.

When everything fell silent, I stood up. My throat

was dry and I was sweating so much my shirt was sticking to my back and arms, despite the chill in the air. My heart continued its fretful pumping and my mouth tasted like sawdust.

The principal rushed to Sameer Lukuvi. He felt for a pulse and shook his head. Lucky wouldn't make it home to Zanzibar. The same for poor Phil Loveless. Later, when they moved him, his head flopped around like a discarded glove puppet.

Within two minutes several street marshals came running down the side of the main buildings, dressed as usual in their full protective suits. They glanced at the bodies lying on the ground then kicked the rifles to one side to make sure they couldn't be used. Two wounded boys tried to crawl away, but one of the street marshals picked them off from near point-blank range. They were taking no risks. The lead marshal approached us. "What the hell happened?" he asked. His voice sounded like he had his head inside an empty fish tank. Which, in effect, he did.

The principal explained how we thought we had all the live ammunition, but clearly hadn't. There was no accusation in his voice. As he was talking, a further shot rang out and Bill McCormick, the small hockey-player who had stood up to Bruiser Williams in the showers, staggered backwards, hit the chapel wall, and slumped to the ground. His hockey days were over.

"Back in the chapel," the principal screamed. The boys all turned and began to run.

Another shot sounded and another boy was hit. Rob Harrison, a gifted scholar destined for great things in the field of computer science, stumbled with a hole through his thigh. The principal pointed up to the top of the tower. "Up there. I saw the muzzle flash."

As the pupils all ran inside for safety, I picked up Sameer Lukuvi's rifle, which still had three rounds in the magazine. I hadn't been counting them; I just knew he hadn't fired off all ten rounds. I took aim at the top of the tower and waited for a sign of any movement.

George Armstrong, our principal, stayed where he was and gave clear instruction to the street marshals how to find their way through the reading room to get to the tower. "Then up the stairs on your left," he said as another shot rang out. It missed him by a hair's width and hit the ground near my feet. "Keep going right up, past the dining hall. But for God's sake take care. The staircase is winding and whoever it is can ambush you at any point." While the principal was talking, I hadn't seen any sign of movement at the top of the tower. I fired off a round just to let whoever was up there know that we had them in our sights. I spotted a spray of splintered stone as the round hit about five feet below the parapet. I didn't have time to adjust the sights; I just had to make a point of aiming higher on the next shot.

Two of the marshals ran off to take down whoever was shooting. The others, like me, took aim at the top of the tower and fired volley after volley to keep the sniper's head down. The stone walls of the tower chipped away as bullets punched into them. When everybody was safely in the chapel, all firing stopped. A few minutes later, two muffled shots rang out. The marshals had shot Ffynlo Cranston, a fourteen-year-old acolyte of Bruiser Williams, twice in the stomach. He didn't survive.

As Mr Spock would say, some years later when Star

Trek hit the screens, "Without followers, evil cannot spread".

I looked down at the brave Bill McCormick. He looked so young in that moment. His round, innocent eyes shining back as if looking for answers to life's complicated questions. But they were eyes that no longer saw the world. Eyes that would never again experience life and friendship. Damn Bruiser Williams to hell. And damn his stupid followers too. They may have only been fourteen-, fifteen-, sixteen-year-olds, but even at that age you should know the difference between right and wrong. And for God's sake, damn the goddam fucking virus too.

CHAPTER TWENTY-FOUR

Later, when the street marshals took away the bodies that lay strewn between us and the entrance to the reading room, they also collected up the rifles. They discovered that most of them did indeed have blank rounds in their magazines. We could only assume that, when they had broken into the armoury, Bruiser and his young zombies had discovered a small box of maybe twenty or so live rounds. They had possibly loaded blanks in the delusional hope they would somehow scare us into submission. Or maybe to give them some Dutch courage. But the live rounds were enough to kill three boys and leave the rest of us stunned into silence. When Jack and I discussed it later with the principal, we could only assume that Mr Flanagan had kept some live rounds in his desk in the armoury. Jack and I were both certain that we had taken everything except the blanks from the double-locked steel armoury cupboard. The only other explanation was that there must have been some live rounds mixed into the boxes of blanks, but that seemed less likely. The principal accepted the explanation without comment.

Rick Tanner's wound on his upper arm was painful but not life threatening. Mrs Maxwell, who had trained as a nurse, helped him back to health. But it was an unhappy health without his close friend Phil. Rob Harrison's thigh wound was clean and would eventually heal. Sameer Lukuvi, Phil Loveless, and Bill McCormick were beyond help and I felt desperately sad for all three. Lucky and Phil had done what they could to defend our position but it turned out badly for them. Bill was just an easy target. As if to rub salt into the wounds, we were required to carry their bodies to the edge of the zone and allow the street marshals to take them away with the other dead students for burning up in the hills. It was like adding insult to injury, but there were no other choices. I had to simply accept that the dead would live on in our memories.

Bruiser Williams was amongst the sixteen dead and he would not be getting up again. If the first bullet in the abdomen didn't kill him, the second one in his chest certainly did. I was glad. He had brought it on himself. They burned his body, along with the others, on the hillside that same night. I wished to God that Bruiser had never been allowed back into College after he had been expelled the previous term. I knew that the principal had been against it, but he had been outvoted by the trustees. That decision had cost many lives - not just our three, but the dozens who had followed Bruiser and been mowed down with real bullets, not blanks. The anger welled inside me, with nowhere to go. I could feel it eating away at me. I knew if I didn't find a way to release it, it would destroy me. I tried to calm my pulse but my heart was so heavy with agony for the whole community. Inside College, those who hadn't taken part in Bruiser's rebellion still had to face a killer virus. It would be a long time before things got any better.

Everybody wanted to hold meetings and discuss what had happened, how College had fallen apart. The principal encouraged people to open up and not to bottle up. Jack and I kept well away from all that. We weighed things up between ourselves and let the facts speak for themselves. It is, after all, the grain of sand that finds its way into an oyster's shell that makes the pearl, not pearl-making seminars with other oysters.

"You realise you're a hero now, don't you?" Jack said.

I grunted. "Heroes are like labourers, my friend. You know what you get for shovelling more shit than anyone else?"

"Pushed into it face first?"

"No," I replied. "They just give you a bigger fucking shovel."

Jack chuckled. "I think I'd rather shovel shit than listen to the constant Utopian ideology that some of our fellow students are spewing out in an endless loop."

It was true, Strong words were lobbed like grenades. Not everybody agreed with our actions, it seemed. Donald McIntyre, the vicar who would end up in prison for inappropriate sexual contact with children said we should have negotiated. Some nodding heads agreed with him including Thomas Arnold, the budding alcoholic who would choke on his own vomit. I heard that same argument years later when the Argentineans invaded the Falkland Islands. The Socialists said we should sort it out with a friendly chat over a cup of tea. Thatcher decided, as was usual for her, that it was best to negotiate from a position of strength and sent a flotilla of war ships to sort it out. That lady had more balls than the whole Labour Party put together.

Okay, I know that's not a view that will find much favour with the chattering classes, or the politically correct, or the self-appointed leaders of fashionable opinion, or so-called progressives, or liberals in general. But it's a view that would have seemed normal and middle-of-the-road when I was a young man. Which makes it anathema today, when mis-called 'right wing values' are derided.

Okay - I'm back off my high horse.

That evening minutes turned to hours. I tossed and turned. My mind was unable to rest. I thought about what I had seen and done. I could hear other lads' restless turning on their camp beds. Nobody would get much sleep that night. And I realised I still hadn't told Jack about Michelle. Maybe the virus had already infected us all. Maybe our own quarantine had been a waste of time. I made the decision to say nothing. If it turned out that she was infected, we'd all know soon enough.

As my watch eased its way towards midnight, I threw off the blanket that covered me, pulled on a shirt and trousers and made my way outside. The cold air caught beneath my collar. The moon was bright and the night was clear and fresh. I soon put an end to that. I lit up a cigarette as soon as I was beyond the outer doors, and blew the smoke skywards. I sauntered towards the cricket pavilion, nodding to the patrols as they passed me. We didn't have much to say that evening. After the short exchange of fire, the street marshals had taken away all the remaining rifles from the armoury and extended their patrols to cover the whole school. We felt safe enough to drop back to three teams of two boys rotating every fourteen hours. I found myself nodding and saying 'hello' to a pair of street marshals as I passed them by on my side of the yellow tape, while they were on the other. They were mostly army lads, some no older than me. They were stretched to the limits covering everywhere on the island, and I didn't envy them their jobs. They had trained for warfare, but not against an unseen enemy.

At the pavilion, I saw a man's outline and another glowing cigarette in the darkness. As I approached, I was surprised to find it was the principal. "I thought you only smoked one cigar a day?" I joked.

He waved his hand in the air. "I do, Nick. This is a cigarette."

"I thought you'd given those up."

"So did I."

We lapsed into a comfortable silence until he said, "I need to move. Let's mooch. This bloody virus is killing us all, even if we don't catch it ourselves. This whole situation is beyond my worst nightmares."

"You know about Michelle?" I asked.

He just nodded. I looked at him and nodded back. I held his eyes with mine and I saw something that I hadn't seen before. There was more dread and uncertainty swirling inside him than I had ever thought possible. But he had dealt with it. George Armstrong was our fearless leader who wasn't afraid of taking on the largest issues that yielded the biggest consequences, good and bad. But now that all our lives were on the line, he could either play it safe or continue to push the boundaries until we were through the viral threat. I was just happy to know Armstrong had our backs and I wasn't ready to let him see any weakness in me.

I wasn't ready, but when it came, I couldn't help it.

I stopped and turned in a semi-circle with the strange sense of being watched. Holding my breath, I listened for sounds while my mind raced. Had the mob returned? Did we have to fight another battle? Were more innocent lives to be taken? I shrugged and moved to the seaward side of the pavilion alongside the principal. As we strolled onto the open area of playing field that we'd cordoned off, we maintained our silence for a while, but I couldn't shake off the feeling of being watched. When we reached the yellow tape that defined the safe zone, I felt my muscles shudder; I didn't have a good feeling about this. But I couldn't place what or where that feeling was coming from. My lips turned dry and I felt the ball of goo that had been floating around in my stomach all day since the morning battle suddenly harden into stone. Looking back now, I realise it may just have been my mind playing tricks on me, but it was as real to me then as the pages of the book I had been pretending to read that afternoon.

The stone ball in my gut rose and lodged in my throat. I thought I was going to be sick and struggled to swallow it down. "They didn't stand a chance," I mumbled.

The principal looked at me. "There is only one way to fight, Nick, and that's dirty. I learnt that very quickly on the battlefields of Normandy. Clean gentlemanly fighting will get you nowhere but dead - and fast. Take every cheap shot and every low blow you can. By all means kick all hell out of people when they're down, and maybe you'll be the one who walks away. Most of us walked away today because you and a few others did what was right and necessary. You didn't question whether those boys stood a chance. You just knew that if you didn't act, we would be the ones who wouldn't stand a chance."

"But we even kept firing as they retreated."

"And so you should. Many still had some live rounds in their rifles. They could, and probably would, have come back again later. They could have taken pot shots at us from the school windows." He looked towards the hills where fires burned bright. "If you and the other young men hadn't done what you did, it would be us they would be burning up there. Pray for the dead by all means, but fight like hell for the living."

"I just feel so guilty."

"Voltaire said, 'Every man is guilty of all the good he did not do'. You have done good things, Nick. The guilt is not yours to bear."

"But that's how it feels."

The principal looked hard at me in the bright moonlight. "Maybe there's more we all could have done, but we just have to let the guilt remind us to do better next time. I feel guilty for leaving the praes inside the school. I knew the risks, but it was a decision I had to make. Self-reproach is a luxury none of us can afford at the moment. It might catch up with us later when we all get out of here, but right now, you have no reason to blame yourself for —"

A loud voice cut across George Armstrong's. "Looks like we've got two of the big noises."

As we had chatted, we hadn't seen their silent approach. Simon Wigglesworth and Adrian Chadwick stood on the other side of the tape, just a few yards away pointing rifles at us.

CHAPTER TWENTY-FIVE

"Thought you'd got rid of us, did you?" Wigglesworth snarled. "Thought it was all over, did you? Well you might have won a battle, but you didn't win the bloody war."

"How did you get here?" the principal asked in a sharp voice.

"Adrian and I sneaked over the wall behind the art school under cover of darkness. We just kept our heads down and walked round to here on the airport side of the wall. We've been training for something like this for weeks."

I was reminded of Jack telling me about how Rhonda had seen a group of boys walking in the airport after dark, safe in the knowledge that our boundary with the airport wasn't patrolled. Wigglesworth and Chadwick could have been waiting there for hours without being seen. "You mean Bruiser style training?" I said. "Like walking down the main runway after dark? What a load of utter dummies."

"We're not the dummies here," Wigglesworth snarled. "Bruiser had it right all along. He trained us for this, and now we're going to even the score a little."

The principal sliced his hand through the air, sharp as a knife. "Wigglesworth, put that rifle down and stop with this nonsense. It's over. It's finished."

"It's not finished," Chadwick said. "It's not bloody

finished till I say so." Blood sloshed in my ears as he levelled his rifle at my chest. "Like Bruiser said, you lot have deserted us and left us to catch this bloody virus while you all shelter here in your safety zone. Well we're here to level things up a bit. If we're going to die, we're going to take some of you bastards with us."

"No you're not," said Lance Clooney from our left. "Do as the principal says and lower your weapons."

Adrian Chadwick spun round. He swung his rifle towards Lance, but Lance cut him down before he had chance to shoot. Blood spurted from Chadwick's back as the round passed right through him. The rifle fell from his hands and more hot blood splattered onto his hands, pouring down his chest. His lungs deflated and his knees gave way as he fell to the ground, lying on his back, staring up into that bright moon.

A second shot rang out as Simon Wigglesworth squeezed the trigger, shooting at the principal at almost point-blank range. The rifle flash punched a hole in the darkness but the principal didn't even flinch. He didn't know that the round was a blank, but he still didn't cringe or cower.

Lance swung his rifle at Wigglesworth. "Drop it," he shouted. "Now! Or you'll end up the same as Chadwick."

Wigglesworth worked the bolt to chamber the next round, maybe hoping it would be a live round, but he never had the chance to fire it. Lance cut him down as effectively as he had Adrian Chadwick. One .303 round was enough. I heard myself scream. A deep tremor quaked in my bones as I watched Wigglesworth's head explode. His body slumped like a puppet with broken strings. He lay limp on the ground with his brains splattered in a thick fan on the grass in front of me. It glistened black in the light of the moon. I blinked and hyperventilated as I looked around. The air had been knocked right out of me.

I took several deep breaths and pulled myself together. I stepped forward to pick up one of the rifles in case there were others out there who were armed, but I stopped myself, remembering Jack's warning about the plastic supermarket bag a few days earlier. In any case, who knew if the bullets were real or not? Two street marshals came running on the other side of the yellow tape. I think it was the two I had passed a few minutes earlier. Pete Scott raced round the back of the pavilion.

"What happened?" one of the street marshals asked.

Lance explained. "While the main mob were shooting at the front of the chapel this morning, I waited here because I had a feeling it could have been a double bluff by these two. I didn't think they would just quietly go away. They crept back straight after the shooting while your guys were clearing up. I warned them off again. When we resumed patrols, and you men were guarding the other side, I thought the danger had passed."

"So how did you know they were here tonight?" I asked.

Lance laughed, though there was little humour in it. "I didn't. I'm not psychic, Nick. I came back on patrol again about an hour ago and I got caught short. I stopped for a pee behind the pavilion while Pete carried on walking slowly, waiting for me to catch up. As I was buttoning up, I saw this pair climbing over the airport wall carrying rifles. I thought it might be best to take them away from them."

"For which Nick and I are very grateful," the principal said

Lance looked down. "I wish they'd just dropped the bloody rifles. I didn't want to kill anybody. Maybe all that either of them had were blanks. Knowing those two, they probably wouldn't even know the difference."

"You couldn't take that risk," George Armstrong said. "None of us want to kill, Lance, but as I was just explaining to Nick, these are difficult times and we have to do whatever is necessary to protect ourselves."

One of the street marshals bent and picked up Wigglesworth's rifle in his gloved hand. He ejected the round that was in the chamber. "It's live," he said. "The idiot hadn't even checked that his live rounds were at the top of the magazine." He looked at Lance, who was looking pale and shaken. "Your headmaster is right. None of us want to kill people, but none of us want to be killed by them either. You did the right thing, my friend." He turned to the principal. "We'll get this situation here cleaned up. Meanwhile, I suggest you reduce the size of your safety zone a few metres at this point to exclude this area where the bodies are. There's blood here and it may well be contaminated."

The principal nodded. "I'll get it seen to. I think we can shrink it down much closer to the pavilion now."

The street marshal nodded and got on his walkie-talkie to summon help.

The principal took Lance to one side and spoke quietly with him for a few minutes. I'm sure he was giving him a similar talk to the one he'd just given me about fighting hard, and being on the winning side. As they spoke, I walked slowly back to the cricket pavilion and left them in private. The shock of what had just happened had sent my heart into overdrive.

I wasn't ready for what happened next. A felling of total inadequacy came over me. It was like I was suffocating and being crushed under the weight of it all. I stepped back and dropped down like a dead weight onto one of the wooden benches on the pavilion verandah. The sky was clear but the open verandah was shaded by the pavilion roof, so I didn't expect to be seen by anybody. What began as a quake deep inside my core soon spread to each of my limbs. I lifted my hand and watched my fingers tremble. My lungs breathed short, hungry rasps until black splotches blinked in front of my eyes. I felt trapped, like I was losing control of something I should have had a tight grip on.

The first of my tears squeezed out. Then the floodgates opened and I couldn't stop the river that flowed down my cheeks. I grieved for the victims, wept in silence for those of us who remained, and cried for myself because I was exhausted. But, mostly, I was just scared. I was scared for my life, for what might happen next, and for the bloody virus that might already have us in its grip because of Michelle. I hated feeling helpless. And, on top of everything, I still felt guilty that I had been the cause of Braxton Boddington's death with our childish trick on the linen store handle. It was a heavy burden to carry and the weight of it had finally caught up with me.

I remember even thinking how bloody unfair it was that people I knew in England didn't have to suffer like we were. I think the absence of hope removes all empathy. Then all you want is for the rest of the world to suffer like you do.

After a few minutes and several deep breaths, I wiped my cheeks dry with the back of my hand. I felt a hand rest on my shoulder. "Don't worry, Nick. Things will work out. The past has gone, and we need to focus now on staying safe." My heart skipped a beat when I realised it was the principal talking. He finished with, "And, Nick, stay strong. You're an asset I can't afford to lose. You and the other young men with guns kept us all safe today. No matter what you are feeling right now, you can be proud of that for the rest of your life." Then he disappeared like a phantom into the darkness. I smoked another cigarette with shaking hands, then pulled myself together and made my way back to the chapel. I wanted to know that things could only get better but, with Michelle's illness, it would be a few more days before I began to feel more optimistic.

CHAPTER TWENTY-SIX

Only having to patrol every fourteen hours again eased the burden on the patrols. It also meant that, a few days later, when Michelle got over her illness, she and I could spend some more quality time together. Angela Maxwell suggested that her fever and headache may have been psychosomatic, caused by the stress that we were all feeling. Many weeks later, when things returned to normal, Michelle saw a specialist who agreed with that diagnosis. It was, he said, almost certainly psychogenic fever - a stress-related, psychosomatic condition that manifests itself in a high body temperature. It was caused by exposure to emotional events or to chronic stress, he said. That made sense, bearing in mind what we were all going through. Personally, I didn't care what it was as long as it wasn't Coviman-12.

After our first love-making session, I asked, "You feeling better now?"

"Oh yes. Sex pretty much cures everything," she answered with that cheeky grin on her face. "Sex is friendship with less clothes, which makes it far more interesting."

Olakunle Onikoyi, the Nigerian student who later died in a bloody coup, must have thought the same. I spotted him leaving Mrs Maxwell's room that night, and several times later. We never commented. He just smiled and winked at me. Mrs Maxwell's mood improved considerably as the weeks went by, as did her figure. It seemed from what Rhonda told me, she had put herself on a diet so she could be more attractive to other men now she didn't have a husband. She already seemed to be doing quite well with Olakunle without changing shape.

Henry Miller, the American writer said in his book Tropic Of Cancer, 'What holds the world together, as I have learned from bitter experience, is sexual intercourse'. Well said, Henry, except that my experience in 1967 was not in the slightest bit bitter. I loved every minute of my time with Michele. Rhonda too, from time-to-time. Never once in my whole life have I regretted my relationship with those wonderful, spontaneous, sensuous ladies from the dining hall. To this day, I love them both to bits.

Meanwhile, another bit of news both cheered me up and depressed me in equal measure. A few days after the battle with Bruiser's zombies, the principal told Jack and me that Matron had now fallen victim to the virus. It seemed that imminent death was like entering the confessional box. She had told George Armstrong that it was she who had let Mr Maxwell know about his wife's extra-curricular linen store activities.

"So he didn't find out about Boddington because of the door handle?" I asked.

The principal shook his head. "Ease your conscience, Nick. It was Matron who told him. She didn't like being blackmailed by Mrs Maxwell into giving her a key to the linen store. She thought she would stir up trouble for her. She certainly succeeded in that."

I can't help admitting that, sorry though I was for Matron, I felt huge relief at that news. For many days, I had dwelt on the fact that an innocent prank had a cost a boy his life. Now at least I could wash my conscience of that particular area of guilt. I had plenty of others queuing for my attention. Night-times were the worst. That was when visions of the boys I'd shot crawled back into my conscience. I struggled to get to sleep at nights. Then I was impossible to live with during the day. You don't embrace darkness; you stumble into its welcoming arms. It gets you settled, then tightens its embrace, bares its fangs and starts to bite. I didn't know that then, I was trying to cope with something way bigger than me and I was lashing out blindly. The only person I hurt was myself. Jack and the girls stayed loyal and supportive until I sorted my head out.

Our quarantine lasted four more months. After no new cases of Coviman-12 had come to light for a period of four weeks, the authorities declared the emergency over. But we remained enclosed in our cocoon for a further five weeks as every building, street, beach and rabbit hole was sprayed with a noxious-smelling disinfectant. Gun shots sounded regularly as the street marshals eliminated all animals on the island, domestic, wild, or farmed. There was a suggestion that they might have been responsible for Coviman-12. So, even after the emergency was officially ended, the fires on the hills still blazed bright at night as animal carcasses were destroyed. Later, when we discovered that the bio lab opposite the airport had been shut down and burned, we suspected that the true source was going to be hidden forever and that the culling of the animals was just a cover. To this day, you'll find no foxes, badgers, otters, deer, moles, squirrels or snakes on the Isle of Man.

In addition to soldiers destroying all the animals, the naval blockade continued to keep people away from the island. But the boats also collected up many dozens of floating corpses. It seemed that a lot of infected people had stepped out of their houses expecting and hoping to be shot by the street marshals but had not been challenged. In their pain and their frustration, they had walked into the sea and drowned themselves.

During that time of quarantine relaxation, restrictions on the use of the phone were eased and we all had the opportunity to contact our parents from the privacy of the principal's living room. I'm not ashamed to say that a lot of tears were shed on both sides.

With the pressure off, conversations in the chapel became more normalised. Would Tottenham or Chelsea win the first 'Cockney Cup Final'? To save you looking it up, Spurs won the match 2–1, thus winning the FA Cup for the third time in seven years and the fifth time in all. Would the famous TT races be run this year? No, and it was cancelled in 2001 because of an outbreak of Foot and Mouth in UK. And again in 2020 due to Coronavirus - a pale imitation of Coviman-12, even though it killed many thousands worldwide. If Coviman had been allowed to spread worldwide like Coronavirus, it would have decimated half the world's population.

As the end of quarantine approached, the question for some was would Yorkshire win the Cricket County Championship. Yawn - yes they did, so I'm told. The principal's efforts to try to make us rise above this intellectual hardening of the arteries met with limited success. Chaucer and Homer could go suck themselves. If they'd lived through the quarantine and the fear that we had, they probably would have done exactly that.

It was early June before we were told it was all clear and we could go about our business. The yellow tape came down and the principal got us all to clear away the detritus in the chapel, and screw back the pews that had lain in the chancel for months. The school buildings were empty save fifty or so students who had somehow survived. There was an air of sanitised abandonment about the whole edifice, a hopelessness that permeated every room, every study, every corridor. One can only imagine the carnage inside where Bruiser and his zombies had run riot before trying to shoot their way into the chapel. The study Jack and I had shared had been torched, presumably by an angry Bruiser. For some reason, he held Jack and me responsible for all the world's woes. I was amazed that he hadn't set fire to the whole school.

As Bruiser's mob had run riot, the surviving pupils had grabbed whatever supplies they could and barricaded themselves into the gymnasium until things had quietened down again. Survival tactics, and nothing more. Those who lived looked ill and worn out. One boy had actually contracted the virus and lived. He looked like a man emptied out of all vital organs and all emotions. But the hospitals were full, so there was nothing that could be done to help him. I heard much later that even some of the survivors who had remained free of the virus had died at an early age. They had developed medical and psychological complications due to the stress of suffering a living death for so long.

I think that was when the real anger set in. So many of my friends and fellow pupils had died because of a stupid virus that didn't even have a brain. I don't believe there's a God, but nonetheless I cursed him for allowing Coviman-12 to exist. It's natural to feel angry once in a while, but it becomes a problem when you regularly get angry in routine situations at home or in the office. When the anger becomes frequent and flares up at the slightest provocation, it is an indication that all is not well in your life.

Frequent and uncontrolled anger is a symptom of a fragile state of mind, which manifests itself at the slightest adverse situation. I was that fragile person for a long time, until the vivid memories began to fade a little. But even now, the voices of my dead friends echo between my ears and I don't know what to make of it or how to handle it.

When I got back home, my parents needed to believe I was okay. For a long time I tried to convince them that I was. I tried to convince myself too. But I was a much tougher sell because I knew the truth. I was so very not okay. I realised that I was going to feel shitty either way. I was almost certainly going to feel shitty for the rest of my life. A life many of my friends were not even living. So I got angry. Then I got very angry. Then I got angrier still. Then I healed.

You can only go so long being angry before you learn to say 'what the fuck' and just get on with your life, because there's no other choice. So I said, "Dear God, thanks for screwing up the world, what the fuck," and got on with the job of living.

Out of the fifty or so pupils who were housed in Lower School only six young boys survived, along with Smoothie Jones, my English teacher. He survived Coviman but smoked himself into an early grave with his 60-a-day habit. Gallaher's took Senior Service Extra Strength off the market a few years later. Too late for Steven Jones. But I remember him fondly, above all else as a human being with human faults. I thank him for being understanding, and supporting all our idiosyncrasies with little resistance.

I recall one day when he lost his temper a bit with a pupil. He'd asked him to describe his feelings having read a chapter of 'For Whom The Bell Tolls' by

Ernest Hemingway. It's a beast of a book that graphically describes the brutality of the Spanish Civil War. When the boy couldn't describe how he felt, Steven Jones lowered his eyes to the open book. He took his time reading aloud a particularly graphic excerpt from the chapter in question before looking up at the boy. In a calm, quiet voice, he said, "Bargery, do you think that, if you have a feeling you can't describe, you might just be, I don't know, kind of like, my sense of it is, maybe in the wrong fucking class?" We all roared laughing, and we respected him all the more for his restrained outburst. I salute you, Sir. Old as I now am, I can still tell you that an antecedent is a noun, noun phrase or clause referred to by a pronoun. I can also spell 'onomatopoeia'.

In the chapel, life-long friendships were made. Those of us who are left still exchange Christmas cards. For Jack and me, for many years, that included Michelle and Rhonda. But every year one or two more have to be taken off the list as they don't respond, or we have no news of them. My list no longer includes Jack, Rhonda, or Michelle.

We mostly did okay in life. Jack became a doctor - a damn good one. Like the rest of us, he had to take his A levels one year late, but we all got there in the end. I took mine at a local grammar school in England since I was a scholarship boy at College and the school remained closed for some while. To make ends meet Bishop's College merged with the Lady Burnside School for Girls from the local town and renamed itself 'Island School'. Like College, the Lady Burnside School for Girls had been almost wiped out with Coviman-12. College wasn't co-ed in my day, but Jack, Pete and I didn't miss too much action because of it. Nor, it seemed, did Olakunle Onikoyi. I guess college life could even be more interesting nowadays. In my experience, boys are predictable. As soon as they think of something, they do it. Girls are smarter - they plan ahead. They think about not getting caught. There's probably quite a lot of 'not getting caught' going on at Island School nowadays.

Angela Maxwell disappeared into the ether. Her husband, who had set about Braxton Boddington with a hockey stick, had fallen foul of the virus and his body was burned on the hillside with thousands of others. There are several discreet sites on the island's hills with memorials for 'those who perished to the virus of 1967'. No names or numbers, just a granite slab with a brass plaque. There's a rumour that any bits of body that hadn't completely burned were scooped up and shipped to the crematorium in Douglas. I guess it's easier to deal with a few hundred arms and legs than several thousand people. The government never owned up to how many died, but for sure it was reckoned to be over 20,000.

There were never any inquests into the deaths of Cedric Patterson, Braxton Boddington, Sameer Lukuvi, Phil Loveless, or Bill McCormick. Nor for Bruiser, Cockroach or their followers who we had shot. They were just a statistic of people who had died thanks to Coviman-12. I guess it was easier for everybody that way.

Pete and Lesley, as I already mentioned, lived happily in a small market town in Norfolk, sharing themselves around with whoever pleased them. They're probably wife-swapping right now with a group of incontinent old wrinklies with walking sticks and no teeth. Last time we met, Pete told me that George Armstrong had been aware all along that he, Pete, was meeting with his wife. Just as Cordelia had been aware that the principal was knocking off Lesley Parkes. When Jack and I found him bonking Lesley, the principal had never been worried about their marriage, just about his job and his reputation. Was it something they regularly did? I somehow doubt it, but who knows. As I had discovered for myself, you can't pre-judge anything and it takes all sorts to make a world.

Poor old Phil Loveless never did get the chance to rebuild his valve radio. But at least Rick Tanner found another guy who made him happy. When The Marriage (Same Sex Couples) Act came into force in March 2014, forty-seven years later, Rick and his lifelong partner Eddie were amongst the first to get married. Jack and I turned up at their wedding and discovered that a few more of our old comrades in arms had been invited. Andy Pemberton, the boy who Bruiser Williams had smashed with his hockey stick, was there. He walked with the help of a stick, but at least he walked. We had a monster piss-up followed by some monster hangovers. The hangovers are worse as you get older.

Lance Clooney, our only remaining prae who warned us about the witch's curse, became a dentist on the island, eventually retiring to Cyprus where, as far as I know, he spends his days painting and testing the local wines. We stay in touch on Facebook now. He was a good, straightforward guy, and he saved my life. The world could do with more like him; people willing to take responsibility and act when required.

The principal's final words to Jack and me as we left college for the last time were, "It's going to be a long road to making sense of this, lads, but stay strong. You'll find a way to turn this into a positive."

It was the only time I knew George Godfrey Armstrong to be wrong.

EPILOGUE

You might be interested to know that Margaret IneQuaine's curse that Lance warned us about seems to have ended. There were no more major catastrophes at College on the two following generational anniversaries - 1992 or 2017. Maybe she decided that the deaths of over 319 boys and masters from Bishop's College was enough. That figure included day boys whom we never saw again, and masters who were outside College grounds. On the other hand, it was reported that not one of the island's vicars, priests, and pastors escaped with their lives. The churches and chapels stood empty for a long while. Many of them still do. Maybe it was that which finally satisfied Margaret IneQuaine's search for revenge. Many people came to realise that hands clasped together in prayer were useless against Coviman-12.

It took a while, but the Isle of Man got over the events of 1967. The virus destroyed the tourist industry as surely as Brazil is now destroying the Amazon rain forest. Holidaymakers soon discovered cheap flights to sunny Spain. Over the years, the island reinvented itself as a tax haven, then grew up, behaved itself, and became an attractive place to do business due to a legitimate low tax regime. The island's population before the virus was 52,000. Today, it's 84,000. Life has moved on. As you drive the island's roads, you don't see many mansions. They're there alright, but they are hidden behind granite walls or high hedges. It's a discreet independent offshore gem, right on the UK's doorstep. It has come back to life, but it was a long, uphill struggle.

The sexual revolution that first appeared with 'Flower Power' in the 1960s was a social movement that challenged traditional codes of behaviour related to sexuality and interpersonal relationships. Sexual liberation included increased acceptance of sex outside of traditional heterosexual, monogamous relationships. The normalisation of contraception and the pill, public nudity, pornography, premarital sex, homosexuality, masturbation, alternative forms of sexuality, and the legalisation of abortion all followed. I think Jack and I beat most of the 'Flower People' to it. Trail blazers - that was us. With the help of Lesley Parkes and the Owen sisters, of course.

Our last four months in quarantine were a love-fest of ridiculous proportions. On one occasion, I actually turned down an invitation. I needed the sleep. Even Jack admitted to me once that he had stumbled back to his camp bed with the stooped posture of an exhausted marathon runner. Mostly, Jack tended towards Rhonda and I tended towards Michelle. But that didn't stop us from changing bedrooms from time to time. A change is as good as a rest, as they say. Apart from good sex, mutual fulfilment, and consideration for your bed fellow during our post-coital tender moments, Michelle taught me to stand back and observe myself. She taught me to unpick each tangled rope of emotion, however painful, and then to deal with it. It was, she told me, how she and Rhonda had lived through their childhood with abusive parents.

Our last love-making session was tender, slow and gentle, unlike most of our frenetic coupling. We just wrapped ourselves in each other and took up an easy, gradual rhythm. There was a lot of kissing, and a few tears. But it wasn't the last time I saw Michelle.

After we all left College, the girls went back to Blackpool from whence they had come. Fifteen years later, while on a week-long business seminar I looked up Michelle who was still on my Christmas card list at the time. She hadn't changed much, other than a few extra laughter wrinkles at the corners of her eyes. She was still a hungry MILF and I'm ashamed to admit - well maybe not very ashamed - that I was jolly unfaithful to my second wife for several days. I'm as pure as driven slush, me.

The years had been kind to Michelle. Her lips were still full and inviting. She still had the same infectious laugh and glassy cackle in her eyes that she had at College. And that 20,000 volt sexual charisma that beckoned me all those years ago on the Isle of Man had not dimmed. The last time I saw her, she was standing on the bed wearing banana-yellow socks with the smiley face logo on the sides - and nothing else. She looked darn good too. After our final romp together, her bedroom looked like a freshly trashed playground for gorillas.

As I threw my clothes on, Michelle said, "You're not leaving me, are you?"

"Sorry, but I have to run. Got a train to catch."

"Think of me, will you?"

I waved and smiled. "Kiss my dick," I shouted over my shoulder.

"Already have," Michelle replied with a huge grin on her face.

And so she had.

I suppose sex is like oxygen - it's not important unless you aren't getting any. And sex without smiling is as unpleasant as vodka and tonic without ice. God, I miss that woman. Hardly a week goes by without me thinking of her and our time together. It wasn't love. It was never love. After all, why drown in love when you can have so much more fun swimming in lust? What we had was a deep, deep friendship. A closeness of spirit that supported us both during a time of need and which lived on afterwards. Michelle was my first crush and my first lust. But she was never mine to have. She belonged to herself and her world.

While I was in Blackpool, Rhonda called in to say hello, but she was dating a married man and had an appointment to go and meet with him, so she kept her clothes on. They say it's a man's world, but men are easily controlled by women. Particularly women of Michelle and Rhonda's pedigree. Of the two of them, Rhonda was the one who had changed the most. I was struck by how tall she seemed, and boyishly slim. But still with all the right curves in all the right places. Her hair was different. She had elfin-short ash-blonde hair, which I could see had been expensively highlighted with three different shades.

They may well both be dead by now, Michelle and Rhonda. They were about fifteen years older than Jack and me, and I'm now heading into serious old age. But they led interesting, fulfilled lives. I wouldn't mind betting that they're up there somewhere seducing little Martians or skinny dipping in moonbeams to make themselves laugh. They'd have stuck a pitchfork up the devil's bum if he tried to stop them.

I last saw Jack Parsons almost ten years ago, a week before his death. At school, Jack was awarded school colours for athletics. Quite how that happened I don't know considering the number of cigarettes we both smoked. But in his teens, he was a fit, fast, guy. I managed to kick the nicotine habit a good few years back, but Jack continued to battle against the addiction all his life. It was suicide by instalments and he lost the battle. But he took it all in his stride. When I visited him in the hospice, he had trouble breathing, but he still chuckled and chortled as we reminded ourselves of our romps with Michelle and Rhonda. And our 'manning-up' as he called it, courtesy of Lesley Parkes. When I commented on the fact that he could never quit smoking, he shrugged and said, "I've not missed the house I never had."

I looked at him puzzled.

Jack laughed. "I worked out the other day that, during my life, I have spent enough on cigarettes to buy a luxury house. But I've never missed it."

Later I checked his maths and discovered he was right.

Jack's final words to me were, "You do know, don't you, Nick, that after the shoot-out outside the chapel, I've always held you up as my hero? You were just fucking awesome." I made to answer him but he added, "Keep hold of that thought, old man." I smiled and waved as I went out of the door for the last time. Just two grown men saying goodbye, though a tear rolled down my cheek as I left the hospice. When I heard of Jack's death, it crossed my mind that I could kill a bad guy, but I couldn't save my friend. I was no hero. I was nothing more than a killer. A killer who sat and cried afterwards. Guns make small men feel big, and I'd always believed they were the tools of the poorly educated. We didn't have that excuse. We were at a private establishment that charged most of our parents an arm and a leg for us to be properly educated.

You may find it easy to read this and think badly of Jack for smoking all his life. For a non-smoker, not smoking is not an achievement. Like virginity, not smoking comes as standard in the original package. But once you've started to smoke, it's a bastard to give up. After all, how many women can grow their hymen back once it's gone?

Smoking was always a blissful experience, and I understand how people find it impossible to quit. Despite having given up many years ago, if someone told me today that I had only three months left to live, the first thing I would do would be to go out and buy a pack of cigarettes. It's a lifelong habit that never really leaves you alone.

Jack and I had been friends so long, I've forgotten which one of us was the bad influence. He was like a brother to me, but too smart for an eighteen-year-old. His brains were always getting us in trouble, and he learnt at some point - probably after I blew up all the electrical fuses in College with a dodgy toaster that we found on the rubbish tip - that it was usually possible to get his mate Nick to join him on the master's carpet when trouble was in the wind. Jack never asked me to shoulder the blame for his often brilliant fuck-ups - he was neither a sneak nor a coward - but on several occasions I was asked to share it. Which was, I think, why we both got in trouble when I tested the fire alarms three nights running. And for the record, the fire alarms worked just fine.

Jack was a character, and his friendship has always been very special to me. Together, we remained strong, even in the face of adversity. He was as rare as a unicorn. You know, a friend like no other. Rarely in life do you make a true, lifelong friend, so I feel privileged to have known Jack Parsons. Jack was special - a one-off. I still miss him.

But for me, the hero of 1967 has always been our principal, George Godfrey Armstrong. Jack and I caught him with his trousers down, but he forgave us our intrusion into his privacy and led us all safely through the awful events of 1967. Most of us would not be alive today had it not been for him. He was a man of some extraordinary wisdom, knowing when to be firm and when to turn a blind eye.

Pete once let it drop that Lesley had entertained George Armstrong in her bedroom a few times while we waited out the lifting of the quarantine. It didn't surprise me, but that was something between him and Lesley. After the island opened up its doors again, and Cordelia Armstrong came home, they lived together until his death from a sudden heart attack at the age of 88. She died just weeks later. Until that point, like my other close friends, they had been on my Christmas card list.

After the Internet and Wikipedia invaded our lives, I looked up George Armstrong and found that he had, indeed been a war hero. He had never made it known to us at school, but in his early twenties he had been awarded the Victoria Cross. The night before D-Day, Armstrong led a raiding party up a Normandy cliff to capture a shore battery that could have wreaked havoc with the invasion ships. He saved his platoon from a German machine gun, at some very considerable risk to himself.

In 1967 we learnt the lessons of leadership from a master of the art - George Armstrong. Go in peace, Sir. You were a good man. A damn good man.

As for me, the years have been just full of surprises, and a lot of fun. When I left school at eighteen, I had premature grey hair. So did many others who'd shared the chapel with me. Everybody reckoned it made me look distinguished. I dismissed the idea as borderline fruitcake, and ignored whatever colour my hair decided to be. I naively thought that happiness would be something I would wake up to every day once I could legally smoke, drink and fornicate. But I discovered that it comes with a price tag. I had to accept that I was just a simple guy. I loved Bacardi, sex, and women who said 'no' but looked as though they meant 'yes'. I hated paedophiles, political correctness, hypocrisy, and pink blancmange.

At thirty, I decided to give up on my pipe-dream of being an itinerant sperm donor, to set up my own building business. I was an accounting technician at the time, but no smoking was becoming a thing in many work places. On a building site, every bugger smoked. I actually did give up smoking a few years later.

I have wandered my way through life dodging from one thing to another and from one woman to another. Sex doesn't satisfy for a lifetime, the more you have it, the more you want it. Maybe I should try and blame Michelle and Rhonda for that bad habit, but I'm fairly certain I would have been the same had I never met them. "I am what I am," as a friend of mine called Jack Parsons used to say. He also used to say, "Life is but a bowl of cherries," though I had to disagree with him over that after living through those first few months of 1967.

My first wife was a treasure. We're still good friends and our two lovely sons have their own families to raise. My second wife taught me the difference between the three types of sex. One - new sensation, spontaneous kitchen table sex. Two - safe bedroom sex with the light off. Then number three - doorway sex, when you pass each other going out of the door and tell each other to 'Fuck off'. Then, just when I thought I had about mastered the art of not getting too close to anyone, I finally anchored my wandering feet to the ground twenty-five years ago with a lady who is rather special. We argue a lot, but we move on quickly and we're good together. Forgive her. She can't help being French.

My life has taken me to different countries and with different jobs. From bank clerk, to digging holes in frozen clay, to herding pigs in a cattle market, to running a construction company, to scuba diving instructor, to webmaster, to business analyst in an international corporation. A life well wasted, as some of my more ambitious colleagues might say. But I've enjoyed it, and I've made a lot of friends. In my old age, I have taken up writing. I've written yuppie thrillers. My stock characters are two police women who always stumble into bizarre murder mysteries. I wonder what real-life figures inspired them? At least I didn't call them Michelle and Rhonda. And there's no way I could realistically describe their love lives. The books are mystery thrillers not pornography.

Slowly, unevenly, like a house-mover trying to wrestle a piano up a narrow staircase, my memories of 1967 have begun to fade. Some facts are beginning to disappear into the mists of time. Some have undoubtedly slipped my mind altogether. Which is why I have written down the story of Coviman-12 as best as I recall it, before my memory goes completely. Soon I shall end up as dust and nothingness and nobody will know how much our principal leaving his lounge curtains open affected our lives and subsequent actions.

As I look back on the events at College that year, I see that we entered the school gates that term as angst-ridden adolescents kicking against authority. We left six months later as young men with a history to tell. We had gained considerable sexual experience. We had lived through the terrors of a deadly virus hammering on the door, trying to get its claws into us. I had shot and killed people, and to this day have never doubted the justification for doing so. But it bugs me nonetheless. I can still see Toby Cochrane's chest exploding as I pulled the trigger on an ancient Lee-Enfield .303. I see too, fifteen-year-old David Newbold as he slithers down the school wall, leaving a trail of blood behind. I don't see the others. After those first two, I was just culling the herd.

Mental scars have the power to remind us that our past is real. It's never dead. It's not even past.

In so many ways, all of us suffered a living death. We had all felt our souls being squeezed from us. I know some of the young men who were in that chapel with me who were old men at fifty. Chewed-up, spat-out, like an old pair of trainers you give to the dog to drool over. I refused to be old before my time, but my time is now fast approaching. The clock is ticking, the hours are going by, the past increases and the future grows smaller. I may not be much, but I'm all I have, and there's not much of me left.

All these thoughts, all these memories, are amongst the first things on my mind when I wake and they're often the last thing that flits across my consciousness before I fall to sleep each night. I realised a long time ago that what happened is never going to go away. Ever. 'It will get easier,' Jack once told me. But you see, it doesn't get easier. Killing people never gets easier. The strength of feeling, the horror, the thought that I have ended people's lives - no matter how much they deserved it. It never goes away but you do kind of get used to having it around. You begin to accept that you will never feel happy or at peace.

Now, having arrived at the final sentences of this account, I feel some form of release. I read somewhere that each of us is a book waiting to be written, and that book, if written, results in a person explained. I have told the world what happened on the Isle of Man in 1967 and in doing so, I hope that I have, to some extent, explained myself. At least the telling has at last released me from my some of my guilt. I hope to God nothing like it ever happens again.

THE END

The following books by Graham Hamer are also available or will be published shortly

THE CHARACTERS COMPILATION
Chasing Paper – Characters Compilation 1
Walking on Water – Characters Compilation 2
Tommy Gee – Characters Compilation 3
The Zone – Characters Compilation 4

THE ISLAND CONNECTION
Under the Rock - Island Connection 1
Out of the Window - Island Connection 2
On Whom the Axe Falls - Island Connection 3
China in Her Hand - Island Connection 4
Devil's Helmet - Island Connection 5
The Vicar's Lot - Island Connection 6
Chicken Rock - Island Connection 7
The Platinum Pirate - Island Connection 8
Picasso's Secret – Island Connection 9
Travellers – Island Connection 10
Flint - Island Connection 11

THE FRENCH COLLECTION
Web of Tangled Blood – French Collection 1
Cenotaph for the Living - French Collection 2
Jasmine's Journey - French Collection 3
Taken on Face Value - French Collection 4

THE ODDBALL ODYSSEY
A Little Bit Odd – Oddball Odyssey 1
Odd Gets Even – Oddball Odyssey 2
A Little Bit Odder – Oddball Odyssey 3

You can find out more about the author and his books at
http://www.graham-hamer.com

Printed in Great Britain
by Amazon